SWAMP PRINCESS

CRIMINALS AND CRITTERS
BOOK 2

TARA LUSH

COVER DESIGN BY ALEXANDRA ALLEN

COVER IMAGES: SHUTTERSTOCK.COM

TYPESET BY TYPO-GLYPHIX

ISBN: 979-8-9893269-3-8

To Marco,
who doesn't believe in Bigfoot,
but has always believed in me.

Swamp Princess

Chapter One

It was March in Florida, which meant bright blue skies, no humidity, and weather so perfect that it made one almost weep at the thought of the stifling inferno to come in just a few short weeks.

This was precisely the kind of day I'd normally spend outside. Hiking, kayaking—hell, even hanging out on the porch under the live oaks with a sweet tea and a romance novel. Instead, I was indoors in an airless chain-hotel conference room eating a foot.

A pinky toe, to be precise.

"How does it taste?" My twin sister Vera's nose wrinkled as I swallowed.

"Like a pretzel. Salty. Pleasantly doughy with a buttery crust. Here." I held out the baked treat sprinkled with salt. "Take the big toe. Just rip it off."

"It seems weird."

"Vera, we're at the Fifth Annual Sunshine State Bigfoot Conference. It can't get any weirder." I popped a chunk of the foot-shaped pretzel into my mouth and chewed, while I surveyed the large banquet hall that served as the convention's vendor alley. This place was like Comic-Con for conspiracy theorists.

Folks in Bigfoot and Sasquatch T-shirts milled about,

perusing adorable stuffed cryptid toys, plaster casts of feet, and DVDs of paranormal encounters. At least one booth offered human-sized Bigfoot outfits. A plethora of themed snacks were also for sale, including cookies shaped like Nessie the Loch Ness Monster, Chupacabra tacos, and something called Ogopogo Pie, whatever that was.

I had my eye on a six-pack of Bigfoot Brew that a local craft brewer was hawking in the corner, complete with complimentary beer coozies that said BELIEVE IN YOURSELF, EVEN WHEN NO ONE ELSE DOES.

"What's an Ogopogo?" I asked my sister between bites. The pretzel was delicious, with just enough sea salt to make me want a beer. But it was only 11 a.m., and it was probably best to stay sober in this crowd. Plus, I had to work soon, if walking in the woods with some Bigfoot hunters was considered employment.

She shrugged. "I guess some kind of Canadian cryptid. Although I think it was also the last name of one of those guys I matched with on Tinder last year."

Vera shuffled a stack of paperbacks, her pin-straight blonde hair swaying with her movement. She was here as the owner of Straight From the Heart, her romance bookstore, selling mostly monster romance novels, a genre that both confounded and intrigued me. Were real human men so terrible that people felt the need to fantasize about monsters?

Apparently so, because this crowd couldn't get enough of the stories. Vera had almost sold out of her stock on the first day of the conference. There had practically been a fistfight over the last Orc erotica anthology, she'd said. That was yesterday, and today she was better prepared.

Her booth was possibly the cutest and most appealing here as far as I could tell, with a delicate, almost fairy-forest decor. Lush fake vines and small twinkling LED lights entwined the edges of the table. In the center, a miniature, moss-covered wishing well was surrounded by colorful silk wildflowers.

My sister had a keen eye for aesthetics, and always seemed to know how to decorate or dress based on where she was and who she was with. Today she was in a long, hunter-green maxi dress and sported a crown of flowers. Her blonde hair was loose, and I thought she looked like a pretty woodland sprite.

I was nowhere near as adorable, and was only here because one of the co-sponsors of the event—the North America Bigfoot and Cryptid Symposium—had asked me, Maggie Andrews, to give a presentation on the flora and fauna one might encounter in Florida while tracking critters in the wild. At first, I'd thought the email invitation was a prank and had laughed so hard that tears had streamed down my face, but the organizer had insisted that she wanted an alligator expert to explain the dangers of wading through swamps in the Sunshine State.

Seemed like pretty obvious information to me, but I'd learned in my twenty-five years on Earth not to assume people possessed common sense.

It had been a last-minute invite for both me and Vera,

but as new, local business owners, we'd jumped at the chance to peddle our wares, so to speak.

I'd given plenty of talks in my old job as the assistant to the assistant director at the Boston Zoo, but those had been to the general public. Back then, I'd fielded questions such as "What do crocodiles eat for breakfast?" "How can you tell a male reptile from a female?"—and, my personal favorite at the gator exhibit, "Do they bite?"

Since the Bigfoot group had chosen the small yet eccentric town of Wahoo, Florida, for its days-long annual conference, it had seemed like a no-brainer for them to ask me, the local gator trapper, to speak. I had taken the gig because Vera said I should—and I was thrilled to be in the presence of so much weirdness.

The two-thousand-dollar speaking fee didn't hurt my mood, either.

"I can't believe all these people believe in Bigfoot," I said, taking a sip of Vera's Alien Limeade, which tasted suspiciously like Mountain Dew Baja Blast. "I also can't believe they're paying me this much to tell people to stay away from gators. Then again, folks never listen."

"Is Bigfoot even in Florida?" Vera straightened a stack of romance books involving the Loch Ness Monster and a sexy cryptozoologist. She wore a slight scowl, which meant she was worried about something. I knew this as her twin.

I shook my head and swallowed. "Skunk Ape. That's the creature in these parts."

"Oh, right, I remember Dad used to talk about that . . ." Vera's words trailed off as she stared over my shoulder, toward the far end of her booth. Her blue eyes, identical to mine, were clouded with worry—as they often were. Vera was much more of a worrier than I was. "Hey, do you think the reporter on Monday will be nice? Or is this some sort of investigative report? It's stressing me out."

I swallowed a fluffy wad of dough. "Is that why you've been quiet all morning?"

She nodded. Last week, while I was helping out at the bookstore, the editor of the local paper—the *Wahoo Sentinel*—had come in. Of course, I didn't know her from Bigfoot, but I had helped her choose a few historical romances. That's when she'd introduced herself and said she was going to send out a reporter and photographer to do a feature on the store. The interview was scheduled for Monday, three days away.

"It's the *Sentinel*. Not the *New York Times*. They're going to write about a local business. No biggie. We've got this. Don't ruin the weekend worrying." I bit into the heel of the pretzel.

"Can you be in the photos?"

"Vera, no. You're the official owner. And this is your baby. You deserve all the credit and recognition."

She shook her head.

"What?" I asked. "Is it your skin?"

"Whatever," she grumbled. "Don't want to talk about it."

Her nonanswer meant yes. Vera had vitiligo, an autoimmune disorder that caused her skin to turn white. She was already fair-skinned and had mad makeup skills thanks to online videos—but she was still incredibly self-conscious about the white patches on her face. Had been since it bloomed and spread, starting in high school.

Of course, I thought my sister was gorgeous. We weren't identical twins, and with her delicate features, giant eyes, and curves, she'd gotten the better end of the genetic spectrum. I was somewhere between plain and "interesting-looking," which is what my ex-boyfriend had said when he first met me. (That I still dated him after that statement was not my best decision.)

Because I knew my sister better than anyone on the planet, I understood that she didn't want to talk more about this topic, and I respected that.

I turned back to the crowd. Three people had come to a stop about five feet from the table, and one woman—a blonde in a tight, olive-green jumpsuit and designer-looking black combat boots—was glaring at a rugged-looking dude. He had a foot pretzel in one hand.

A second woman stood by, wringing her hands.

"I can't believe you're getting upset about this," the man pleaded. He reached for her arm, and she slapped him away.

"I should have gotten top billing in the program," the woman hissed. "I have more followers than you."

"She's right," the second woman said. "So perhaps Kristi can get the bigger spot in the Atlanta program?"

The blonde glared at the other woman, then at the guy. He smiled and reached for the blonde's arm with his free hand.

"Kristi, I'm worried about you. For some reason you don't seem okay." The man gestured with the foot pretzel. I stifled a snicker.

"I'm fine, Grant. Why are you always so condescending? Geez." The blonde rolled her eyes in the direction of the other woman, who smiled weakly and nodded.

From my stool behind the table, I tore off another toe and watched as I chewed. I adored drama if it was someone else's. I imagined that the two had hooked up at some point. Their enemies-to-lovers-to-enemies energy had all the hallmarks of two people who had gone down to bone town.

I spun an entire narrative within seconds. Their relationship had been borne out of the drama and danger of tracking completely made-up characters. It was like a reality TV show come to life. I definitely wished I had one of those Bigfoot beers now.

The trio stood and bickered for a while, and I pretended to study the pretzel as I listened.

"You know people are here to see me," the blonde said, then coughed.

"You're not feeling well," the man replied.

I glanced up, just in time to meet the man's eyes. He was that close. He winked.

Eww. Pig. I ducked my head and focused on the pretzel.

"I'm feeling fine," the blonde said, her voice rising an octave. "You're being sexist. Not wanting a woman to be in the spotlight. You've always been this way, Grant. It's tedious."

I raised my head again, impressed that the woman was so direct, so assertive, so . . . bitchy. That dude probably deserved it, though.

"Maggie. Psst." My sister's voice pulled me away, but I didn't have any remorse about watching them. Something about being behind a table made me feel invisible, as if I blended into the table's pretty decor.

"What?" I whispered, slightly annoyed that she'd spoiled my fun.

She pulled me toward a chair at the opposite end of the booth. "That's one of the organizers of this whole shindig. Grant P. Sanders."

"Oh yeah?" I munched thoughtfully on my pretzel as I watched. The woman in the jumpsuit had one of those trendy water bottles, the kind that held bladder-busting amounts of liquid. The thing was hot pink.

Grant Sanders leaned into the blonde with a simpering smile. His dark hair was close-cropped. His muscles bulged, barely kept in check by a tight black T-shirt. He looked older than me—easily in his mid-thirties—with cargo pants and a rakish, I'm-in-charge-here vibe.

He was exactly the kind of man who annoyed me, and precisely the kind my sister adored. Was that a whip coiled and attached to his tool belt? Sketchy.

The ensemble might have worked if he hadn't been holding the giant Bigfoot pretzel.

I bit back laughter.

"What time do you give your talk?" Vera asked, her voice peeling me away from eavesdropping.

I checked my watch. "I need to be at the meeting point in the lobby in a half hour. Not enough time for me to enjoy a Bigfoot Brew, but enough time to get a cookie. And tomorrow's the talk. Today's the walk."

The conference had booked me for two speaking engagements. One was tomorrow, a formal talk with a PowerPoint presentation in a smaller conference room down the hall. That was all about the American alligator, of which there were 1.3 million in Florida alone.

Today was a more informal session. The hotel had been chosen because of its close proximity to Sawgrass Park, a gem of a county park. Boardwalks and trails stretched through vast swaths of swamp, and a beautiful path paralleled the Wahoo River. Gators, birds, and turtles were commonly spotted there, and I thought it was the best place to show off the area's natural beauty.

I was supposed to lead a group out of the conference and into the (tame) wilderness, pointing out various plants and critters of interest along the way. I was hoping we'd spot a gator, even.

Again, I eyed Grant Sanders and the blonde. He handed her the pretzel. They glared at each other, he murmured something in her ear, then each went in a different direction.

Definitely a lovers' fight. Which made his wink all the more skeevy. Vera and I glanced at each other. "Glad it's not me," I said.

I polished off our pretzel while Vera shuffled more stacks of books. My attention drifted again to the crowd, and I noticed several people wearing shirts with an unfamiliar slogan and what looked like the furry face of a Bigfoot.

"Hey, Vera?"

"Yeah?"

"What does 'bromie' mean? Is that some kind of cryptozoology lingo?"

She looked up and shrugged. "Who knows? Where'd you see that?"

"I keep seeing it on T-shirts."

"Dunno." She put her hands on her hips. "I'm going to call Diego and ask him to bring more books. I didn't think I'd sell this many, this early."

"Good plan," I called out.

Diego Viernes was a twentysomething animal rights activist and computer hacker. He'd moved to Wahoo to investigate a report of animal abuse and stayed after helping Vera and I catch the killer of another gator trapper.

Diego also was a lover of paranormal romance, and when my sister opened her bookstore, he'd asked if he could work there a few hours a week. It was a little odd—a young, tattooed, vegan guy in a romance bookstore—but so far, the customers adored him, probably because he had excellent recommendations.

He especially loved gay werewolf shifter romance. Today he was manning the store while Vera was at the conference, although she'd said that Diego and his boyfriend were going to swing by the conference later because they, too, were curious about Bigfoot.

I balled up my napkin and threw it in the trash. "I'm going to roam. If I don't come back by three, send out a search party. There's no shortage of amateur sleuths here. And listen, the booth looks incredible. You've done an amazing job. I'm super impressed."

"Thanks!" Vera giggled and did a little finger wave. "Oh, wait. Maggie?"

I turned back. "Yeah?"

"I almost forgot. We need to talk about something important. Now isn't the best time. Remind me when we're both at home tonight, okay?"

I tilted my head. My twin was a bit flighty, and tended toward the dramatic. She was sometimes difficult. Often forgetful in odd ways. This could be about adopting a new pet (we had two already—Catsy the kitten and Harry the rescue iguana). Or it could be about something more important. Who knew, with Vera.

"Sounds good," I said, not wanting to give in to her theatrics. "See ya."

With less than a half hour until I had to meet my group, I had enough time to take a lap or two around the convention floor. I couldn't get enough of the crowds of seemingly normal folks casually rifling through tables full of Bigfoot-themed merchandise.

Although now that I looked a little closer, a lot of the conference attendees were dressed in camouflage, flak jackets, and those tan vests with multiple pockets that only fishermen, pro photographers, and eccentric older men wore. It seemed as though everyone here was ready to dive into the swamp and wade through muck— or go on a nice weekend camping trip with the family.

Everyone needs a hobby, I guess.

Chapter Two

I paused at a large booth filled with handmade wallets in the shape of furry Sasquatch faces. A couple nearby was gushing about the craftsmanship.

"See, they've used quality fake fur," the woman in the couple said, then she turned to me and pointed at one satchel that looked more like Willie Nelson than a cryptid. "That's a nice purse."

I reached out to trace the googly eyes stuck on the side of the bag. "It's . . . unique."

"Darned tootin' its unique," the woman behind the table said. "Nobody else sells Sasquatch wallets."

"Are you the . . . creator?" *Artist* seemed to be a bit of a stretch, considering the wallets seemed to be made of fake brown fur glue-gunned to a piece of virgin vinyl.

The woman took a swig of Gatorade and nodded. "I go to all the cryptid conferences."

I blinked. Truthfully, I had only a vague idea of what a cryptid even was, and I definitely didn't believe in them. A smile started to spread on my face, and I was dangerously close to laughing. It was something I did when I was nervous.

"There's more than one conference?"

"Oh, honey, you must be new in these parts," the

woman said, and everyone in earshot chuckled. "This is a whole traveling show!"

I was about to ask her if she actually believed in Bigfoot, but she was called away to answer a question about a pair of handmade Bigfoot slippers, so I moved on.

Most of the booths offered books and DVDs about the elusive creatures. I stopped at one, which sported bedazzled Bigfoot water bottles, Mothman pepper spray holders, and adorable stuffed toys for pets.

"Is this one filled with catnip?" I asked, holding up a small toy that looked like a dung-brown version of those old Pac-Man monsters.

"That's a baby Sasquatch, and yes, it is," the woman behind the table chirped. "My cats love those. They go wild."

"I'll take one," I said. Vera and I were the proud owners of Catsy Cline, a fluffy white kitten. Well, perhaps "owners" wasn't the best description. We were more like servants of a four-pound, jarringly adorable feline. Who had never tried catnip.

It was time to introduce the kitten to the hard stuff, I decided while paying for my purchase. I declined a bag and the woman smiled.

"Thanks for saving the environment," she said.

She was about fifty, with a bob the color of dishwater. She had a pleasingly plump, curvy shape, and wore a tan sweatshirt with a giant Bigfoot silhouette on the front and leopard-print leggings. Her teeth had obviously been whitened, because they were almost blue and glowed when she smiled.

A large vinyl banner hung on a divider behind the table. In large letters, it read: *Giggles-N-Ghoulies Boutique*.

There was no one else at the booth, so I decided to take a chance and ask her the question I'd been pondering for hours.

"Maybe you can help me with something," I said in my friendliest tone while I shoved the catnip toy in my small backpack. "I'm new to this world. Do people here actually believe in Bigfoot, or is this just a fun hobby, or what? I'm not trying to be mean, and don't intend to be disrespectful. I'm asking out of genuine curiosity. The whole scene is fascinating to me."

She giggled. "I know. It's hard to believe that all these people believe in Bigfoot."

I nodded. "I'd always thought of him—er, *it*, as a myth. Or something out of those supermarket tabloids. You know, like Bat Boy."

"That's what most folks think. Have you seen any of the shows on YouTube or Netflix?"

"Can't say I have."

"You should check out Grant P. Sanders's work. He'll be speaking later today."

Ooh. Mess! Grant was the guy I'd seen arguing with that blonde woman. "Wow. Is he interesting?"

She bit her lip and glanced to the side. Then she leaned over the table in my direction. "Interesting? He's incredible. He's dreamy. Easy on the eyes, if you know what I mean. And so smart. My gosh, he's the best. Grant explains complex things in ways you can understand."

I wasn't sure how one would have difficulty grasping

the concept of a giant, furry being stomping through the woods, but I nodded anyway. "I'll be sure to look out for his session."

"I'm like his personal cheerleader. During every one of these conferences, Grant is so sweet and takes me out for coffee. We went out last night." She giggled like a teen. "We joke that I'm his stalker. We're all Bromies here."

My face lit up in recognition. "What is a Bromie, anyway? I keep seeing that on people's T-shirts."

She laughed. "Oh, that's Grant's word for his fans. He always calls us that. It's a combination of 'bro' and 'homie.' As in, Bigfoot Bromies. It's an inside joke with all of us. See?" She turned, and on the back of her shirt was a furry face and *#1 Bromie* in gothic letters.

"Oh, okay." I tried to pretend to understand, even though I was really thinking about whether it was cool for a middle-aged white guy to co-opt a word like "homie." Or even use the word "bro," period. A split second later, I decided it wasn't cool in any way, shape, or form.

The woman stuck her hand out, and I couldn't help but notice her long, white nails. Each had a tiny decal of Bigfoot—the same silhouette that was on the front of her shirt. "I'm Michelle Newman, by the way."

"Good to meet you. I'm Maggie Andrews." I explained that I was here to give a talk about real-life critters.

"We don't use terms like 'real life,' just so you know. I don't mind, but some might. They get offended if you suggest the creatures aren't alive. People take this quite seriously. Did you get a brochure?"

I felt properly chastised, even though she was smiling.

"Oh, good point. Thank you. Well, maybe I'll run into you at Grant's talk. And no, I didn't get a brochure. I arrived here a little late because of work."

What I didn't tell her: I'd had to take a detour on my way here to check on Chubbs, a giant alligator on a local golf course. The creature had been lumbering around for months, and today I wanted to see if it had moved from the water trap on the seventh hole. It hadn't, which meant Chubbs was safe for now.

Michelle handed me a pamphlet. "You can have this one, I picked up extras. Plus, there's a great photo of Grant on page two." She winked. "He took my advice and wore the dark green T-shirt."

"You *are* his number one Bromie," I pointed out with a smile.

She said something about how Grant *just loved* his fans. Considering how he'd winked at me, I was sure he did.

I flipped through the glossy booklet, stopping on page two, where Grant smirked in a giant photo.

"Isn't he hot?" Michelle said, tapping the paper.

If one was attracted to Great Value Indiana Jones. "Sure," I agreed.

I continued to peruse the booklet. On page four was a photo of the angry blonde I'd seen earlier. Sure enough, her picture wasn't as large as Grant's, and she had to share a page with another Bigfoot "researcher."

"Kristi Klaus—so that's her name," I murmured as I read her bio, which included the detail that she'd reached a million YouTube viewers.

Considered one of the world's preeminent Bigfoot researchers, Kristi has tracked cryptids on four continents and has even come face-to-face with Sasquatch in the Pacific Northwest! Her soul connection with nature only deepens her love of Bigfoot and the extra-normal world.

I was wondering what a "soul connection with nature" was when Michelle grunted, "Ugh. Don't believe a word of that."

I looked up, surprised.

She shook her head. "I can't stand that woman. She tries to get free things from the vendors all the time. She's a real bitch. And she's always after Grant. She's not his type. He'd never be interested in her, but she hasn't gotten the hint. She'll get hers someday soon. I believe in karma."

She ended her diatribe with a manic laugh. Eek. Kinda weird. Or not. I wasn't sure if my definition of "weird" was the same as it had been a few hours ago, before I stepped into this convention.

I grimaced and considered telling her about what I'd seen just minutes earlier. But it wasn't nice to gossip, even among weirdos. Also, I wondered if there was a bit of jealousy surrounding Kristi: she was a gorgeous and successful woman, two things that often set people off.

Now that I thought about it, Kristi and I had a lot in common. We were both women in male-dominated fields. We both spent time in the outdoors. Both of us loved cute outfits.

It occurred to me that perhaps I should introduce myself to Kristi and maybe get a photo for social media. Vera was always after me to "think of the 'gram." I almost never did, since I loathed social media. But considering Kristi was so popular, it couldn't hurt to get a picture. It would make Vera happy.

Maybe Kristi was around here somewhere.

I said goodbye to Michelle and wandered off, pausing at an empty chair in the corner to take a photo of the catnip toy and send it to Vera. She responded with a gushing, emoji-filled text of happiness. I also quickly checked my messages, hoping that no one had texted, called, or emailed with an emergency.

Fortunately, they hadn't. In my line of work, I never knew when someone would contact me. That was the life of a wildlife trapper. I'd learned the business from my father, who had been known around our hometown of Wahoo as the Gator King.

When he was on his deathbed, I'd promised him I'd continue his legacy and take over his business as the Gator Queen. Since my degree was in zoology and my former job was as an assistant in the reptile exhibit at the Boston Zoo, I possessed unique expertise about reptiles, and Florida critters in particular.

But I'd never dreamed I'd be imparting my wisdom to a bunch of Bigfoot enthusiasts. This was a first. Although, now that I saw how much money was exchanging hands here, maybe I had a future on the cryptid circuit.

I'd probably have to get a better outfit, though. Today I was wearing my nicest skinny jeans, a long-sleeve, button-down, pale green sweat-wicking shirt, and a pair of sneakers. Alarmingly, I blended in with everyone here.

I went through all my messages again, wondering if I'd missed something, and sighed.

Unfortunately, the one person who I wanted to hear from hadn't texted: Jack Bianchi. He was a criminology professor writing a book on serial killers and was taking a six-month writing sabbatical in Wahoo. He rented a cabin on the property owned by Vera and me, which meant that I was his landlord.

He had jet-black hair, tattoos that marked the time he was bitten by a shark *and* when he was struck by lightning, and sexy dark stubble. He made delicious lasagna. He was single. And he wasn't here permanently—eventually, after finishing his book, he'd return to his teaching job in Miami.

The perfect man, really.

I harbored extremely lustful thoughts about him, and with any luck, this weekend we'd take our friendship to the next level, with some benefits.

But first, Bigfoot.

I still had twenty minutes to kill, so I refilled my water bottle and studied the official program, all while looking for Kristi. If I found her, maybe we could bond over hiking. Or hairy men.

If I didn't find her now, perhaps this evening. There was a "meet and greet," and I wondered who we would be meeting. Bigfoot himself? I needed to ask Vera if she wanted to go. Kristi would almost certainly be there.

As people buzzed around me, I read on, both fascinated and skeptical.

Who even knew that there was a North America Bigfoot and Cryptid Symposium? Not I. This was definitely in the realm of "learning experience." My father, rest his soul, would have asserted that this kind of event "builds character." I wasn't so certain about that, but I would have lots of new stories to tell.

I noted that there was a "late-night hike on Saturday" and on Sunday, a "5K Fancy Feet Run" through downtown Wahoo. I had to hand it to these folks: they embraced the outdoors. I guess they had to, given the subject matter.

I closed the program, shoved it into my bag, and continued to mill around.

I wandered into separate, smaller conference space, where a reed-thin bald man with a white beard was speaking into a microphone at the front of the room. I leaned against the back wall and tried to figure out what he was talking about. I peered at the projector screen behind the guy.

Was that a picture of Charlton Heston? I only recognized him because Dad had loved the old actor. Oh dear. I wasn't sure where this was headed.

"As you can see, the family tree of the hominoid looks familiar," the man said.

Another slide flashed onto the screen. It showed a family tree of sorts, with Charlton Heston, a plus sign, an ape wearing a pink bow on its head, and an equal sign. There was nothing after that.

"Has anyone seen the genital anatomy of a female Sasquatch?" the man asked.

A few people raised their hands.

Wait. Was he talking about Sasquatch cooch? Human-ape breeding? I glanced around, shifting only my eyes, but no one else seemed horrified. Yikes on bikes. I wasn't sticking around to find out the answer to the question, so I grabbed my bag and scrammed so I could laugh without anyone noticing.

For a few seconds I paused in the main hall and giggled to myself so I could tap out a text to Vera. Her announcement that she wanted us to chat later had been flitting around in the back of my mind like an unwanted ghost. My finger hovered over the letters on my phone as I wondered whether I should press her for more details.

Finally, I decided against it.

Did you know that Sasquatches are possibly the result of human-ape breeding?

She quickly responded with a barf emoji.

I snorted and checked my watch. It was time to lead a group of Skunk Ape seekers into the Florida swamp.

Chapter Three

There was already a cluster of folks waiting for me in the lobby, which was the designated meeting point previously emailed to people who had signed up for the walk. Outside, the bright sunshine and blue sky beckoned and teased. I couldn't wait to get outdoors and into the non-air-conditioned sunshine.

I walked over to the group. "Hi! Are you here for the walk? I'm Maggie Andrews, the presenter."

An older man with a black fishing hat stared down at me, over the tops of his reading glasses. He pulled out one of the glossy brochures, unfolded it, and studied it for a second. Then he looked up. "There are two outdoor sessions. 'When Bigfoot Hunting Turns into Gator Trapping,' and 'Florida Man Meets Florida Cryptid: True Tales from the Trails.'"

"Uh, the gator one." After that Sasquatch sex session, I shuddered to think of what the "true tales" were.

The man beamed and motioned to the half-dozen people standing nearby. "Yeah, that's us here. I think the other session is being held at the picnic tables near the pool. They're probably going to order tropical drinks, but we'll be out in the wild."

"Excellent, and yes, we will be." I waved at everyone

excitedly while they smiled. I had to say, folks sure were pleasant here.

"I thought there'd be more people than this," the man said apologetically. "I suspect many already know about the flora and fauna in the swamp. And I'm more worried about a momma Sasquatch than a gator."

While he smiled earnestly, my nervous chuckle faded. Good God, he was serious. I nodded sagely in response.

"We'll wait a couple more minutes in case there are any stragglers." I pretended to type out an urgent message on my phone. In reality, I was checking to see what time Cheesy Does It, the grilled cheese restaurant, closed on Fridays. Screw the meet and greet.

I was in luck. If I could get out of here by four, I'd just make it. The place had recently added a new sandwich, a Gruyère with caramelized onions and rosemary butter. My mouth watered at the thought of all that gooey cheese and pungent herb flavor.

Five minutes passed and I gathered my small group into a loose huddle. There were four women and three men, including the man in the black fishing hat who sported a T-shirt that said KEEP IT SQUATCHY.

The rest were also wearing various cryptid-themed T-shirts: a Bigfoot on a Harley-Davidson, Bigfoot carrying an American flag, Bigfoot walking over an LGBTQ+ rainbow. A man and a woman wore identical tan, long-sleeved shirts that read *Bigfoot Hunters of Iowa*.

I assumed those two were a couple. I tried to imagine Jack and I wearing those shirts and muffled a snicker. Wait, why was I fantasizing about matching outfits with the guy? We'd only met a couple of months ago, and we were . . . well, I didn't know what we were doing. We were keeping things light and simple, interspersed with hot makeout sessions.

All I knew was that Jack was sexy, smart, and sported tattoos of both a shark and a lightning bolt. Since he also had a wicked sense of humor, I was certain that he'd find this conference as weirdly fascinating as I did. Maybe we could stop by tomorrow, if he wasn't busy.

The man with the black hat and the KEEP IT SQUATCHY shirt clapped his hands. "Okay, what's the plan? We headed out to look for some critters? Does anyone have any Quarter Pounders?"

Everyone laughed. Everyone but me, that was. I raised my eyebrows and smiled. "I'm not sure why we would bring McDonald's on the walk? But I can tell you where the nearest one is. It's not far."

"We'd bring burgers because that's what we use to lure the creatures," the woman in the Iowa shirt said in a girlish voice. "Bigfoot loves hamburgers!"

I scratched my neck. Was she joking? Part of me hoped so, but it also made sense in an odd way. Who didn't love hamburgers?

"Okay, um. Right. Well, today we're going to be looking at real—er, potentially harmful critters that you might encounter while hiking in Florida. Today's walk is pretty low-key, it's less than a mile, and we won't be getting wet or going off-trail. We'll be on dirt paths only."

"Bummer," said the motorcycle-shirt guy. He was about sixty, with a buzz cut and a gray handlebar mustache. He held up a pair of tall green boots. "I brought my waders along."

"Yeah, we have our dry bag." The woman with the high-pitched voice waved a red bag, the heavy vinyl kind that folded over at the top and was often used by people on dive boats.

"I'm glad you're all so prepared," I said, marveling that they'd toted all this stuff to a conference. The woman in the American flag shirt held up a pair of binoculars and I pointed at her, nodding slowly. "Very nice."

I took another couple of minutes to explain where we were headed (out the door, across the back parking lot, then down a short, paved path to the park), and reminded everyone to top off their water bottles since it was warm. While folks did that, the motorcycle-shirt guy stashed his waders behind the hotel's front desk.

As we were about to leave, the door from the convention hall was flung open. The blonde in the green jumpsuit that I'd seen earlier burst into the lobby, carrying a selfie stick with a phone attached.

"Oh my goddddd, is this the alligator walk? Wait for me! Wait for me! I'm so sorry I'm late."

As she swept up to us, everyone in the group either gasped or grinned.

"Kristi Klaus," the motorcycle-shirt guy said, in a reverent voice most people would use for royalty and certain A-list celebrities. "You're joining us? Wow. This is the place to be."

Everyone murmured and nodded. Even I had to grin. Kristi had an infectious, upbeat vibe.

"You know me, I won't ever turn down a chance to get dirty." She winked at the guy in the fishing hat, who blushed scarlet. "Who's leading this session, anyway? Or am I going to have to take charge?"

I held out my hand to my new bestie. "Hi, I'm Maggie Andrews. I'm leading the walk. I'm a gator trapper here in Wahoo—"

"Amazeballs." She beamed. "That's my catchphrase, you know. Or maybe you don't, if you're not familiar with my work . . ."

Her words dissolved into a cough, and I stepped back, not wanting to be sprayed with germs. "You okay? Need some water?"

She patted the side pocket of her jumpsuit, which was bulging with a plastic water bottle, and shook her head. She pulled the bottle out and we all watched as she struggled to uncap it. Oh dear, she seemed a little drunk and shaky. Instead of the pink cup she'd been clutching earlier, this was the kind you'd buy in the supermarket—a brand of bottled water called Aqua de la Florida.

I hated the stuff, because the company drained Florida's aquifers, preventing wildlife and plants from accessing the water. To me, the company represented everything that was wrong with my home state: greed and relentless consumption.

But that was of no importance now. I had to wrangle this clown down the trail.

I glanced around. No one else seemed alarmed, so perhaps this was normal for Kristi. Maybe it was her stage persona, or her schtick.

While she took a sip, I seized the moment and the spotlight.

"Let's go look for some gators," I said. Everyone except Kristi replied with little whoops and cheers. The energy in the group seemed to have ratcheted up by several notches since she'd arrived, which wasn't a bad thing. I loved when folks were enthusiastic about wildlife—Florida wildlife especially. We had one of the most unique ecosystems in America, and I felt that more people should take interest in the place.

"If they learn about it, maybe they'll save it," Dad used to say, and I couldn't have agreed more.

I was halfway out the door when I realized that Kristi was now taking selfies with the group. Stifling a sigh, I went back in and waited until they were finished. This took at least ten minutes, since everyone had to gush over her and post the pictures to their social media. I noticed she kissed all of the men on the cheek during the selfies.

"This is like meeting a rock star and the president all in one," one of the Iowa Bigfoot hunters declared.

My odds of eating a gourmet grilled cheese were dwindling. Then again, I could endure anything for two grand—even buy my own Gruyère at the Publix down the street.

I studied my group. This was going to be a weird walk, I could feel it. Still, I had hope that I could grab a cute photo of Kristi and me. Maybe she'd even give my sister's bookstore a shoutout on her social media.

Vera would be beside herself with joy. A picture of us on the trail would be perfect.

We set out under a bright Florida sun. Ahh. It felt like I was breaking free from jail, going from the stale air in the conference hall to the clean, grassy smell of the nearby park. I could feel my muscles relaxing with every step I took toward nature.

As we ambled toward the park entrance, we introduced ourselves and said where we were from. Everyone was from out of state: Iowa, Montana, Nevada, and Texas. All mentioned that they'd spotted Bigfoot in their part of the country.

I considered asking if they had any proof, like videos or photos, or physical evidence, but I remembered those earlier words of caution. It wasn't any of my business if these people thought Bigfoot was real, and I wasn't being paid to talk about that anyway.

"Have you ever Squatched?" one of the women wearing a LGBTQ+ Bigfoot T-shirt asked me.

Was this a new social media platform? A dance on TikTok? "No, I can't say that I have."

She grinned, revealing a diamond in her front tooth. "Do you even know what Squatching is?"

I laughed, genuinely. "Not really. Wait, did you say 'squashing'?"

Everyone stopped and gathered around. Grabbing my arm, Kristi leaned in and slurred, "You don't know what Squatching is?"

"Squatching," said the man in the black hat, "is the term for when you hunt Bigfoot. Or Sasquatch."

"Or the Skunk Ape," someone chimed in.

"I see. Well, let's go Squatching." I grinned, thinking

about how I'd tell Jack every detail of this, and how he'd sound so hot with that low, easy laugh of his.

We quickly arrived at the park. The main path ran along the Wahoo River. At the trailhead, I paused.

"It looks like any other suburban recreational area, but there are predators lurking—"

"We are here at the trail and going to hunt some gatorsssss," Kristi yelled. "And maybe we'll play hide-and-seek with some cryptids, too! Squatch stroll! We've got a gator nerd with us. Her name's . . . ah, oh hell. Amazeballs!"

All of us whirled in her direction. She was holding her phone, attached to her selfie stick, in the air. Her expression was somewhere between manic and utterly oblivious to the fact that she'd just interrupted the talk. We all watched as she shimmied her upper body in a little dance for the camera.

I froze. This was not the kind of social media exposure I'd wanted from her. "Um. Excuse me? Kristi?"

"I'm going live," she said, then angled the camera so it captured me. "This is Madge, and she's a gator trapper? I'm not sure?"

When she spoke, it sounded like every sentence ended on a question.

"Maggie. My name's Maggie." I folded my arms over my chest. I was all for girl power, girlbossing, and girlfriends. But this witch was now getting on my last nerve. No one disparaged my gator business.

Yet she ignored me and continued to talk to the camera. How could anyone be so rude, so inappropriate, so . . . selfish? As I studied her, I noticed something else.

She was sweating. Not just profusely, but like a water-fall. Her mascara was creeping down her left cheek. To me, she looked unhinged. This was the world's pre-eminent Bigfoot researcher? Was she okay?

But I wasn't here to ask questions.

"Say hey to my fans, Midge!" She shuffled over to me and wrapped an arm around my shoulders, doing a duck face for the camera.

I raised my hand in a little wave and let out a manic, soft chuckle. This was supremely awkward. "Hey. I'm the Gator Queen."

"Come on, girl, be more enthusiastic! Sell yourself! You're live with thousands of viewers!" Kristi elbowed me in the ribs. She was close enough that I could smell her—she gave off a powerful stench of gin, sour body odor, and a heavy coconut perfume.

I fought back a grimace. Part of me was totally repelled by her, but another part felt terrible that she was out here with her ass hanging out, so to speak.

Something was clearly wrong. No one should be sweating this much on such a beautiful, seventy-five-degree spring day with no humidity. Then again, no one should be hammered on gin at this hour, either.

"Have you ever seen Bigfoot?" she asked me in a mock-serious tone, her eyes wide.

The group stepped closer, possibly to hear my response. Or they wanted to be in the live shot.

"Um, well, I don't think so." This wasn't the time to explain that I mostly hated social media and that whenever someone pointed a camera at me, I froze like a deer caught in the headlights of a fast-approaching eighteen-wheeler loaded with boxes of awkwardness.

Do this for Vera.

"You don't think so, or you don't want to say?" She raised an eyebrow. "Hmm? What secrets of the swamp are you keeping to yourself?"

Everyone was silent while they waited for my response.

I nodded and frowned, biding my time so I could hopefully come up with a coherent answer. "When I'm trapping gators," I said in a low, conspiratorial tone, "it's safety first. One wrong step and I can lose a limb. I can't take my eye off the gator, otherwise—SNAP."

I made a motion with my hands, clapping loudly, like the fans did at the University of Florida Gators football games. Everyone jumped a little.

"But I've never been bitten." I smiled triumphantly, proud that I'd steered the conversation away from Kristi's attention-hogging antics. "So, no, that's probably why I've never seen a cryptid. I'm too laser-focused."

"Amazeballs," Kristi slurred, little drops of spittle hitting my face. It came out more like "Amaze-ballthhhhhsss."

I edged away from her and tried to regain my bearings. I wasn't usually nervous about leading groups—heck, I'd had lots of contact with the public when I'd worked for the Boston Zoo, and had even given tours of the Slimy Scaly Spectacular, a popular reptile exhibit.

But this, out here in the park with an unmoored Bigfoot YouTube celebrity, was a new and troubling experience. As I tried to ignore that Kristi was filming me, I turned back to the group. Should I say something about her? To her? Ugh, maybe not. I didn't want to cause a scene and upset these fans, who clearly adored her.

I clasped my hands. "The American alligator is native to Florida. You can distinguish them from their cousin, the crocodile, by their wide, U-shaped snout. The croc has more of a V-shape, so their snout is narrow. Generally alligators can be found in almost any body of fresh water here, which is why you should be careful when trekking in and around rivers, lakes, ponds, swamps, marshes, and streams. One notable thing is that they have an elaborate courtship ritual during mating season—"

"That's what I'm talking about!" Kristi yelled into the camera. "A man's gotta show you what he's worth. Isn't that right, Marge?"

I glanced around, unsure of what was more alarming: that she would act like this, or that no one in the group seemed to think anything was amiss. In fact, several were laughing.

"Even gators do a better job at courtship than human men," I quipped.

Kristi seemed to love that, because she cackled. Then her laughter dissolved into a fit of coughing, and I seized the opportunity to usher everyone onto the trail. She straggled along behind us, chattering and coughing into the camera.

As we stepped onto the path, she thankfully kept quiet, but she aimed the camera at me while I explained some facts and history about the Wahoo River.

"We'll be taking this trail parallel to the river, and at

various points there are lookouts where we can see the riverbank. That's our best bet for seeing wildlife. We're going to be searching for gators, turtles, fish, and wading birds."

My sneakers made a soft crunching noise on the gravel path. It would have been a peaceful walk, if not for Kristi's continued, rambling monologue. She was now being so annoying that if I could, I would slingshot cat poop at her. Still, I struggled with whether to interrupt her chatter.

She was a celebrity in this crowd. Probably best to ignore her.

About a hundred feet down the trail, there was a small, wooden bridge. It was the kind that arched, and since there was only room for one or two people at the top of the arch, I went first and stopped.

The rest of the group was on one side of the trail. Mercifully, Kristi shut up and stood silently with the rest of the group while I spoke.

"This is a great example of a Florida creek. Even though we're in a park that's maintained by the county, the place is still wild, as you can see. We're not all that far from the hotel, but we might as well be miles inland. We can't hear cars or people." I paused to let the hush of the forest sink in. "Water is where you'll find a lot of critters. In fact, I see one right there."

"A gator?" someone asked excitedly.

I pointed at a medium-sized log that was partially submerged in the stream. "There's a freshwater turtle over there, about five feet away. Do you see it? Stand carefully on the bank of the stream. It's atop that fallen log."

Everyone clustered around. "Oh, there he is," one woman said excitedly. "We don't have those in Montana."

"That's a snapping turtle. Now, remember, if you're in Florida and see a turtle in the road and want to rescue it, great. Put it on the side of the road. Don't put it in water! A little-known fact is that most of the turtles you see on land are actually gopher tortoises that don't live in the water. So don't put those in a stream or pond. Snapping turtles like this little nugget hold their breath underwater. You can tell the difference between the two in a few ways."

I went on to explain that snapping turtles were larger, had webbed feet for swimming, and had a beak-like nose.

"They can do some serious damage if they bite you, so I'd stay away from . . . Kristi, no!"

The woman was wading into the creek, selfie stick in hand, talking to her viewers. "Who wants to see me pet that turtle?"

I took a few giant steps down the slope of the bridge, but the man in the fishing hat grabbed Kristi's arm and pulled her back to land.

"Fun stealer," she said to him, sticking out her tongue.

"We aren't going to touch any wildlife today. This isn't a petting zoo. These are wild animals and are unpredictable." My voice was sharp.

I couldn't wait for this walk to end. As far as I was concerned, two grand wasn't enough for babysitting a drunk viral internet star.

"Kristi? Do you hear me? We can't touch the animals."

"Fine." She stuck out her bottom lip, like a child, then

turned back to the camera. "They're trying to steal my magic."

Magic or not, nothing turned my crank more than people messing with wild animals. Feeding gators, touching turtles, trying to trap birds, riding manatees . . . it all made me angry. I had no issue with people rescuing critters from traffic and dangerous situations, but for some reason, tourists liked to come to Florida and molest our wildlife. Sometimes the results were tragic, for both human and animal.

Mounting manatees should be a death-penalty crime, in my book.

I shoved my rising anger down and motioned for everyone to follow me over the bridge. We continued on. The woman with the diamond in her tooth asked me about snakes. While we walked through the swampy woodlands, I explained that we probably wouldn't see any today.

"They're most active between April and October, when the weather's hot. But don't worry. This isn't the Everglades, so you probably won't stumble across an invasive python."

The woman shuddered.

The temperature cooled as we walked on, the forest growing dark and lush. At a clearing, I stopped. Behind me was a gentle embankment that went down a couple of feet, then the river. But that wasn't what I wanted to point out.

"Okay, everyone! What do you see down here? Please be careful and don't go down the dirt slope. It's best not to erode the trail or the river embankment."

Everyone respectfully stayed on the path and peered at the water.

"A river," someone said.

"Trees."

"Wait, what's that in the grass, right near the water?"

"Excellent. Very good. You spotted it."

I pointed to a small depression in the grass that looked almost like a puddle. It was about fifteen feet from us.

"Is it a sinkhole?" said the man in the black hat, lowering his glasses and squinting.

"No. That is a gator hole."

Everyone gasped in delight.

"Gators, like all reptiles, are cold-blooded. When it's warm out, they like to sunbathe. When it's not, they dig holes in mud in order to trap heat and stay comfortable. And stay alive. Wait, Kristi, no!"

She was scrambling down the small embankment, toward the water. *Oh, hell.*

"What is that thing over there?" She sloppily gestured toward the water. Or something. I wasn't paying attention because she was leaping down the small slope.

"No. Kristi, absolutely not," I repeated, sharper this time. I could handle her disrespecting my talk, but I simply would not tolerate her walking through delicate wetlands. "That's terrible for the environment, to go off-trail. Plus, it's dangerous."

"I know all about danger, girl. It's my middle name. Watch this—"

Her foot slid down the embankment, and she coughed the entire way.

"Whoa, whoa, whoa," said the guy in the black hat.

Kristi tried to regain her balance, brandishing the selfie stick in the air. But the ground gave way and she tumbled toward the murky water, with the gator hole only about ten feet away. She flailed wildly, arms and legs making wild, jerky motions. The plastic water bottle in her pocket popped out and rolled a few feet.

"Kristi!" I yelled, rushing to the edge. The stick and phone soared into the air and landed with a splat on the wet earth. I scrambled down the bank, ignoring the dirt accumulating on my clothes. My heart thrashed. I needed to reach her and help. Something in my gut told me that this was an urgent situation, a crisis, even—and not just a garden-variety drunken stumble.

"Are you okay?" I asked, but she didn't respond. She was on her back and, to my horror, began to jerk and spasm. Her eyes rolled back in her head.

"Oh, crap," I whispered. As much as she'd annoyed me by interrupting the talk, she didn't deserve whatever was happening to her now. Yikes.

I glanced at the gator hole. More than likely it was empty—it was far too warm for a gator to burrow—but there were solid odds that the creature was nearby.

By now Kristi was convulsing and frothing at the mouth. We had to get her out of there and to a hospital. I put my hand on her forehead. Her skin was oddly clammy. *Crap, crap, crap.*

"What happened?" I asked her as I frantically slipped off my backpack. I had a small first-aid kit, but nothing that would help me with . . . whatever was going on here.

She didn't answer. In fact, she'd stopped moving entirely. *This can't be good.*

I repeated her name several times, but she was silent. I shook her arm and clasped her hand. It was limp. I gently patted her cheek. She didn't stir. Finally, I pressed my fingers to her carotid artery.

Nothing.

Panic seized me, making my breath come in shallow gulps. I looked up to see the entire group of Bigfoot hunters gaping down at me, their faces frozen and horrified.

Within an instant, everything imaginable was deeply uncomfortable. My skin bloomed with unwanted sweat. My once-cute jeans were suddenly so tight that they felt like sausage casing. And I was hyperventilating because I was *holding what was possibly a dead woman's hand*.

"Does anyone know CPR?" I hollered, trying to squeeze her fingers to see if she'd respond. She didn't.

Seven pairs of giant eyes stared back at me.

"I learned CPR when I was a lifeguard, but that was thirty years ago," Black Hat said.

"Well, get down here." I was done being nice. "Wait, no. Let's get her up there. Away from the . . . No. Let's do it here. We don't want to waste time. Someone call 911."

This was my walk, and I needed to take charge.

I checked the gator hole, then looked back at the group. One of the women whipped out her phone and pointed the camera at us.

"No. 911," I snapped. "Now."

The woman fumbled with her phone, almost dropping it, then started to tap on the screen.

"I'm going to get help," said one of the LGBTQ+ Bigfoot people, and she dashed away.

Black Hat jumped down the embankment. He rolled up his shirtsleeves and promptly attempted mouth-to-mouth with Kristi.

While my mind swirled with a thousand horrible possibilities, my chest grew tight as I watched him try to resuscitate her. After the third attempt, he put his ear to her mouth, then her chest. He straightened his spine and shook his head.

I crossed my arms and rubbed my elbows, overwhelmed. Part of me didn't want to look at her or the guy resuscitating her. It seemed too intimate, too intense. I crab-crawled over to Kristi's phone and selfie stick, which were a few feet away. She'd definitely want her phone when she felt better.

The thing was still broadcasting, a steady stream of comments scrolling away.

R U OK?

What happened? I can't see anything?

Did a Squatch get you?

My face filled the screen, and it dawned on me that I was broadcasting myself, double chin and all.

"Dammit," I whispered as I took the phone off the stick, ended the live video, and shoved it in the back pocket of my jeans.

"Paramedics are on their way," shouted one of the women. "They said it would be five or ten minutes, max."

I mumbled a thanks. My gaze darted to Kristi. Her blonde-bombshell beauty was still evident, but in a ruined-doll kind of way. Mud caked her golden hair. Poor thing, she must have suffered a seizure or some medical condition. I couldn't bear to look anymore, so I stood.

A collective gasp from the group on the trail made me look up.

"Margie, over there," one man said in a low voice.

"Maggie, my name's Maggie," I replied, now irritable. "Over where . . . Oh, shit."

Coming out of the water was exactly what I'd feared.

A gator.

Chapter Four

Fortunately for all of us, it wasn't an adult gator. This one was a manageable three feet or so, which meant it was about two or three years old. Fun fact: gators grow about a foot a year until they turn six—then their growth slows, but they aren't done until they're about twenty.

If this was a regular walk, I'd tell the group these details. But I had bigger fish to fry at the moment.

I wasn't even sure if this gator had seen us. The cold-weather creature was stepping out of the water slowly, probably wanting to soak up the sun on the riverbank. Honestly, it was far enough away that we could probably coexist peacefully. I'd kayaked much closer to far larger gators.

Easy-peasy, lemon squeezy. But Dad always said to never let your guard down around gators, and I lived by that rule.

The creature turned its head and I saw its left eyeball practically zoom in on Kristi and the man trying to revive her. It took a hesitant step in our direction.

I let out an exasperated sigh. There would be no peaceful coexistence today. This seemed like a lot to deal with in one afternoon.

The alligator took another step, its foot smacking against the wet riverbank.

My eyes flitted to the group. All of them looked horrified, except for the two who were filming the scene with their phones. They wore expressions of utter delight. Dicks. I then glanced at Black Hat and Kristi. She was the same as before—motionless. Black Hat was shaking, probably seconds away from peeing his pants. His hands were still on Kristi's sternum, but he wasn't pumping anymore.

"What's your name?" I said to him.

He whimpered something in response. I thought he said Joe. Perhaps Joe was strong enough to carry her up the embankment, but I decided we probably shouldn't chance it, from the way he was quaking in his new-looking hiking boots.

"Listen, Joe, it's going to be fine. I've dealt with a lot bigger gators. But if I tell you to run, you run, okay? Your safety's my priority. You run and leave Kristi if need be, okay?" I felt terrible about saying this, but I feared Kristi's situation was above my paygrade.

Joe let out another unintelligible, high-pitched whine.

"Okay, folks," I called out. The gator fixed its eerily hard gaze on me and advanced. "Normally I'd advise to back away slowly and then run like hell, but that's going to be difficult with Kristi here. This is the gator's territory, so I'm going to try to scare it away."

Angling my body in the creature's direction, I raised my arms, stood on the balls of my feet, and tried to make myself look bigger. This often hadn't worked for me in the past, since I was only five-three. And the other times I'd tried it, Dad—a six-foot-four guy with a lumberjack build—had been with me as backup.

"Just be as fierce as you possibly can. Channel all your anger toward it," he'd advised.

I thought about Kristi calling me Midge as she interrupted my walk. I remembered how upset my ex-boyfriend had made me when he chewed with his mouth open. I was reminded that I probably wouldn't be eating a tasty grilled cheese tonight.

When I opened my mouth, I unleashed a banshee scream.

The gator didn't budge. Instead, it took two halting steps—toward me.

"Oh, it's on, dude," I said.

I bent my knees and crouched, circling the thing, trying to channel Dad and my Uncle Bert. They'd taught me how to wrestle a gator.

The thing kept following me, shifting its head. I'd take a step, and it would mirror me with a step of its own. I'd done this dance dozens of times before. I wanted to warn the group to never try this, but I needed to focus.

My yell had failed to deter the determined critter, and it was closing in fast. I had managed to lure it away from Kristi and the guy at least. We were about twenty feet from them now. The gator and I circled one another a few times. I wanted it to twist itself into a half-circle shape.

When it did, I lunged, aiming for the back of its neck.

My heart raced as I reached out, my hands closing around the tough hide. The gator snapped its jaws in my direction, but I managed to evade its bite. Gripping firmly, I used all my strength to clamp my hands around its throat.

Surprisingly, the gator froze. Its body tensed under my grasp, and I could feel the power in its muscles. The group stared in shock as I wrestled with the creature, trying to maintain control. My other hand went to its neck and I lifted it up in the air.

The little guy was about five pounds soaking wet. It was a cutie, and I wished Vera was here to see it.

"Stay back!" I shouted to the onlookers for good measure, my focus solely on the small gator. I never underestimated the stupidity of people around wild animals.

"You don't have to tell me twice," someone from the group muttered, and a few others laughed nervously.

Adrenaline surged through me as I wrestled to keep its jaws away from my body. It thrashed its tail wildly, but only the very tip flicked my body. No biggie.

After a short struggle, the gator seemed to recognize defeat and decided I wasn't worth the effort. It stopped resisting and relaxed under my grip, going limp as a noodle. Slowly, I stepped toward the river, still holding the gator high in the air by the throat, away from my body.

I waded into the water to my knees, then hurled the gator into the river with everything I had. Thank goodness I'd been keeping up with my weightlifting routine since moving home. The gator landed about three feet away with a smack, then swam off with the current, away from us. "Sorry, little guy," I said. "Swim free."

Letting out a big exhale, I turned back to the group, most of whom were sweating and incredulous. Dammit, people were still filming?

"Normally I wouldn't do that. I don't like to throw gators, or any animal. But this one was small, and needed to be redirected." I brushed off my hands. "It'll be fine, and I'm certain it didn't feel any pain. Alligator skin's tough, you know."

Breathing heavily, I checked on Kristi. She still wasn't moving. Black Hat Joe had a mix of awe and relief on his face. He quickly went back to pumping Kristi's chest.

"That was bananas," he grunted.

"Sometimes you've got to show them who's boss." I pressed my hands into my hips.

The group erupted into a mix of applause, murmurs, and nervous chuckles. Ignoring them, I stood over Kristi, sweat covering my face. I wanted nothing more than to wipe the perspiration away, but not after I'd touched the reptile.

The sound of urgent footsteps on the dirt path soon drowned out the sound of the burbling river.

"Kristi? Kristi! Someone said you were—" The woman practically skidded to a stop at the edge of the embankment. "Oh. My. God."

In my confusion, I recognized her, but I didn't know from where. A second later, it hit me: this was the woman I'd seen earlier with Kristi and that Grant guy.

Now she was bent over, gulping in breaths. Shocked, like all of us. Hoo boy. Another sticky situation to deal with.

I reached for my backpack and went to the bottom of the embankment. Someone extended a hand and helped me up the small slope. Another person muttered something about EMTs and groused about how they were taking so long.

I glared at a woman aiming her cell phone camera at Kristi's body. "Have some respect. Please."

She didn't respond and continued to film. Sometimes people just weren't decent, as Dad used to say. Shaking my head, I went over to the woman who'd just arrived.

"Hey," I said softly, putting my hand on her back. "Are you Kristi's friend?"

She unfolded herself. "I'm her assistant."

"Oh, no. I'm so sorry." I chewed on my lip while I watched her tremble like a blade of grass in a gator-infested swamp. She was about my age. "What's your name, anyway? I'm Maggie."

She wiped her nose on the back of her hand. "I'm Alice. Alice Oates."

I squeezed her upper arm, trying to offer a little comfort. "Was Kristi sick? Did she have epilepsy or something? Or was she on some kind of, er, medication? Substance? Booze?"

I immediately regretted asking so many questions, because Alice's red eyes filled with tears. She shook her head. "Kristi was totally healthy. She was a workout fanatic because she wanted to look hot. When she got a BBL she couldn't exercise and she was going out of her mind."

"BBL?" I scrunched up my face. "What's that?"

"Brazilian butt lift."

My mouth contorted into an O. This was information I did not need, ever. "Okay. Oh. Right."

The scene around us remained an unpleasant blend of urgency and shock, disbelief and impatience. I tried to console Alice as she sniffled and wept, but my mind reeled with questions.

The wail of a siren cut through the tension, offering a glimmer of hope amid the chaos. The trail was wide enough for an ambulance, and the vehicle eased down the dirt path. Finally, the EMTs were here, a breath of relief in this surreal nightmare.

But unanswered questions still gnawed at me. What had caused Kristi's sudden collapse?

"Oh my God," whispered Alice, and I went over to console her.

She took a few shaky steps toward the embankment. Weird. She looked like she was going to jump down. What was with her and Kristi?

"You don't want to go down there," I said softly, thinking of the gator and the possibility it might return. "Let's let the paramedics handle it."

Without saying a word, she jumped down and went to Kristi. Joe, who had given up on Kristi and was pacing by the river, whirled around.

"What are you doing?" he yelled, breaking into a quick jog and reaching Alice in seconds.

"I need something," she said, reaching into Kristi's pocket. "She always keeps her phone with her and I need to let everyone know she won't be able to . . . to . . ."

Alice burst into sloppy tears, shaking her head. She

plucked a lip gloss out of the pocket on Kristi's leg, then reached for the other pocket, extracting a small wallet. She went through every pocket.

Kristi's phone. Which was in my back pocket. I opened my mouth to say something, but a feeling in my gut told me not to. Alice was snaking her hand underneath Kristi's body, as if to check her back pockets.

"That's a bad idea," I called down to her. "Leave everything. The police are going to want that as evidence. Especially if she's—" I didn't want to say the word "dead" aloud.

"Maggie's right," Joe said. "I wouldn't move anything. I wouldn't jostle her, either, on the off chance she's, uh . . ."

It was more of a hope at this point than reality. *In case she's still alive.*

Alice ignored us and emptied Kristi's pockets, stuffing everything into her own bag. "This is what she would've wanted me to do," she said, with more than a touch of defiance.

I looked to one of the people in the group and we exchanged a horrified glance. I didn't have time to try to stop Alice, because the EMTs were now scrambling down the embankment, shouting orders at each other.

They told Alice in sharp voices to get back on the trail and away from "the victim." Just hearing that word sent chills racing through my body.

This time, Alice complied. I pulled another paramedic aside and told him about the gator. He thanked me, nodded once, and leaped down the embankment.

As they worked on Kristi, I walked over to Alice,

hoping to shield her from watching the EMTs perform another grueling round of CPR on poor Kristi. Alice glanced down the trail, toward the hotel, as if thinking of taking off. Probably someone should keep her here until the police arrived.

"Hey, it's okay. Take a deep breath. This is a lot to deal with, and I'm really sorry you have to see this. Did Kristi mention feeling unwell before this happened?"

Alice shook her head, her voice cracking. "No, nothing. She was fine, just nervous about this conference and doing her Bigfoot talk. She was super excited for this walk, kept talking about how she'd livestream some alligators."

My thoughts spun into a tangle. Excitement about gators and Bigfoot didn't equate to collapsing by a river. Something didn't add up. But people of all ages had heart attacks and medical issues all the time. Right?

Before I could probe further, the paramedics motioned for everyone to step back. A flurry of activity enveloped Kristi as they hoisted her onto a stretcher, preparing to take her away. I wondered why they would bother if she was already dead, but perhaps this was protocol.

I reached out again to touch Alice's arm. But she recoiled slightly, her gaze on the trail. "Oh, shit, it's the cops," she whispered.

A police cruiser roared up and out jumped a familiar, square-jawed face: Detective Alex Holt. This was a painful reminder that this was the second time I'd seen Alex at the scene of a tragedy.

The first time had turned out to be murder.

Fortunately, this time I wasn't a suspect, and hopefully this wasn't a homicide. I was no less curious about what had happened, though.

And today, I knew exactly what would prod Alex into giving me information about Kristi's death.

My sister.

"I'll be right back," I whispered to Alice, who didn't acknowledge me.

I found refuge under an oak tree a few feet away and whipped out my cell. My phone was blowing up with texts, all from my sister. I scrolled back to read from the beginning.

I just heard that someone collapsed here at the conference. Wait, it wasn't inside here, it was outside. Parking lot, maybe

OMG Maggie where are you?

MAGGIE WHAT IS HECKING GOING ON I'm hearing Kristi collapsed on the trail during your walk R U OK

Someone who bought a historical Loch Ness Monster romance said they are closing the trail because of Kristi. Please tell me you are okay!

Instead of responding with a text, I decided on the nuclear option: a phone call. Vera was notoriously averse to talking on the phone, but this was an emergency if there ever was one.

As I was about to tap into my contacts, I heard an EMT shout, "Nope, nothing. Let's keep her here and wait for the ME."

Oh dear. The medical examiner? I stood up to get a better look. Yikes. It seemed like they weren't even bothering to take Kristi to the hospital.

Because there wasn't anything anyone there could do for her. With shaky hands, I pulled up Vera's number and dialed.

She answered on the first ring. "Maggie! I've been so worried. Where are you?"

Facing the tree and speaking in a low voice so the others wouldn't hear, I explained everything. How Kristi had been acting drunk and obnoxious, how she'd smelled of gin, how she'd collapsed. "Oh. And your boyfriend just showed up."

There was silence on the other end for a few beats. "Why is Henry Cavill there? Does he love Bigfoot? I'm confused."

I rolled my eyes. Sometimes my sister could be dense. "Your real-life boyfriend. Detective Alex Holt."

"He's not my boyfriend. We haven't even been out on a date. I don't know why you keep harping on this."

"Because he walked up to me not that long ago and asked if he should ask you out on a date. Wait, why are we talking about this again? I just saw a woman collapse and maybe die." I added a few choice swear words, which I knew would annoy my sister.

"That is unhinged," Vera whispered. I knew she was serious because she wasn't telling me to watch my language. Even though we were twenty-five, she never approved when I sounded more like a long-haul trucker.

"I didn't even tell you about the gator that I hurled like I was in the Florida Man Olympics. Can you come down here? I really need some moral support." I reduced my voice to a whisper. "Everyone's strange. I need some sanity around me."

She groaned. "I can't. I'm sorry! The booth is super busy. Hang on."

I listened to her ring up a customer.

"I'm back. The sessions have been cancelled, I guess because of Kristi, so everyone's shopping."

"Has anyone made an announcement about her?"

"No, they said the sessions were on hold due to an emergency. I have to go, but I'll come if I can. Oh, hello ma'am, yes, you can buy that special edition of *Alien Love Triangle*. Aren't those sprayed edges gorgeous? That will be thirty dollars . . ."

She hung up.

I heaved a sigh and turned, slumping against the rough bark of the oak tree. The ambulance pulled away, and Alex stood in the middle of the trail, hands on hips, surveying our shell-shocked and ragtag group.

"I'm going to need all of you to give a statement, so you'd better get comfy here," he said gruffly.

"Detective Holt?" I called out, intending to give him Kristi's phone. "I have something to—"

"Andrews, pipe down. I see you over there. I'll get to you." He glared at me before turning his attention to the group, pointing at them. "All of you? Break up. I need to interview each and every one of you, and I don't want you talking amongst yourselves."

The group, who was clustered together, seemed to recoil as a unit, then dispersed to various trees and shady spots.

To them, Alex Holt was probably intimidating because of his muscular frame. I wasn't fooled, though. I'd seen him melt into an awkward puddle of goo simply standing next to my sister, who seemed to have put some sort of spell on the man.

I eased my butt onto the ground with a heavy sigh and leaned my back against the tree. There was no way in hell I was getting my grilled cheese sandwich tonight.

Chapter Five

Minutes, then hours, crept by. This was taking so much longer than I'd anticipated.

It was late afternoon, which meant that the mosquitos were about to descend for a feast of my exposed skin. I paced, waiting to be interviewed by Alex.

My sister never showed up, and further texts to her were met with apologetic answers.

Busy.

I'm so sorry

I should be finished in an hour but people are swarming the table. How did she die?

I tapped the shrug emoji and sent it.

As much as I wanted my sister's emotional support, I couldn't begrudge Vera her book sales. She'd worked so hard to get her shop up and running, and now, to have a convention where people were clamoring for her books? Well, that was incredible.

Still, I was bored and anxious here on the trail while waiting for Alex to interview me. I suspected I was next, since the group had chatted with him one by one. Now only Black Hat Joe remained. And Alice, who was slumped against another tree about twenty feet away.

Her behavior near Kristi's body was still disturbing to me. Why had she needed to empty Kristi's pockets so badly? Had Alice really been looking for Kristi's phone? I had to tell Alex about that, in case she hadn't been searching for something else.

In an attempt to pass the time, I cleaned my hands, face, and arms with some wipes, then reapplied sunscreen. Then checked to see if Jack had texted (he hadn't), whether anyone had posted random crap on the Gator Queen Facebook page (they hadn't), and whether anything had been posted about Kristi on the local newspaper's website (it hadn't). Another five minutes were spent scanning the *Wahoo Sentinel*'s web page because I wanted to see if they had any news about Kristi.

They didn't, but I passed a few entertaining minutes reading a story about a man in Fort Lauderdale who had dressed up as a pirate and attempted to commandeer a crise ship.

I considered texting Jack, but decided to put the phone away because my battery was low. Then my left butt cheek felt an odd tingle. Hunh? Oh, right. I had Kristi's cell. I kept forgetting that.

While reaching behind me and pulling it out of my pocket, I looked around for Alex. He was chatting with a gaggle of paramedics. Kristi's phone buzzed again.

Naturally, I checked it. There was a text from someone named Mac M.

Kristi? Are you okay? I'm hearing some strange things happened on that walk. I'm worried about you. Can you message me back, please?

I tapped on the notification, thinking that perhaps I should contact this person, since they seemed so concerned. Maybe it was her husband, or a relative. Probably the phone was locked, but . . . No. It wasn't. For a conspiracy-minded Bigfoot hunter, Kristi apparently wasn't big on tech security.

My stomach clenched. Should I message this Mac from her phone? Out of sheer curiosity and a little boredom, I scrolled up and scanned the previous texts.

"Holy craparoni," I whispered as I settled back against the tree, absorbed in what I was reading.

I won't be able to give you money this week, Mac had texted. The message was from yesterday. *I had a lot of unexpected expenses with the car this week.*

I don't give a crap about your stupid car, Kristi had texted back. *I need that money now. You promised. Don't be a dick. You're already putting your family over me.*

My eyebrows shot up. Kristi sure seemed demanding of Mac M. What was their relationship?

Please don't be upset, he'd responded. *You know why I'm doing all this.*

All what? I wanted to shout. But I didn't.

If I can't rely on you than what are we doing here? Kristi had said.

You know I adore you. You're my princess. Just let all this drama blow over. Please? I love you.

Go to hell, she'd written back.

"Whoa," I muttered. "A bit harsh."

That was her last text to him, at approximately eight the previous evening.

Mac had texted at least a dozen more times. Most were of the *R U OK?* and *Hey, U mad?* variety, but one sent chills up my spine.

If you don't text or call me there's no telling what I'm going to do. I'm going out of my mind.

I chewed on my bottom lip. Yeesh.

Because I was nosy—and because Alex didn't seem all that interested in chatting yet, I took a quick peek at the rest of Kristi's texts.

Most were recent, from people asking if she was okay, if she knew what had happened on the trail, if she'd heard about someone collapsing. There were several in this vein from Alice. The rest were ads, compliments on her videos, and a warning that her electricity bill was coming due.

I glanced up, checking the bustle of the crime scene. It felt like I was doing something very wrong by snooping into Kristi's phone. But no one was paying any attention to me, so I peeked at her photo gallery. Surely that couldn't hurt.

Instead of pictures of Bigfoot, there were plenty of her butt. In various stages of undress. "Yikes," I whispered. No shame in sexting—many had done it, to some degree—but it made me sad that women felt like they had to show their bodies in order to be noticed.

It was something I knew in my core; that if I went on camera and looked a certain way, I'd be way more popular as a trapper. Vera had even encouraged me to show off more on social media, to be more flirtatious and engaging, but something about it made me feel icky.

As I scrolled through endless photos of Kristi sitting by a pool in a miniscule bikini, a shadow fell over me.

"You always seem to find trouble, don't you?"

I looked up. The object of my earlier lusty thoughts was standing over me, looking like a snack.

And holding one, too. Jack Bianchi, criminology professor and serial killer expert, was toting a bag and a box sporting the logo of my favorite donut shop downtown.

Trying and failing to be dignified and ladylike, I climbed to my feet, shoving Kristi's phone into my back pocket again. "Hey, you. Or does trouble always find me? Hmm?"

He handed me the bag with a grin. "Thought you might need some sustenance."

"Oooh, yesssss." I opened the bag to find my favorite donuts: strawberry-frosted. Three of the delicacies looked at me expectantly from the bottom of the bag. I reached for one, bit into it, and groaned.

As I chewed, I nodded and smiled, then offered Jack the bag.

He shook his head. "I ate one on the way here."

Finally, I swallowed. "Thank you. This is the highlight of my day."

I took another bite, then a thought occurred to me. I washed the donut down with some water from my bottle and wiped my mouth with a napkin I found in the bag. "How did you get down here, anyway? I heard the cops roped off the trail entrance because so many conference attendees wanted to gawk at the crime scene."

Jack raised one dark eyebrow. "I have connections."

I held the donut in midair. "Detective Holt called you?"

"Well, your sister texted me first. Said you were out here alone and that she couldn't come to support you. Then I called Alex and he suggested I head over and give my professional opinion on the case. Thought I'd bring him and his officers some snacks, too."

This was the thing about Jack. He was hot and smart and thoughtful. A truly dangerous combination for a man.

As I savored another bite of the donut, Jack sat on a nearby fallen log. "So, what have you gotten yourself into this time, Maggie?"

I shrugged, attempting nonchalance with a mouthful of pastry and probably some strawberry sugar on my chin. "Just witnessed a Bigfoot hunter collapse and die during a leisurely gator walk. You know, the usual for a Friday afternoon."

He chuckled, a low, rumbling sound that sent a pleasant shiver down my spine. "I should've known better than to expect anything ordinary when it comes to you."

"Hey, it's not like I planned for this to happen. Dead bodies seem to have a knack for finding me."

"Or maybe you have a knack for finding them," Jack said. There was a serious tone in his voice. Because it was true.

"Touché," I conceded, grinning despite the gravity of the situation. "So, Professor, any insights into this mystery?"

He leaned back, crossing his arms. "Tell me what you know, Ms. Andrews."

Before I could retort with something flirty and informative, a familiar gruff voice cut through the air. "Yeah, Maggie, mind filling me in on what happened as well?"

Speak of the devil, and Detective Alex Holt shall appear. I swallowed the last bite of my donut, wiped my chin, then waved my hand toward the box that was in Jack's hands. "Donut?"

Alex looked at the box with a hint of appreciation before focusing back on me. "Hey, man, glad you could make it," he said to Jack. "Thanks for these."

Jack opened the box and Alex took out a plain donut. That summed him up, I felt.

"I thought you were going to ask my sister out," I said while he munched.

He fixed me with a steely glare. "Working my way up to it. I'm shy, you know? And busy. I sure as hell didn't need this today. I'm up to my ass in alligators."

"That's my line," I snorted. "So do y'all want to hear my version of what happened?"

The two men nodded. Alex polished off the donut in two bites and reached for a notebook in the pocket of his khaki pants.

I brushed the crumbs off my fingers, suddenly self-conscious under their scrutiny. "Here's the rundown . . ."

As I recounted the minutes leading up to Kristi's collapse, Jack occasionally interrupted with observations and grave nods of his head. Alex listened intently, his brow furrowing with each detail as he scribbled in his notebook. When I was telling them about how Kristi had been acting odd and smelled like gin, Alex held up a hand.

"Hang on. I can't write that fast."

Slowing down, I explained about Kristi's weird behavior and added one additional thing that had been bothering me.

"Earlier, I saw her with a hot-pink water bottle. The Stanley kind. She didn't have that on her during the walk, but there is a plastic bottle near where her body was. The kind you buy in the store. I think that's hers." I craned my neck in the direction of where Kristi had collapsed. "It's probably still there."

"Interesting, I'll ask the techs to take it as evidence." Alex mused. "Did anyone mention anything unusual happening before she went unconscious?"

"No one said a word, although I'm not sure they would, since everyone seemed to treat her as a goddess. However . . ." I paused for dramatic effect, and both men leaned in a few inches. "I did see Kristi and a guy arguing about a half hour before the walk."

I explained all of the details of that encounter, then held my index finger in the air. "But, wait! There's more. Come a little closer."

Alice was still leaning against a nearby tree. I wasn't sure if she could hear our conversation or not, so I wanted to keep it down. "Something weird happened. Kristi's assistant, Alice, ran up and freaked out.

Understandably. I'm not sure of the time frame, but maybe about twenty minutes after she collapsed?"

"Wait, how did she know where Kristi was?"

I let out a long breath. "I figured it was either because Kristi was livestreaming and her feed got interrupted when she fell, or because one of the other women in the group filmed it all and put it on social media. Also, Vera said word of Kristi's collapse spread like wildfire at the con."

"Filmed all what?" Alex asked, clicking his pen rapid-fire.

"Kristi's death."

The men looked at me in horror.

"Yeah, I know. Tacky."

"Ghoulish," said Jack, obviously disgusted.

"Back to Alice. She insisted on going through Kristi's pockets. She didn't take the plastic water bottle though, and I wasn't about to point it out." I shrugged. "That's all I've got, Detective."

"Goddammit," Alex said. "I'll be right back. Maggie, you're free to go, but don't leave town."

He took the final bite of a donut, chewed three times, and was about to walk off when I stopped him by calling his name. I reached into my back pocket.

"What now?" Alex sighed.

"Here's Kristi's phone. I picked it up while Joe, the guy in the black hat, did CPR. Pay special attention to the texts from Mac."

I handed the cell to Alex. His scowl lines deepened. "You went through her phone? I could arrest you for evidence tampering."

"No, I didn't go through her phone. A text came in and I checked it. That's all. I didn't respond. And I tried to tell you I had the phone when you first got here, but you told me to sit down and shut up." I folded my arms.

He grunted and turned to Jack. "Let's chat later, man. I'd really like your opinion on this." His footsteps were heavy as he made his way toward Alice.

Jack and I looked at each other.

"Sometimes in Miami I'm called to consult on cases, but typically not this early in the game," he said. "Something seems pretty weird about this one."

"What's weird to you?" I took a seat next to him on the log.

He lifted a shoulder into a shrug. "Her age, for one thing. She's what, thirty? Thirty-five? I took a peek at her bio while walking here."

"Probably around that age, yeah."

"Most healthy folks in their thirties don't just keel over."

"True."

We sat in silence for a few seconds.

"What are you doing now?" Jack asked. There was a sexy hint of mischief in his eyes.

"What do you have in mind?" My gaze met his, and I could feel the heat rising in my face. I was hopeful he'd say dinner. A movie. More.

Forgetting about this craptastic day was priority number one.

"Going back into the convention hall and seeing if we can find out more info on Kristi Klaus. I saw the program and apparently there's some events tonight. If they're not cancelled because of this, we should go and poke around. Just for funsies."

Jack had helped me solve the murder of a rival gator trapper not long ago, so it wasn't out of the realm of possibility that he'd want to chat people up about Kristi's murder. Honestly, his plan sounded even better than dinner and a movie, and didn't preclude going to bed together later . . .

"I like how you think, Mr. Bianchi." More than that, though, I marveled at why he thought the way he did. Most hot guys didn't want to spend a Friday night sleuthing "for funsies." While Jack and I had spent some time together over the past couple of months, I didn't know much about him, or what made him tick.

Kinda hard to do when dead bodies kept appearing and interrupting our budding romance.

As we were gathering the empty donut bag and my backpack, we stopped to gape as Alex loudly ordered two officers to guard Alice.

"She's in some deep shit," I whispered. We watched for a few more seconds then faced each other.

"Hey, you mentioned a text from a person named Mac. What did you see? What did it say?"

I paused and looked over. "Nothing gets past you, does it?"

Jack shrugged casually but a small smile played on his lips. It was hot as hell, because understated confidence was sexy.

"If you don't text or call me there's no telling what I'm going to do. That's what Mac wrote. Also some stuff

about money." I recounted exactly what I'd read. "Now that I say it aloud, it seems pretty . . ."

I scrunched up my face.

"Damning?" Jack asked.

I was about to answer in the affirmative when I heard my name. Or rather, my business name.

"Gator Queen!" The name cut through the air. It was Alex's stern voice. I stopped and whirled, only to find everyone within earshot was staring at me.

Alex jogged up to us. "Hey," he said in a low voice. "Sorry to yell. Uh, the reason why I haven't asked your sister out is because my mom's been sick. I've been going back and forth between here and Clearwater, and it's been rough."

My face fell, and so did my earlier, uncharitable feelings about the man. "I'm sorry to hear that. Do you need anything?"

"Yeah, man, I can make you a lasagna or something, so you have food," Jack added. A guy who was secure enough in his manhood not only to offer to cook, but for another man? Without being all toxic about it? I practically swooned right there.

"Nah, I'm good, bro. I appreciate it. Yeah, Mom's going to be okay. She's pulling through. Heart issues," Alex said, his voice uncharacteristically gentle. "I told your sister that, and she said she understood."

Huh. Vera hadn't mentioned this to me. Sometimes she could be dramatic and a tad self-pitying, so it wasn't a surprise that she'd interpret Alex's actions as different from reality.

"Well, I'm glad your mom's better. Hey, we're headed

to see Vera now. She's inside, selling books at the convention in the vendor hall. I'd ask you to come, but you've got your hands full."

Alex's eyes widened for a second. "She's here? She didn't mention that in our last round of texts."

I shrugged. "My sister can be funny about professional stuff."

"I see. I'll probably run into you later, I suppose. See you around."

Jack and I exchanged raised eyebrows before we set off down the trail. There was more than one mystery brewing, apparently.

Chapter Six

We were a solid thirty feet from the entrance to the hotel when we heard the buzz of gossip. People were talking about Kristi. Openly. Folks were clustered on benches and around trees, chatting to each other, smoking cigarettes, and staring at their phones. As we walked past, we heard snippets of conversation.

"I can't believe Kristi's really gone. She was a rock star."

"The Bigfoot community has lost a legend. I'm glad she died doing what she loved."

"I thought she looked better before her butt implants. Didn't you? Her butt was so big. Too big."

Again, Jack and I locked eyes.

"I didn't think her butt was that big," I muttered.

He shrugged. "They need to talk about something, I guess."

I would've thought people had enough to discuss with her Bigfoot work, but I guessed when you were female, and pretty, your ass implants took precedence over tracking a large, hairy, fake creature. Figured. I wished I knew more about Kristi, and whether she'd have wanted to be remembered for her new butt or her Bigfoot research.

Personally, I'd be horrified if I dropped dead and all people talked about was my body. Then again, I'd be dead, so maybe it wouldn't matter. I was about to explain these thoughts to Jack but we were inside now, headed toward the convention.

The vendor hall was closed, but we were waved through due to my VIP badge by a large security officer, who was repeating an announcement in a loud voice. "The convention hall closes to vendors in an hour. And the meet and greet is cancelled tonight. So is Sunday morning's 5K Fancy Feet Run. The only event still on is the happy hour in the bar."

"Seems pretty serious if they cancelled the fun run," Jack deadpanned, and I let out a little snort-laugh in response.

We found Vera doing inventory of her books. Relief washed over her face when she saw us. She wrapped her arms around me in a quick hug.

"Oh, thank goodness you're here. Are you okay? I was worried there for a while. I'm really sorry I couldn't come out."

"That's okay, you needed to be here. I guess I'm fine. It was pretty weird."

"I'll bet." She studied me with pursed lips. "You get into the weirdest situations, I swear."

"Says the woman selling Bigfoot erotica."

She sighed. "Well, I'm just glad you're okay."

I paused, wondering if she'd be so charitable when I broke it to her that Jack and I were going to poke around. She didn't notice my hesitation, because she burbled on. She did this when she was nervous.

"Few of the real-life historicals are selling, so I'm taking one box of those back to the store. People seem to want anything that has to do with the paranormal. Tomorrow, I'll bring my entire monster romance stock. Can you believe every copy of every Mothman book sold out?"

Jack picked up a box set of a BDSM romance that I'd read months ago. It was so steamy that I couldn't even look at him holding it without thinking X-rated thoughts. I shifted to face my sister instead of thinking about him reading one particular shower scene.

"What's going on with the"—Vera looked around and lowered her voice to a dramatic whisper—"dead woman?"

"She's still dead. Your boyfriend's out there investigating. Your real boyfriend, not Henry Cavill." Come to think of it, Alex and Henry shared some physical characteristics. I preferred my men a little rougher around the edges, a little less . . . beefy.

My sister tucked a lock of blonde hair behind her ear. "Oh. Well that makes sense. That's Alex's job."

"Oh yeah. Also. He said he told you why he hasn't had time to go on a date, and it makes total sense." I leaned against the table. "*You* didn't give me the full picture. I thought he was ghosting you, and I glared at him like he'd done something wrong. Turns out he has a legit excuse. Vera, don't be insecure. The man's obviously captivated with you."

"Whose side are you on here?"

"Yours. Always yours. But cut the man some slack. His mom had a heart attack."

"I know. But I get the feeling he's not interested after all. This always happens to me. A man shows interest and then he ghosts me."

He's not ghosting, I wanted to scream. But Vera was in a hurry to find love and her feelings of insecurity were valid, considering her past relationships. Her biological clock was ticking, whereas mine was permanently frozen. I snuck a glance at Jack, who had opened one of the BDSM books and was frowning as he read.

"What's your plan for the rest of the night?" I said to Vera.

"I'm headed back to the store with these. Want to get dinner after?"

I tugged at my ear and pretended to organize a stack of business cards. "Jack and I are going to hang out, I think."

My sister's face fell. "What are you . . . Oh, hey!" Suddenly her expression was positively sparkling, as if she'd just turned into a vampire in a teen romance novel.

I didn't have to turn around to know why.

"Hi Vera. How are you today? Did you have a good day at the conference?" It was as if Alex had assumed a sexy, Barry White baritone.

Vera giggled and fiddled with the wildflower crown atop her head.

"Wow, you look really pretty—er, nice, today," Alex stammered while shoving his hands in his pockets. It was as if he lost every ounce of bravado and cop attitude around my sister. It was a marvel to witness, and a bit embarrassing because he was so painfully awkward.

This left me no choice but to sidle up to Jack, who was

still perusing the smutty book. I spotted the words "BEG ME" on the page and cleared my throat. He snapped the book shut and looked up.

"Hey, tater tot," he murmured. Normally I'd hate such a nickname, but something about the way he said it made me turn to mush. Funny how that worked.

"Hi. Vera and Detective Loverbro are going to flirt and giggle for a while. Shall we strike out into the great unknown and look for some cryptids or something?"

A grin spread on Jack's face. "Let's do it. I think the happy hour here at the hotel is our best bet."

I told Vera I'd get a ride home with Jack. We waved goodbye to her and Alex, who barely acknowledged us because he was looking at my sister with googly eyes, and walked into the lobby.

"Over there," Jack said, gesturing toward the far end of the room. A makeshift sign read *Sasquatch Sips*, with an arrow pointing toward a heavy-looking wooden door designed like a ship's hatch.

Jack opened the door for me, and I stepped inside. As we entered the bar, our intentions of having a quiet discussion about Kristi's death were promptly thwarted by the shrill sound of microphone feedback.

I stopped in my tracks, clapping my hands over my ears. Jack, who was behind me, stopped abruptly as well. His hands found my waist.

"What the—" he muttered. We both stared straight ahead, beyond the tables and people. I leaned back into Jack's chest as he gently squeezed my hips.

While I'd normally be into him getting handsy, I was

too focused on something else to notice: the four people on stage in Bigfoot suits.

"Holy shit," he whispered in my ear. "These people really are bonkers."

As we were staring at one of the Bigfoot (Bigfeet?) trying to wrangle a guitar and strap around his body and the costume, a hostess bounced up to us.

"Hey there! Welcome to the Ship's Galley. Would you like a booth, a table, or the bar?"

"Bar," Jack said in a commanding tone, then lower, into my ear, "Better view of the entire place."

We slipped into the tall chairs and the bartender came over. "We've got a special on the Thunderbird Tea. It's like a Long Island Iced Tea but with cherry juice."

"Yeah, I'll take that," I said.

"Make it two," Jack added.

Normally I didn't mind being a little dirty and unkempt in public—I was a wildlife trapper, after all—but even I was suddenly feeling a bit self-conscious about my physical appearance after scrambling around in the dirt at the park. I probably smelled like swamp ass. I told Jack I needed to freshen up and toted my backpack to the bathroom. On my way, the band's singer announced they were having technical difficulties and they would play shortly.

Oh, goody. I couldn't wait to hear those tunes.

In the bathroom, I did a quick sink bath. Something I'd learned during my years of handling reptiles was that a solid hygiene kit was a necessity. I always carried wipes, deodorant, and a little rollerball bottle of my favorite perfume, and today I used all three liberally. After I swiped on some lip gloss, I looked in the mirror. Taming my curly hair wasn't happening tonight, so I'd have to go with the boho look.

Still, it was a vast improvement on before, and I didn't have to sit next to Jack smelling like gator (which had the distinct odor of fish, swamp, and sometimes rotting meat—not exactly an olfactory aphrodisiac). I popped a mint in my mouth.

I returned just as the bartender was setting our drinks down. Jack stopped me as I was about to grab the tall glass and hop into the bar seat. Still seated, he gently reached for my forearm and spun me so that I was standing between his legs.

"Maggie, you didn't tell me about the gator. You bad girl." His smirk was so smoldering that I thought the bar might catch on fire.

"What? Oh. The gator? Normally that would be the most exciting thing of the day, but not with the Bigfoot hunter dropping dead. How did you find out?"

He held up his phone then set it on the bar. "It's already trending on social media."

"Oh no," I groaned. "Really?"

He pulled me closer, which made me forget, well, everything. His hand cupped my jaw and little tingles flowed through my body.

"That was incredible, what you did. Tossing that alligator into the river like it was an Olympic sport. Damn. I'm impressed."

My gaze locked onto his. Jack had the most expressive

dark brown eyes, framed with long lashes. Eep. I wanted to know so much more about this man.

"It was nothing," I murmured.

"It was sexy as hell." He leaned in and planted a soft kiss on my mouth. I held onto his arm with one hand and the chair with the other, otherwise I thought I might lose my balance and keel over.

After a few, too-short seconds, I reluctantly broke away. "I don't think I can handle that right now. I'm a little overwhelmed. No offense. I really want to kiss you, but maybe after a meal and a shower and a toothbrush."

He chuckled. "Let's get some food, water, and booze in you. Then we'll see about the shower."

"I like the sound of that."

We didn't bother with a toast, instead taking bracing swigs of our drinks. They came not only with hot-pink straws but bird-shaped swizzle sticks. We ordered nachos, then swiveled our seats to face each other, giant cocktails in hand.

"Tell me again how everything went down on the trail. Don't leave out any details this time." Apparently Jack thought I hadn't told him everything, but instead of being annoyed, I loved that we were here, chatting about what had happened.

While we drank and ate, I went over every detail, from the time I saw Kristi and that Bigfoot guy arguing, to the moment Jack came up the trail.

"It's interesting that you thought she was drunk." He popped a tortilla chip into his mouth.

"She seemed unhinged, honestly. But then again, maybe that's her schtick. She committed to the bit and that's how she acts—or acted—in public." I lifted a shoulder into a shrug.

Jack swallowed and wiped his hands. "One way to find out. Let's hit the Googles."

"Ooh, yeah, good idea."

I flicked on my phone and navigated to one of Kristi's social media channels. "Here we go."

Jack stood so that he was close to my leg. He casually wrapped an arm around me and I fought back a grin. His nearness made me nervous in a good way, and I fumbled for the volume buttons. It wasn't loud in the bar because the band hadn't started playing, and still we strained to hear Kristi on the video, as she traipsed through some forest with an incredulous look.

We watched as Kristi picked her way through a densely wooded area, gesturing excitedly as she spoke. While the video was a little shaky, her voice had the strong resonance of someone who had done community theater, or who had taken public speaking courses.

"Many in the Bigfoot research community believe these beings arrived on Earth thousands of years ago from another planet. I mean, look at them! Over seven feet tall, incredibly strong, able to evade detection. They're practically superheroes! It's totally plausible that they came here to study weaker life forms like humans."

I paused the video and turned toward Jack, who wore a thoughtful expression.

"She thinks that Bigfoot is an alien? Is this a joke?"

He shrugged. "Not the weirdest idea out there."

For the first time, I started to question his sanity. My eyebrows shot up.

He licked his bottom lip, all sensual-like, and smiled. "I've read a lot of conspiracy theories. This doesn't even rate as one of the strangest."

"Okay, then." I tapped the play button.

Kristi gazed up at the tall pines surrounding her. *"And get this: there are reports of UFO sightings in conjunction with Bigfoot encounters. That can't be a coincidence. I think the aliens keep tabs on their creatures, making sure the Squatches are staying safe from humans who might harm them. Why else would it be virtually impossible to capture them on camera? They're beings with higher consciousness."*

"Hoo boy," I whispered. "Maybe they haven't been captured on camera because they don't exist?"

She stepped over a mossy log, continuing her monologue. *"Of course, the government denies the existence of both Bigfoot and aliens. But we know better, don't we, fam? When I capture definitive proof of Sasquatches, I'll reveal the truth of their extraterrestrial origins. I've got some proof that will blow your minds."*

Kristi grinned triumphantly at the camera. *"My ground-breaking research is going to expose the biggest coverup in human history! Now remember to like, follow, and comment, and if you want more, head over to my private subscription site, which is just $19.99 a month . . ."*

The video ended with a closeup of her curvy butt in tight jeans as she sauntered down the trail. I tapped the screen to stop the video.

"Well. That was something. But it does answer our question about whether she acted drunk for her videos prior to today. She was perfectly clear and articulate in this one," I said. "If not totally unhinged. She was rational in her insanity."

We scrolled through a few more videos, all of which showed an excited, yet perfectly composed Kristi. She was a natural talent on camera, I had to give her that. It made me a little envious, honestly. As much as I disliked social media, I knew my trapping business would take off if I could embrace video like she did. I'd probably get more speaking gigs, too.

But that was a thought for another day, because just then the guitarist onstage strummed a loud chord. Jack and I turned our attention away from the phone and toward the stage. This time, however, the musicians were clad in furry, brown Bigfoot costumes only from the waist down.

"I guess they discovered it was difficult to cosplay cryptids and play instruments," Jack murmured in my ear, sending a wave of pleasurable tingles through my body.

The lead singer, a middle-aged guy with sandy hair and a chubby face, tapped the mic.

"Good evening, Squatchers! We're the Mysterious Beats Society. Thanks for bearing with us during our wardrobe malfunction. Since we're coming on a little late, we wanted to play our first song and get right to the main attraction: the dance-off! Now, I know it might be a little strange to hold the dance-off, considering what happened today."

A few people clapped, and a couple of others hooted. The singer continued.

"I knew Kristi Klaus. Not well, but well enough. She was a great gal, and I know she'd want us to party in her memory. Kristi never missed a conference party." The man shook his head. "May she rest in peace after she died doing what she loved. Let's dance in her memory. One, two, THREE!"

The band launched into a song that sounded like the kind of music my grandpa used to like: he'd called it swamp rock, but I knew it as southern rock with a touch of country twang. You know, Lynyrd Skynyrd, the Charlie Daniels Band, the Allman Brothers.

By now, several more people had come into the bar, and many of them whooped and hollered at the first few bars of the song. I hadn't noticed how packed the place had gotten, probably because I'd been too busy enjoying the feeling of Jack's arm around me. And checking out Kristi's videos, of course.

Jack grabbed my hand. "C'mon."

"What?" I looked at him with wide eyes.

"Let's dance."

"You don't think it's inappropriate because of Kristi?"

He shrugged. "No one else seems bothered. I mean, it's sad what happened to her, but the Bigfoot hunting goes on. People do die of natural causes. You didn't know her. Besides, you'll never regret entering a dance contest. And clearly"—he turned to the dance floor that was filling with people, then back to me—"everyone's dancing in her memory."

Although I highly suspected that some people did indeed regret entering dance contests, I allowed him to pull me onto the floor. We were one of at least a dozen couples, and somehow I wasn't the only one who looked like she'd just been hiking in the woods.

Apparently, this was just a warmup, because halfway through the song, the band quieted and the singer made an announcement.

He explained that a judge—someone named Dr. Jess Daws—would tap dancers on the shoulder if they were moving to the next round, Jack and I awkwardly stood facing each other.

"It's probably a bad time to tell you I can't dance," I said.

"It's okay. I've got you. Took years of salsa lessons in Miami."

Gah. We were seriously competing? I tamped down my panic as the first beats of a new song soared through the air.

Then I doubled over with laughter. "Footloose," by Kenny Loggins? How weirdly wonderful. Any guilt I had about partying after Kristi had shuffled off this mortal coil was dissipating. This was a crowd that not only embraced the unknown, but thumbed their noses at death itself.

Cool, I guess.

As the infectious rhythm of the old '80s tune filled the air, Jack and I launched into our respective dance moves. Jack's Miami salsa skills clashed hilariously with my awkward, robotic shimmying.

Yet, instead of feeling self-conscious, I embraced the

absurdity of the moment. I rotated my hips. He did a little disco move straight out of *Saturday Night Fever*. I mimicked him. He took me in his arms and spun me around. Somehow, disco-ball sparkly lights rained down on the dance floor just as we were hitting our stride.

It was like a music video. Or a montage in a comedy.

With Jack leading the way, we attempted an eclectic fusion of salsa steps and wild, manic movements. Laughter bubbled up as our steps became more of a comedic spectacle than a display of skill. The crowd, entertained by our ridiculousness, cheered and clapped.

In the midst of this chaos, I caught glimpses of other couples engaging in equally quirky dance moves. A woman who I assumed was the judge observed everyone with a grin. It was an oddly sweet moment, especially after so much awfulness. Maybe this was exactly what I needed.

As the song reached its climax, Jack twirled me in a salsa-inspired move that ended in a playful dip. The crowd erupted in cheers, and the judge—an older woman—tapped both our shoulders, signaling that we were moving to the next round.

The song ended and I fanned my face. The temperature had ratcheted up in the bar by at least ten degrees, and not only because of Jack's presence. I think the AC was a little spotty. The lead singer announced they'd play a couple more tunes, then round two would start.

"Let's get another drink, then dance more," I yelled to Jack over the din.

Chapter Seven

Another drink and five songs later, Jack and I were breathless and one of three couples left in the contest. Our unique dance style had morphed into an unspoken, shared competitiveness.

"We're in it to win it," I hollered at one point, pumping my fist in the air.

The band's guitarist let it rip, launching into a cover of Poison's "Talk Dirty to Me." I knew the song because my dad and Uncle Bert had been big '80s rock lovers. I'd always thought it embarrassing when growing up, but now I was grateful to know every riff and beat.

I could play air guitar, dance, and sing along. Probably I looked sillier than a flamingo in a snowstorm, but I didn't give a crap. Jack and I shout-sang the lyrics to each other, and at one point, we were visibly, gloriously, dirty dancing.

Jack could really move his . . . pelvis. This was information I was happy to possess. I couldn't stop grinning. Or shaking my boobs. Thank God Vera wasn't here, because she'd have been scandalized. I had always been the wilder twin, the one who didn't care how she looked—or what people were saying.

Plus, it felt good to move and let go of all that tension

in my shoulders from the horrible hours on the trail with Kristi and then slumped against a tree.

As the final chords of the song wailed, the judge came over to us.

"Second place," she cried.

Jack held my hand in the air like a prizefighter. First place went to an older couple who were both in blue Mothman costumes—matching tight Lycra leotards, but with wings—and who seemed to know how to actually dance. I'd spotted them waltzing like they were at a Victorian ball.

The band paused to hand out Bigfoot shot glasses to the third-place winners and T-shirts with the conference logo on the front to us. The winners got their drinks and meals comped for the rest of the con, which seemed like a pretty sweet prize to me, considering drinks were nearly fifteen bucks apiece.

By now, I was exhausted. "Let's call it a night," I told Jack once we were back at our bar seats.

He agreed and paid the tab, and as we were about to walk out, I tugged on his sleeve. "I'd better use the facilities before we go."

"Good idea."

We trooped through the crowded dance floor and down the long, dark hallway to the restrooms. There was a line for the men's room, but I went right into the ladies'. When I was done, I waited outside in the dark hallway for Jack.

As I stood against the wall checking my phone, I spotted Dr. Daws, the judge, coming down the hall. She was an efficient-looking woman and unlike a segment of the Bigfoot crowd, she was dressed like a regular person and not in a costume. She wore wide-leg jeans and a classy, nautical striped light sweater. Tan loafers completed the ensemble, and to me, she looked like someone's well-put together mom, or even grandma, with the loose, graying bun at the nape of her neck.

"You were wonderful on the dance floor," she gushed.

"Thanks. I can't say I've ever boogied with Bigfoot, or Mothman, before." We shared a laugh and she pushed open the door to the ladies' room.

I was about to text Vera when I heard a female voice echo in the small hallway.

"I'm not shocked at all. Kristi was . . . problematic."

Frowning, I looked around for the source. Ah. There was a vent about a foot above my head that went right into the women's bathroom. I could hear every word Dr. Daws was saying. From the pauses and *mmm-hmm*s, she was clearly chatting on the phone.

"I couldn't stand the woman, but—"

The men's room door swung open to reveal Jack. I reached for him.

"What's up, buttercup? You ready to hit the road?"

I put my finger to my mouth and pulled him toward my body. "Listen," I hissed in his ear while wrapping my arms around him.

Of course, I told myself that this was all for eavesdropping purposes, but as I ran my hands over his muscular back, I wasn't so sure. When I heard the voice again, I gestured to the vent.

"That woman had the craziest ideas. We have enough stigma without aliens." Dr. Daws snorted. "I wouldn't be surprised if someone killed her, though. She pissed off enough people, that's for sure. God knows she tried to sleep with a lot of married men."

Jack pulled back and stared at me. We kept our eyes fused as we strained to listen.

"No, I haven't talked to the police. Why should I?" Her tone had raised an octave. "Whatever. That situation with us yesterday was nothing new. We'd had that fight a dozen times before, at every conference. She was a scammer, pure and simple."

My mouth formed an O. Jack's eyebrow quirked up.

"Listen, I have to get back out there. Ugh. You know how much I hate this stupid hokey cryptid crap, but contractually, I have to do it. I love you. Bye." The sound of the toilet flushing was our cue to flee.

Jack already had my wrist in his and was pulling me down the hall. We half ran, half walked to his car, holding hands all the way.

"Well, that was interesting," he said when he started the car. "We should probably tell Alex about this."

I made a face. "I guess, but that doesn't mean something nefarious happened to Kristi. All it means is that Dr. Daws is a little snarky, and that she didn't like her. My money's still on drugs or plastic surgery gone bad. I've watched those reality shows. A lot can go wrong, you know."

For the entire ride home, we swapped stories about bad plastic surgery that we'd seen on TV or read about on celebrity gossip websites. We continued bantering as we walked inside the home I shared with Vera.

"Yeah, a lot of butt surgeries end up looking like diaper booty," Jack said, as if he were the world's foremost expert on botched butt lifts.

He followed me inside.

"Nothing worse than diaper booty," I said.

We both stopped, because Vera was standing in the middle of the living room, brandishing a knife.

"Vera, what the hell? Give me that." I stepped forward and took the knife out of her hands. "Don't be ridiculous."

"I'm sorry," she cried, sinking onto the sofa and burying her face in her hands. "I thought you were an intruder, and my mind's been working overtime ever since Alex called."

Jack and I plopped down on either side of my sister. Catsy jumped on Jack's lap. She adored him.

"What did Alex say that affected you so much?" Jack asked. I loved how he could go from snarking about botched plastic surgery to being tender with my sister within seconds—and he hadn't batted an eye when he saw her with the weapon. How had he got to be so unflappable?

"He said Kristi Klaus was murdered, and he's worried there's a killer on the loose. He only called to tell me because he wanted to make sure that I'm safe." She paused to sniffle, then folded over, shuddering in a breath. Sometimes my sister could be so dramatic.

My hand instinctively went to her back, rubbing in a soothing circular motion. Like I used to do when we were kids and she was upset. Meanwhile, I stared at Jack over my sister's crumpled body.

"Funny how I was the one who watched Kristi die, but I didn't get a call from the detective."

#

I shut the back door, still feeling the lingering presence of Jack's lips on mine. After a glass of wine and an hour of talking with my sister and debating who could've killed Kristi—and how—I was beat, and I think Jack was too.

As much as I wanted, well, *him*, tonight didn't seem like the best night to consummate our . . . whatever it was we were doing. Friends with benefits, I guess.

"We'll pick up where we left off another night," he'd murmured against my lips.

Feeling the weight of exhaustion in my bones, I shuffled back to the living room so I could polish off the rest of my second glass of wine. Vera was on the sofa, petting Catsy, who was thrilled she'd gotten so much attention tonight.

"What a day," she declared.

"Right?" I took a sip, finishing half of what was in my glass. "I'm beat."

"Hey, before you go to bed, I'd like to tell you something."

I slapped my forehead. "Oh, crap, I forgot you said you wanted to talk. I'm sorry. I forgot all about it because of everything."

She waved her hand in the air, which caused Catsy to lazily bat at her arm. "You little stinker." Vera nuzzled the top of her head.

"So, what's up?" I asked.

Vera straightened and took a deep breath. "Maggie, this is really difficult for me to tell you, but, well . . . Gosh. I'm sorry. It's just that . . . you're going to be super angry."

"Vera, spit it out. There's nothing you could do that would make me super angry."

Her mouth twisted back and forth. "This is on the level of me hiding your truck."

"Oh God." I groaned. When we were ten, I'd had a remote-controlled monster truck toy. It made the worst noise, one that sounded like a chainsaw. Uncle Bert had given it to me for Christmas and I loved the thing. Vera hated it, and took it one night and hid it in Dad's shed.

I was bereft until Dad finally found it. That was the only time I'd ever wanted to fight my twin sister.

"What is it?" Now I was fully awake and on guard. I went to take another sip.

"I . . . don't want to trap gators anymore."

Her declaration threw me off so hard that I choked while swallowing. This set off a coughing fit, which made Catsy give me a nasty look. I waved Vera away when she tried to thump on my back.

"Wh-what?" I finally sputtered.

"I'm sorry. You know that I've been eating vegan lately."

"Oh God." I rubbed my forehead. Vera had become a vegetarian a few years back and had been flirting with veganism. Dad had always teased her about it, and while I didn't tease her, I privately thought it was just another one of her fad diets.

Vera was always trying to look thinner, prettier, daintier. The opposite of me. How could two people who had shared a womb be so different?

"Maggie, I'm serious. I don't feel comfortable with trapping animals anymore."

"But we don't kill them."

"I know. But do we hurt them? When we trap? And shouldn't they be in the wild instead of captive at Uncle Bert's sanctuary?"

"You know we don't hurt them. We're among the few trappers who don't. Hey, don't cry." I blew out a breath. Seeing her cry sometimes made me want to cry, and I absolutely didn't need that tonight when I was already half-drunk and overtired.

"I didn't want to disappoint you. I know you came home so you could trap and help me, and you expect me to help you."

Well, yeah, I wanted to say. But as always, I didn't want to hurt my sister's feelings. This had been our pattern throughout our entire life. She was the more fragile twin. The one who'd outwardly had a harder time when our mom died. The one who had vitiligo. The one who needed tenderness.

I was the indestructible twin, the one who could handle anything. Sometimes—like when I was alone in Boston all those years, when she was here with Dad and Uncle Bert and everything familiar—I wasn't sure about my future. Or anything. But I never let on, because I was supposed to be the strong twin.

"It's okay. Don't sweat it. I'll work something out." I paused and raked my bottom lip through my teeth. "Do you think you can help if I get calls in the next couple of weeks? It'll take me that long to find someone else who can be on call. Uncle Bert's probably available, but he's hard to count on because of his business."

She wiped tears from her face with her fingers and nodded. "Of course. And I'll help you find someone. I've already been thinking about it."

My shoulders sagged. How long had she been considering this? Even though it wouldn't have made a difference in my decision to leave Boston and return home to small-town Wahoo, it was information I wish I'd known.

"It's fine," I said, pasting on a smile. I leaned in and gave her a quick hug. "Don't worry about it even for a second. I'll work something out. In the meantime, I'm headed to bed. I'm beat."

"Thanks, Maggie. Love you. I'll take care of your glass." She shot me a small, almost apologetic smile.

"Love you too."

When I stood, Catsy jumped from Vera's lap and followed me into my room. Once we were inside, I shut the door and flopped on the bed. Not having my sister around to help me trap critters was a big blow.

It wasn't just an inconvenience, or a hassle to find someone else to help. It was about Dad's legacy, and how I'd hoped we could both carry it on. For some reason, Vera didn't take that as seriously as I did, and as I drifted off to sleep, I wondered if there was a way I could change her mind.

Chapter Eight

The next morning, the sun rose over the town of Wahoo, casting a warm, golden glow over our cute downtown. For the first few weeks after I'd moved home, I'd wondered if I'd been crazy to leave Boston for my hometown.

Then I'd helped solve a murder, trapped some gators, and had a blast with Vera when the bookstore opened. Wahoo was my place. But now that my sister wasn't going to help me trap gators, things felt off-kilter.

Last night's conversation was still bugging me as I drove into town.

No question, Wahoo was home. It felt right in ways Boston never did. Especially on this warm spring morning. Downtown was a happy, cozy reassurance that, despite the events at the Bigfoot conference yesterday, everything in my world wasn't strange.

I was the first to enter when Hannah the barista unlocked the door of the Crow's Nest, the town's most popular coffee shop.

"You're here extra early." Hannah was my favorite employee here at the café, and always worked the morning shift. I saw the bubbly, dark-haired woman several days a week and it seemed like we were forging a tentative friendship.

Unlike lots of others my age in town, I didn't know Hannah. She was a newcomer from Sarasota, and that was all she'd said about her past. She seemed cool, almost too cool for this town, with a full sleeve of tattoos and a pierced nose. She also wore her hair in a rockabilly beehive, and talked about doing pinup photo shoots.

The small, shy part of me hoped we could be friends, but I didn't want to appear too desperate. Still, chatting with her in the mornings made me feel like I was part of something larger—part of a community that actually cared. That was the true appeal of Wahoo.

Still, making friends as an adult—or whatever I was currently, since I sure as hell didn't feel like an adult— was more difficult than I'd anticipated. Boston had been hard enough, and now that I'd been home a few months, I was realizing that I couldn't count on my old high school friends to be my social circle. They'd long since moved away, or had babies and no time.

Meanwhile, Vera and I were adrift in our respective quarter-life crises.

"It's too damn early, Hannah," I grumbled as I walked in. "I've got a wildlife talk today, and it's going to be a doozy. Give me the full IV drip of caffeine."

Hannah went behind the counter and started grinding beans. "How so? A talk about gators? Why would that be hard? You know your stuff. It sounds pretty cool."

"Yeah, but this is an unusual situation." Since we were the only ones in the café at six in the morning on a

Saturday, I took the time to explain the previous day's events at the convention.

Hannah whistled low as she carefully poured the milk into my cappuccino. "You're famous. Bigfoot-famous."

"I dunno about that."

"I do." She handed me the cup. "I follow a lot of cryptid conspiracy sites. Kristi's death is everywhere, and they're all talking about the woman who was there when she died."

"Who's talking? About what woman?" I was confused and perhaps overtired. While I'd hoped to hook up with Jack last night, I'd been so sleepy that I'd asked for a raincheck—and then proceeded to stay awake for half the night, ruminating about my sister, and also Kristi, while feeling terrible that I'd boogied on the dance floor while cops investigated her murder.

"The cryptid conspiracy crowd. And the woman is you, it sounds like. Kristi was broadcasting when she collapsed, and the commenters online said you acted sketchy."

"What?" I yelped. "I didn't act sketchy. She was dying right there in front of me. How was I supposed to act? I was freaked out. Everybody was."

"Of course you didn't kill her. That's ridiculous. I'm just telling you what I've read." She started to wipe the counter with a cloth. "And some people who were on the walk also livestreamed."

"People think I killed Kristi? But how? Why?"

Hannah shrugged. "Any little detail sets off these conspiracy freaks. They think crossed branches are a sign from a Bigfoot creature that it's marking the trail. I don't buy into the theories, but it's hilarious to read about. It's kind of my guilty-pleasure hobby, to be honest." She chattered on about how the creatures apparently used the crossed-stick symbol as a sign of communication in the woods. "It kind of makes sense, I guess, but then again, are they even real? Who knows?"

I sipped my coffee, feeling a mounting panic lodge in my gut. If the cryptid fans thought I was a suspect, what did that mean for today's conference talk?

Visions of an angry mob of Bigfoot enthusiasts at my session danced through my mind. I began to sweat.

"This has been super helpful, actually. Thanks for all that background," I told Hannah. The bells on the main door jangled, indicating that another customer was here. I ignored it and tested a tiny sip of my coffee. Still too hot.

"Anytime," Hannah said. "I love weird crap like that. I don't necessarily believe in it, but I can't get enough of those unexplained-mystery shows. They seem to have a Bigfoot episode every few months." She grinned. "Hey, give me your number and I'll text you if I see anything more about you, okay?"

"You're awesome. Thanks."

"I'll be right with you," she called out to whoever walked in. She put my number in her phone. We chatted more about Bigfoot and murder while she prepared an espresso. I leaned against the counter as I waited for my coffee.

"Who killed who?"

Hannah and I turned at the sound of the male voice.

It was a familiar-looking guy about my age, looking eager to join our conversation. This was the effect Bigfoot—and murder—had on people.

"Oh, hey Luke," Hannah said casually.

"Hey, Hannah. Wait. Maggie Andrews?" The guy looked at me and smiled. "I heard you were home."

My brain started to kick in. "Whoa. Luke Carrington? Is that you?"

I hadn't seen Luke since high school, but there was no mistaking him now. The years had been more than kind. They'd been downright transformative.

Luke Carrington had been the bad boy who used to lean against his locker at Wahoo High with a shit-eating grin, always surrounded by a questionable crowd that liked to smoke weed. His friend group had been a ragtag bunch of goths, punk rock kids, and misfits.

He hadn't been popular, and nor had he been a bully. He'd always seemed far cooler than me or anyone else in school. Although I'd harbored a small crush on him sophomore year, I'd let those feelings lapse when I found out he'd gone to an exclusive listening party of the band Vampire Weekend.

In one disappointing moment, I'd realized that I, Maggie Andrews—then a small, skinny, awkward girl who loved books and reptiles and didn't know jack about cool music—would never be enough for him.

Ten years later, I hadn't even known he was back in town. Actually, I'd forgotten about his existence. A few years ago, Dad—who always kept me up to speed on the Wahoo gossip when he was alive—had told me that Luke was going to school somewhere in the Midwest. Missouri, possibly.

He now stood before me looking as if he'd stepped out of an Instagram street fashion account.

"I heard what happened at the Bigfoot conference. You were there when she died?" he asked, his unsettlingly pretty green eyes shimmering.

"I was." I briefly explained why I was at the conference in the first place.

"Wow. Now I have two things to interview you about."

"I'm sorry, what?" I shook my head, confused.

Hannah slid a coffee toward him. Luke was clearly a regular here. Why hadn't I run into him since coming home? Probably because I never got up this early.

He reached for the cup. "Oh, I guess you didn't know? I recently got a job at the *Wahoo Sentinel* as their general assignment reporter. It's my first job after grad school. I've been assigned to do a story on your bookstore on Monday. And I'm working the crime beat this weekend, so I'm also looking into the Bigfoot murder. That's the life of a small-town reporter. I love this stuff. I wrote the story in the paper today about Kristi Klaus. You should check it out. Here."

He thrust a folded copy of the *Sentinel* into my free hand. I stood with my mouth open for a second longer than was polite. "Oh. Wow. Well, then."

"Want to chat today? I have my notebook with me. We could do an interview now, right here." He reached in the back pocket of his olive-hued skinny jeans, which somehow looked good on him. Usually, dudes in skinny jeans looked terrible. He gestured to a nearby table.

I licked my lips. "This really isn't the best time. I've got things to do. Many things. Gator business."

"Oh, that's right, you took over your dad's trapping operation. You and your sister are going to make the best profile. Gator trapper and romance bookseller. That's so cool." He looked at me intently, rapt, as if I were the only person on the planet. "I always knew you'd do something interesting in life. Kick-ass."

It was way too early for this kind of attention or enthusiasm. "Let's try to catch up later, okay?"

Both he and Hannah seemed a little bewildered when I hastily said goodbye and practically ran out of the coffee shop. I very much did *not* want to do an interview right now. Not only did I not have time, but I wasn't in the proper headspace. When I was tired or overwhelmed, I tended to laugh nervously and blurt out things probably better left unsaid.

I also suspected that Alex and the rest of the Wahoo Police wouldn't want me spilling the beans about murder details to a reporter.

While dredging up memories of high school and Luke—like the time he'd hijacked the morning announcements to read a monologue from *V for Vendetta*—I wondered what Vera would think of this news that he'd been assigned to write the profile of the bookstore. Something told me she wouldn't be happy; she'd always thought of Luke as kind of a loser.

In the privacy of my truck, I unfolded the newspaper. Sure enough, there was a big photo of Kristi in better days, beaming for the camera in a tight camo jumpsuit and pith helmet. I read every word of the article, but it didn't contain any new info about her death.

It did give a few personal details that were mildly interesting.

Klaus leaves behind a sister, 42-year-old Jane Robinson. When contacted by the *Sentinel*, Klaus-Robinson said her sister loved the outdoors and had been fascinated by the metaphysical since she was a kid.

"Kristi had a difficult life, and this news is just devastating," she said, her voice breaking with tears, adding that the family would like privacy at this time.

I screwed my eyes shut. That poor woman, talking to the newspaper about her murdered sister. I couldn't fathom what I'd do or how I'd act if something happened to Vera. The very idea of it made my guts quiver with both anger and fear.

With a deep breath, I opened my eyes and set the paper on the passenger seat, with Kristi's photo face-down. It seemed too sad to look over and see her toothpaste-white smile.

I pointed my truck in the opposite direction of our house. This was part of the reason I'd gotten up so early: I wanted to pay a visit to a potential problem that had been lingering like an alligator lurking beneath the surface of a murky swamp.

Okay, so the problem was actually an alligator, only this one wasn't lurking and didn't live in a swamp.

Chubbs, a fifteen-foot, thousand-pound creature, was Live-Laugh-Loving its best life at the Wahoo Country Club and scaring the pants off golfers.

And if that wasn't bad enough, the creature was also a magnet for idiots.

Chubbs spent most of its time in and around a pond on the course's seventh hole. It came out to sun itself often, and that's when the problems began a few months ago. I had been called in to assess whether to remove the gator, but as a licensed state trapper, I couldn't give the okay.

The gator wasn't doing anything but . . . being a gator. It hadn't threatened or menaced anyone. Yet.

But then one golfer had caught the prehistoric monster on video, and the clip went viral. Now people not only flocked to play the course with the "dinosaur gator," but folks were getting closer and closer as they captured selfies with Chubbs. I was worried people would start feeding it, which was about the worst thing you could do with a wild animal.

The country club wanted to avoid a gory scandal and an alligator attack. So the manager had called me—he'd been an acquaintance of my dad's—and now I was monitoring Chubbs's movements. I tried to check on the thing as often as possible, sometimes once a day.

This morning, I parked the truck in the golf course lot of the country club. Even though it was still early for a weekend, a few golfers were getting ready, clustered around golf carts. I turned off my truck and grabbed my cappuccino.

On the way into the pro shop I ran into Amos, the manager. I'd known him for years, since my dad trapped a giant gator here. Chubbs, however, was larger. This was both a source of pride and a sphincter-puckering detail.

Amos, who was holding a clipboard and wearing a harried expression, gave my shoulder a squeeze. "Mornin', Maggie! Feel free to take any one of those golf carts in the last row. No need to stop into the office."

I thanked him and found a cart, making sure my coffee was secure in the cupholder. A little surge of happiness hit me as I whizzed off. While I had no desire to play golf, tooling around in a cart made me irrationally joyful. I'd come to love these visits to Chubbs, if only because I could drive the electric cart around the course.

Secretly, I wondered if I should buy one, but that seemed exceptionally dorky, even for me.

I zipped around for a while, the wheels crunching softly on the asphalt path. This March morning in Florida was a delightful blend of coolness and warmth, as if the seasons couldn't quite make up their minds. The air carried a faint scent of damp earth, mingling with the freshness of freshly cut grass.

I was no fan of man-made landscapes, but this sure beat being in a windowless hotel conference room—which I'd be in all too soon.

I slowed the cart. The tall palm trees that lined the fairways swayed in the breeze, their fronds rustling and soothing my soul. This was a symphony of nature, the soundtrack to my mission to keep tabs on Chubbs. Of course, being here and looking for a gator only made me think of my sister, and how she no longer wanted to share this with me.

It was almost impossible to fathom. Our dad and grandparents had been trappers. Hell, our great-granddad, too. Mom had helped Dad trap. We were fourth-generation Floridians and this flat, swampy land was in our blood. Why was Vera doing this?

The golf course was bathed in a soft, golden light as the early morning sun rose higher in the sky. The dew on the grass sparkled like a thousand tiny diamonds, and the emerald-green fairways stretched out before me, inviting and serene. The distant chatter of golfers was barely audible.

I rolled to a stop, shoving thoughts of my sister out of my mind. My gaze scanned the pond, searching for any sign of the beast. Chubbs was known for being stealthy, but this morning, I hoped to catch a glimpse of it basking in the sun. The water was calm, reflecting the clear blue sky above.

As I drove a few feet toward the water's edge, I noticed the ripple of movement near a cluster of lily pads. My heart quickened with anticipation. Could that be Chubbs? I inched closer, my senses on high alert.

There, to the right of the lilies. Two eyes popped above the surface and aimed their focused, uncanny gaze at me.

"There you are," I whispered. Soon the rest of the creature's body emerged from the water. It was long, near-black and scaly. Heckin' huge—practically gargan-tuan compared to the little gator I'd easily tossed into the river yesterday.

I suspected Chubbs was a male but couldn't be sure. My hands plunged into my bag, looking for my phone. I liked to note when and where I saw Chubbs. So far, it hadn't ventured beyond this pond.

The sound of birds filled the air, a chorus of chirps and tweets from the surrounding trees. I studied Chubbs, and it watched me back. Finally, the gator silently slipped below the surface without a ripple.

That was the thing about gators. Chubbs could be swimming toward me and burst out of the water looking like a prehistoric monster, or it might be gliding along the depths of the pond to search for a tasty fish breakfast.

I hung out there for several long minutes and my mind drifted back to the conference, and to Luke and his article on Kristi. Who would've killed her? She'd seemed annoying and possibly unethical, but were those reasons to off her? I pondered this while the sun warmed my face and I sipped my tasty coffee.

Chubbs didn't appear again. This was a good sign. It was still scared of humans—or at the very least, wary of their motives.

That made two of us.

Chapter Nine

A Wahoo police cruiser was in the driveway when I arrived home. I tried to reassure myself that it was just Alex finally professing his undying love for my sister, and not because of Kristi's death.

Of course, I was wrong.

Vera, Alex, and Jack were all in the kitchen drinking coffee with serious expressions when I strolled in. Catsy was prancing around, weaving her fluffy body around every available ankle.

"Well, hey all y'all. I'm not used to all this commotion so early. What's going on?" I glanced to Vera, who was wearing a cute pale yellow dress that looked more 1950s housewife than Bigfoot-bonking bookseller.

"Coffee?" Jack pointed to the carafe and winked. "Alex brought muffins, too."

"I'm good, thanks." I held up my cup from the Crow's Nest. Crap. As happy as I was to see Jack, I'd wanted a moment with my sister alone to tell her about Luke and Monday's interview.

Alex muttered hello but nothing else, probably because my sister was regaling him with a story.

"So, like I said before Maggie walked in, I was buying some crickets for Harry . . ."

Harry was our rescue iguana. I'd fished him out of a toilet in a condo on the other side of town.

"... and then I saw a pet sleeping bag! I thought about buying it for Catsy. It said it's for dogs, though. Don't you have a dog, Alex?"

Alex smiled as if my sister had handed him a winning lottery ticket. "I do. Ranger. He's a Belgian Malinois. I can't picture him snuggled up in a sleeping bag."

"Imagine Catsy in a sleeping bag. She'd look like a furry burrito."

Alex chuckled way too hard at that. I successfully refrained from rolling my eyes and gestured to him with my coffee cup.

"Something tells me you're not here for a friendly breakfast and storytime." I reached for a muffin. "Thanks for the snacks."

"Sadly, I'm not here for a social call. And you're welcome." Alex snuck a glance at my sister's bare legs and his mind seemed to derail.

I cleared my throat.

"Yes, yes, I wanted to go over the situation with Kristi with the three of you."

"Well, let's go in the parlor and sit for a spell," Vera said. "Please."

Huh? I tilted my head and looked at her like I'd never laid eyes on her before. She'd obviously been watching and reading too many period dramas, because she had mistaken us, and our station in life, for landed gentry. We didn't have a parlor, we had a TV room/living room/critter playground that I thought smelled a little like hay, cinnamon, and Febreze.

I took a seat across from Harry's tank. He was inside his fake log, with only his tail sticking out.

Jack sat next to me, grinning. "Sleep well?"

I shrugged, wanting to say something flirtatious. But Vera was perched on the edge of a chair with her hands folded demurely in her lap, so I didn't utter a word. Her face was tilted up and aimed at Alex, who remained standing. He glanced at Jack and me and his expression appeared pinched. Annoyed, even.

He turned to Vera and his face instantly softened. It was as if a piece of granite suddenly became a cuddly and welcoming blanket. My sister was delusional if she didn't think this man was in love with her.

Delulu, as the kids would say.

"Well, folks, I have some news and it's not great. There's definitely a killer on the loose, and we need to be cautious. Of course, I suspect this is an isolated incident, but we can't be too careful. I have several suspects but nothing concrete. Yet." He puffed out his chest, probably trying to play the protective alpha male for Vera. She loved that crap. "The circumstances of her death are extremely suspicious, and there are many unanswered questions that need to be addressed."

As he spoke, he glanced at Vera, his eyes showing a hint of concern.

I leaned forward, suddenly more alert. Was it time to put on my detective hat? It sure seemed so.

Vera nodded, her expression grave. "Alex, please, tell us everything you can. We deserve to understand what happened to Kristi, especially if we might be unsafe. Are we?"

I checked my watch. Vera was being dramatic. She also needed to leave in a half hour if she wanted to be there when the convention hall doors opened to vendors. The fact that she was already running late wasn't a shock, since she was late for everything.

But was she really thinking about not attending the rest of the conference because of one murder? Probably it was that Mac guy. That's where I'd start if I were Alex.

"Is it okay to attend the conference today?" Vera asked.

Alex puffed up even more at Vera's question.

This time I rolled my eyes. "Really, Vera? There are hundreds of people at the conference. Half are armed and the other half have been waiting to brawl with Bigfoot for years. It's probably the safest place in town this weekend."

"That unhinged element is exactly what worries me." She looked up at Alex with big doe eyes. He nodded gravely.

"I'd never tell you not to attend the conference. But I want you to be careful." He was addressing only Vera, then shifted his body to me. "And I don't want you poking around."

I gestured with my half-eaten muffin. "Me? Poke around? If this is a cut-and-dried murder, then I have no need to poke around. Unless you need help, of course."

Alex pinched the bridge of his nose. I took a bite of my muffin. Yum. Blueberry.

"Because it's come to my attention that a few of the Bigfoot, er, *fans* believe you might have had something to do with Kristi's death." I opened my mouth to protest, but he held up one finger. "Just so you know, I don't think you had anything to do with her murder. You're innocent of that, at least."

"Oh. Pfft. Well, thanks. Who did kill her, though?"

"If I knew that, I'd be at the county jail right now instead of in your living room." He cast a glance at Vera and smiled. "But of course, I always enjoy visiting with you ladies. And Jack, of course."

"Thanks, bro," Jack said.

"You're welcome in our home anytime," Vera said, blushing. "*Mi casa es su casa.*"

"Do you speak Spanish?" Alex asked, and Vera mentioned her three years of high school classes.

Jack, meanwhile, was cuddling with Catsy and snickering.

I wanted to get this show on the road. "Let's focus. How did she die? Do you know that? Surely some enterprising reporter from the local paper is already asking these questions," I said, thinking of Luke. "I ran into a journalist from the *Sentinel* this morning at the Crow's Nest."

A muscle bunched in Alex's jaw. "We do know that, and yes, we have told the local media the briefest of details."

Funny how Luke didn't mention that. Probably because he was subtly pumping me for information, hoping I'd reveal some crucial detail.

"Okay, well, come on." I waved my hand in a circular motion. "Spill."

"We found traces of tetrahydrozoline in a water bottle we found at the crime scene."

I perked up. "The one I told you about?"

Alex nodded. "It was discovered a foot or so away from Ms. Klaus's body. Several witnesses who were on the walk with y'all saw her carrying that bottle. We did a rush job on analyzing the water left in that bottle and that's when we found the tetrahydrozoline."

"Oh. Ohhh yeah. Yeppers." Jack shook his head and chuckled darkly. Catsy took this as evidence of his affection for her, because she mashed her face against his chin, rubbing herself on his dark and sexy stubble. Oddly, I'd done the same thing once or twice. "That'll do it."

"What? What is it?" Vera whipped her head between the two men.

"Tetra, tet . . . what?" I stammered.

"Visine," Jack piped up.

Alex shifted his weight from foot to foot, and I saw his gaze slide momentarily to Harry's reptile enclosure. "Exactly. It's the ingredient in eye drops that works to temporarily constrict blood vessels in the eye."

"So she drank eye drops? Why?" I wondered if this was a social-media-driven weight loss trend or something equally ridiculous. "Who would do that?"

"I doubt if she drank them willingly. But if a person consumes enough of the drops, it will kill them," Jack said.

"Really?" Vera and I yelped at the same time. Sometimes we did that, as twins, and no one was more embarrassed than me, because my voice always went up an octave to match my sister's.

"People are under the misconception that eye drops will give someone diarrhea, or just make them sick. But that's not the case," Jack continued. "There have been several high-profile cases involving eye drops, many of them fatal. A few ended in homicide convictions."

As Jack told us about various arrests—a woman in South Carolina who killed her husband, a man in North Carolina who killed his wife, a Wisconsin woman who offed a friend—my brain began to work overtime.

"How much does it take to kill someone? A couple of drops? Did someone poison her over time with small amounts of drops, or was it one big dose, just once? How much poison did they use? Who sold or gave her the bottle? What about the rest of the evidence? Did that reveal anything? A lot of people had a problem with her. And what about Alice, her assistant? She seemed sketchy—"

"Maggie." Alex shook his head. "I'm not doing this with you."

"Doing what? Solving a crime? Brainstorming suspects and clues? Using the power of this brilliant collective hive mind to figure this out so we can keep the people of Wahoo safe?"

"Until you go through the police academy, spend a few years on patrol, and then get promoted to detective, I'm not going to entertain this foolishness. Now. I have actual police work to do. I'll be at the convention today, so don't hesitate to text or call me, Vera, if you need anything. And I mean anything."

Vera smiled sweetly at him, then a few seconds later, turned to me with a simpering expression. Like she used to when we were kids and Dad told me I couldn't have a second dessert. I narrowed my eyes and wrinkled my nose at her.

In her infinite feline wisdom, Catsy took this moment to climb off Jack's lap, step over Vera, and come to me. "Yes, you little fuzz bucket. You know I'm right."

Jack climbed to his feet. "I'll walk you out, bro."

"Thanks, man. I wanted to run one detail by you in private."

The two men swaggered out the door, all broad shoulders and testosterone. I stroked Catsy's back and she revved her purr motor.

"You shouldn't be so mean to Alex. He's just doing his job." Vera's tone was petulant.

"He can do his job without being snarky to me. He treats me like I'm a pest."

"If the shoe fits . . ." She took a sip of her coffee.

I huffed out a breath. "And if the slipper fits, Cinderella, maybe you should be at the ball—er, the convention—instead of here, playing Nancy Drew with me."

Vera placed her mug down with a clink. "Oh, please. If we're assigning roles, you're more like Scooby Doo. I'm more of a Miss Marple, thank you very much."

She giggled. I did, as well. As much as I wanted to bring up the gator trapping, I didn't want to ruin this moment. Sometimes my twin and I vibed so well, I wished someone in Hollywood would give us a sitcom.

"Miss Marple? Vera, you're more like one of those characters in those cozy mysteries who stumbles on the clue by accident." I couldn't help but laugh at my own joke.

She raised an eyebrow, her lips curving into a smirk. "And what does that make you? The town gossip who gets it wrong every time?"

"No, I'm the brilliant detective who sees the obvious that's hiding in plain sight. Like how you've got it bad for Alex."

Vera's cheeks turned a shade pinker. "Hello, Captain Obvious. I merely appreciate his . . . professionalism."

"Professionalism, right. Is that what we're calling it now?" I cackled. "And I appreciate Jack's . . . stubble."

"And his butt."

We both dissolved into laughter, the earlier tension melting away with our sisterly banter. It was moments like this that reminded me why, despite our occasional differences, Vera was more than just my twin. She was my partner in crime-solving, and in life.

I decided to wait to tell her about Luke and the interview. And to convince her to continue to trap gators. Those were the least of our worries today.

Chapter Ten

We went to the convention in two vehicles: Vera in her car, and Jack and me in his Prius. I was silent for a few minutes as we drove.

"You okay?" Jack asked, glancing at me with a furrow in his brow. "You're not your usual talkative self."

I explained first about what Hannah the barista had said about Kristi. Then about Vera and her reluctance to trap critters.

"Hmm. That's a lot for one morning. Do you think you can talk your sister into continuing to help you?"

"I dunno. She's pretty stubborn. Maybe I'll just wait her out and see if she changes her mind."

Jack nodded. "As far as the other stuff, the message boards, it's not unexpected, given the crowd. They like to latch onto obscure details and spin them into stories. I've seen this in communities where serial killers have struck. It's almost as though an entire narrative springs up when a tragedy happens. Then myths begin. It's a way to explain the unexplainable. I have a whole chapter about this in my book. Or am planning to. Haven't written it yet."

I smacked my forehead. "Your book! You didn't have to come with me today. You're sure you don't want to stay home and write? I don't want to keep you from your work." We were now driving through town. "I'm sorry. I don't mean to monopolize your time."

"I will gladly take any excuse not to write. Writers procrastinate. But the main reason I want to come is, I enjoy the company." He was smiling as he spoke. "And I can't resist a shitshow like a murder mystery at a Bigfoot conference."

I bit my lip. The feeling was definitely mutual, on all counts.

The one thing I liked about Jack was that he was usually happy. He didn't seem prone to anger, or brooding, or drama. My ex had exhibited a touch of all three—not enough to be dangerous or difficult, but just a sprinkle; enough to be annoying and tedious.

Jack was like a Labrador retriever: cheerful, eager to please, and full of energetic affection. He was the kind of guy who lit up every room he entered with his easy smile and lively banter. My ex could drag conversations into gloomy places, a real Debbie Downer. He'd once launched into a long, depressing monologue about climate change—during my birthday dinner. I was as concerned as anyone about the environment, but I'd felt that I could take a break from worrying at least for a couple of hours while enjoying my favorite pasta.

But Jack, he magically lifted the mood wherever he went. His vibe was light and breezy, like a sunny day at the beach. Cool and effortless. Being around him simply felt good. That he was gorgeous was merely the delicious icing on an already tasty cake.

If I were looking for a long-term relationship, which I wasn't, it would be with a man like him.

"Crap, I never asked you. How did the trip to Miami go? I got so caught up in the murder, and then the dance contest and all this Bigfoot BS."

"Last night was weird, wasn't it? Did I dream that we came in second in a Bigfoot dance contest?" He chuckled and stroked the dark stubble that dusted his chin.

"'Weird' is an understatement. You didn't dream it; we have the T-shirts to prove it. So, what did your publisher say?"

He flipped on the blinker to turn onto the hotel road. "They're happy with what I've written so far. But I'm still not even halfway done. The good news is, they're giving me an extension of three months for the final deadline, and more if I need it."

"Oh. That sounds like an excellent development. It is, right?"

"Extra time is always good when working on a book. I should probably ask your sister, and you, if I can stay another few months. I'm really enjoying the vibe here in Wahoo, honestly. When I was in Miami it seemed so busy. Sensory overload, you know? I tried to get some writing done and I couldn't focus. The solitude here is soothing for my soul."

He slid a glance toward me and winked. My face flared with heat. "I'm sure it won't be a problem if you stay longer. She . . . well, *we* both love having you here."

By now we were pulling into the parking lot of the convention hotel. "I'll tell you more about the trip later.

Some interesting offers came up and I'd like your opinion. No hurry, though."

"Sounds good." I paused because we'd stopped to let a person wearing a Bigfoot mask and wig cross in front of the car. Since the guy had on normal jeans and a T-shirt, the ensemble made him look merely unshaven and disheveled.

I pointed. "That's how I feel sometimes when I wake up."

Jack cracked up.

We parked and walked in, the air conditioning washing over us. Three steps into the hotel, a man stopped us.

"You're Maggie Andrews, right? The Gator Queen girl?"

Ugh, I hated being called a girl.

"I am." I couldn't help but notice how Jack subtly shifted toward me in a protective way.

The man gaped at me, falling over his words as though he couldn't get them out fast enough. "You led the nature walk yesterday? The one at the nearby park?"

"That's me." I was a little confused about why the man seemed so insistent. And his wild blue eyes seemed to be popping out of his head.

"I run a YouTube channel covering the cryptid world. It's called Monster Hunter Media." He handed me a card that had the now-ubiquitous symbol of a Bigfoot silhouette.

"Okay." I didn't like where this was headed.

"I'd love to interview you about Kristi Klaus's death. I have a whole video setup in my hotel room upstairs."

My brows knit together. Going to a hotel room with a random monster hunter? No, thanks. "Interview me?

About Kristi? Why? I only met her shortly before she died. I don't think I can help you much. I'm so sorry."

"Exactly!" He nodded enthusiastically. "An outsider's perspective. And you did find the body, after all."

I shook my head, still not following his logic. "By pure coincidence. She collapsed in front of me. I'd known her for all of fifteen minutes."

Fifteen annoying minutes, I wanted to say.

"Still, very interesting timing." He stroked his chin thoughtfully. "Some say convenient, even."

I stared at him blankly. "I'm sorry, convenient how?"

"Well, with Kristi out of the picture, that leaves room for someone else to take the spotlight." He raised his eyebrows pointedly. "She was Bigfoot royalty, and a lot of people want to take her place. Even people from outside of the community. People like you, who are trying to make a name for themselves."

Bigfoot royalty? Was that even a thing? Was this man on drugs? Comprehension dawned slowly. *Ohh.* He thought I had something to gain from her death. That I wanted attention so badly I would . . .

My mouth fell open in shock. "Wait, are you accusing me of killing her?"

"Hey now, I never said that!" He held up his hands. "But you have to admit, it's quite a coincidence. She goes on your walk, and she dies."

I felt my insides vibrate, which they did whenever anger bubbled up. "I can't believe anyone would think I was involved!"

I glared at the man. This line of questioning was

absolutely absurd. And I refused to stand here a second longer listening to it.

I whirled on my heel. "Come on, Jack. We've got things to do."

We marched toward the vendor hall, and I pulled Jack into an alcove where a water cooler was bolted to a wall. "Can you believe that crap?"

"Sadly, I can. The fact that her final moments were captured live means a lot of people will be morbidly fascinated, and that's a sure path to going viral. And knowing the little I do about how conspiracies form and spread . . ." He grimaced and ran a hand through his hair.

"Are the people here going to assume I had something to do with her murder?"

"I'd say it's almost a certainty. Some of them at least."

Sighing, I slumped against the wall. "I don't want to cancel my talk. I really need the money. They're paying so well. As it is, I'm not even sure they're going to pay me, considering Kristi died during the walk."

Jack frowned. "If the conference hasn't cancelled because of Kristi's death, you shouldn't cancel, either. When's your talk today?"

"Two hours from now."

"I'll be with you. I'm a good bodyguard." He pretended to flex his muscles, probably to cheer me up. The sight of his tanned bicep did boost my spirits. "Seriously. If you don't want to talk to someone, I'll keep them away from you."

"My protector." I grinned. "I like that. What should we do in the meantime?"

He raised one eyebrow. "Maybe ask around about Kristi? See what people know?"

"I'd love to, but . . ."

"But what?"

"Your best bro Alex Holt warned me not to snoop around."

"My best bro Alex Holt also asked for my opinion on the case." His expression turned serious.

"Do you have any opinions yet?"

Jack shook his head.

"It doesn't seem like Alex has many leads. Did he say anything to you this morning?"

Jack paused, and I wondered if he was weighing up whether to disclose what Alex had told him. "He's looking into Kristi's past. That's all he'd say."

"Fair enough."

"It's important we tread carefully if we're going to snoop around. People are already spinning wild theories. We wouldn't want to add fuel to the fire. I also don't want to piss off Alex. He's a good guy."

"You're right." I had to begrudgingly agree that Alex was a decent person. He was also a possible boyfriend for my sister, and given her track record with men, their relationship was probably something I should encourage. Unlike her previous guy, Alex didn't seem destined for a life behind bars. A plus in my book.

"Standing back isn't in my nature. Especially not when there are accusations flying around."

Jack nodded, his demeanor softening. "I know. And that's one of the things I like about you, Maggie. You're not just brave when it comes to wrestling gators. You face life head-on."

I couldn't help but blush at his words. "Thanks. That means a lot, coming from you."

He stepped closer, his voice lowering to a more intimate tone. "You know, if we're going to be snooping around, we might have to blend in a bit more. Maybe act like a couple so we don't draw too much attention."

I couldn't tell if he was joking or not, and didn't much care. He brushed a lock of my hair behind my ear. My entire body lit up like a night sky with fireworks.

"At least we're used to fake-dating."

He laughed and trailed the backs of his fingers down my cheek. "We did pretty good last time, didn't we?"

When a rival gator trapper had been murdered and Vera's old boyfriend was possibly involved, Jack and I had pretended to date in order to more convincingly ferret out information. That had led to the arrest of one murder suspect and several hot makeout sessions between Jack and me.

I smirked, intrigued by the idea. "Pretend to be a couple again? Do you think you can handle being my arm candy?"

Jack chuckled, the sound warm and reassuring. "I think I can manage. But you should know, I'm not just any arm candy. I come with perks. Like ensuring no conspiracy theorist gets too close, and making sure you always have an alibi."

I laughed, the tension easing from my shoulders. "Sounds like you're a full-service bodyguard. That's a popular romance trope, too. Bodyguards. I'm impressed."

"Just one of my many talents."

My face felt like it was melting off; I was blushing so hard thinking about his other talents.

He stroked my cheek with his thumb. "Should we start our undercover operation? Maybe mingle with the convention-goers and see what we can find out?"

"Lead the way, baby," I said in a joking tone. "But remember, if we're going to be undercover, we need to stick close. Hold hands. You know, for authenticity's sake."

"Of course, for authenticity. Wouldn't want to blow our cover."

He leaned in and brushed his lips over mine. "A kiss for good luck," he murmured.

"Here's to investigating another murder, together," I whispered, then went in for another kiss.

Chapter Eleven

My lips were still tingling from that kiss a few minutes later when we walked onto the convention floor.

Jack was alarmingly distracting, and I had to get my mind straight and focus on the tasks at hand: investigating a murder, and talking about alligators.

I took quick stock of the cavernous room. Somehow it seemed less weird than yesterday, or maybe I was getting used to things like plaster foot casts and grainy, blown-up, framed photos of creatures in the forest.

Perhaps because it was still early, there weren't the crowds of the day before.

Or maybe folks had been scared off because of the murder.

"Let's stop in and see Vera first. Make sure she's settled." I grabbed Jack's hand and we walked toward her table.

She and Diego were stacking books as they shouted to each other from either end of the booth.

"This is all the orc erotica we have?" Vera stuck out her bottom lip.

"It's been flying off the shelves. We should've ordered three times as much for this event." Diego readjusted the rainbow headband that kept his curly brown locks out of his face. "Oh, hey, look who's here. The lovebirds."

"Whatever." I let go of Jack's hand and went to my sister. "Everything okay?"

"Other than the fact that I don't have enough monster porn to satisfy the customers here." She made what I called her "sour duck face."

"I mean about the murder. Kristi. Have you heard anything?" I glanced over at Jack, who was yukking it up with Diego.

My sister ripped open a box with her bare hands. "I have bigger and better things to do than investigate a homicide. And I think you do, too. When's your talk? Shouldn't you be preparing for that? Don't be a busybody. Let Alex and the police do their job."

I rolled my eyes so hard I bowled a strike. "I'm just curious. Jeez. No need to be so touchy."

"Listen," she hissed.

I reared back, surprised at the edge in my sister's normally cute, soft voice. Between this and the trapping situation, I wasn't sure what was up with her.

"Alex and I are supposed to go out tonight. I don't want you spoiling it."

"Pfft. What do you mean?" I flipped through a historical romance about an alien and a widowed countess.

"Are you listening to me? I don't want you getting into trouble, or snooping around, or causing a ruckus."

"A ruckus?" I burst out laughing. "Why would I cause a ruckus?"

"Because I know you better than anyone." Vera invaded

my space, wagging her perfectly manicured, Barbie-pink fingernail at me. "You never let things go. And I've heard the whispers around here."

I slammed the book shut. "What whispers? What are you talking about?"

"When I came inside today, two people were talking about how the hike leader who was on the live video with Kristi when she died was possibly her killer. *You* were the only hike leader in her video." Vera put her hands on her hips.

"I didn't kill Kristi." Okay, maybe I said this a little too loud. A few people strolling past stopped and stared. I shifted so my back was to them.

"Of course you didn't. Why would you kill someone you didn't know? That's ridiculous."

"Vera, I wouldn't kill someone I *do* know. Jeez." Sometimes conversations with her went like this. In a circle, in a thick fog, with many twists and turns. It was either hilarious or maddening, and today, in the middle of a Bigfoot conference, it was both.

She snorted in exasperation. "Don't kill anyone. Don't investigate. Just do what you were hired to do and go home."

"But Jack—"

"I don't give a fig about Jack. Tonight's the first night Alex has off, and he promised to take me to Southern Sizzler for dinner."

I lifted my hands and waggled my fingers. "Oooh, Southern Sizzler. Fancy."

"Shut up. I swear to heavens . . ."

Her old-fashioned words made me snicker. "You've really been going hard on the period romance dramas, haven't you? I can always tell, because you talk like a spinster from the Victorian era."

"I swear to *fruitcake* that I will be so mad if you do anything to prevent Alex from having a night off." She went a few steps away, over to her purse.

Now I knew she was serious, because Vera never swore. In her mind, "fruitcake" was as bad as the F-word.

I followed her. "But what if there's an arrest in Kristi's case? I can't help but think you're putting a lot of pressure on the man. And yourself. Things are pretty unpredictable around here. Crime happens, and it won't always happen on your schedule. Think of that when you're fantasizing about an HEA with a detective. Are you prepared to stay home with the kids while he's out dusting for fingerprints at the Wahoo 7-Eleven?"

She lifted her head and shot me a narrow-eyed, pinched-face look. The one she'd done her whole life. I could've ignored it, but being sisters, the only thing I could do was ratchet up the spat and say something that I knew would piss her off.

"You look like a ferret when you do that."

"Shut up," she whispered.

"Fine. I won't tell you something important." We'd now devolved into being ten again. "Something that directly affects you."

She stared at me warily. "Is it about the bookstore?"

I nodded and pretended to study my nails. Unlike

Vera, I never got manicures. My pinky nail was unvarnished and had a smidge of dirt underneath.

"Tell me," she said in a low, threatening squeak.

"I know who the reporter is who's coming Monday."

"Who?"

"Luke Carrington."

Her eyes widened. "From high school? The guy who allegedly dropped acid, climbed the Wahoo water tower, then hung an anarchy flag?"

I nodded. "Turns out he's the new reporter for the *Wahoo Sentinel*. He's been assigned the profile on the bookstore and he's covering Kristi's murder this weekend. Who would've thought, huh? Bad boy Luke turning into a journalist."

Vera's eyebrows shot up, surprise and a hint of nostalgia crossing her features. "Luke Carrington. I remember him. Always in trouble, and now he's reporting on it. That's something."

She straightened her spine and pasted on a smile, probably because Jack and Diego were headed in our direction.

The two guys stopped in front of us.

"Hey!" my sister and I cried in bubbly voices, in tandem.

"That's creepy." Diego shook his head.

"What?" I asked.

"When you two do the twin thing. When you talk at the same time. It's like those little girls in *The Shining*."

"Whatever. We're leaving." I tugged on Jack's arm, then turned to Vera. "Text me if you hear anything, or if Alex stops by or if an arrest is announced. And uh, if Luke comes by, don't give him my number. I don't feel like talking about Kristi for the paper yet."

"Yet? Does that mean you might want to talk to Luke about Kristi at some point?" She scowled. "Remember what I said. No shenanigans, Maggie."

She followed that up by pointing at her eyes with her index and middle fingers. She then pointed her two fingers at me. Our father had done the same thing whenever we left, a half-joking way of saying *I'm watching you.*

I responded with the same gesture, then Jack and I walked off.

"First things first. Where's the coffee? Also, do you have a notebook?" he asked.

"Pfft. Do I have a notebook?" I slapped the strap of my backpack. "I have a notebook, extra pens, a small first-aid kit, a Swiss Army knife, a hunting knife, condoms, and a pack of extra-strength hand wipes."

"Condoms?" The corner of his mouth quirked up.

"You never know."

"Love a woman who comes prepared. Let's get some more caffeine in us."

Once we threaded our way through the maze of tables and found the café area of the convention, we bought giant coffees in Styrofoam cups and settled at a small table in the corner.

While my coffee cooled, I got out my notebook and a stash of pens. I slapped everything on the table. Jack reached for my favorite pen, a rollerball, but I let that slide.

"I asked Diego to poke around a bit," he said.

"Ooh, excellent idea. Although I'm not sure my sister will give him time do anything but shuttle books back and forth from the store." Diego was adept at computers, and hacking. I wasn't sure what all that entailed, and frankly didn't want to know because it was probably illegal.

Which could be helpful in our case, though.

"Hopefully he'll find something. Anyway. Unlike our last investigation," he said, "we're going to try to do things a little more organized this time."

I laughed. The last time Jack and I had tried to solve a murder it had been a chaotic couple of weeks of interviews, research, gossip, and conjecture. In the end, I had been left with the feeling that we'd gotten extremely lucky. Jack apparently felt the same.

"You mean we're not going to be chaos Muppets?"

He shook his head. "In my work life, I don't like chaos. Ever."

I wondered if he had the same sentiment about his personal life. Now didn't seem like the best time to ask, so I opened the notebook and clicked my pen.

"In my line of work, chaos can be deadly," I said. "It can lead to losing a limb to a hungry gator. Should we start out by listing suspects?"

Jack shook his head. "Let's begin with listing what you know about Kristi. While you do that, I'm going to do a cursory search online. One question: do you know if that's her real name?"

I lifted my hands helplessly. "No idea. I'd never heard of her until yesterday."

Jack and I lapsed into a companionable silence, as the

convention hall filled with more Bigfoot aficionados. I wrote down everything I knew, had heard, and suspected about the dead woman, making sure I put an asterisk by the items that I knew were verifiably true.

To my dismay, I didn't know all that much about Kristi. I set my pen down and sipped at my coffee. Jack's face was buried in his phone. This gave me the opportunity to study him without being a creeper.

I replayed the walk in my thoughts and the movie reel in my mind slowed. "Wait. There's something I forgot to tell you. Remember how I said she jumped down the embankment and said, 'watch this'?"

Jack responded with a nod.

"Right before that, she said, 'What is that thing over there?' I don't know what she was referring to."

"You didn't see?"

"Nope. Everything happened so fast."

"Okay, let's write that down. I'll look at her last video in case she happened to film it." He took out a set of earbuds and stuck one in.

After a few minutes, he set his phone on the table and took out the earbud. "No luck. Her last video was pointed directly at her. She seemed out of it, though. Definitely impaired by a substance, or alcohol, or both."

"Crap. I'd like to know what she saw. Maybe it was nothing."

"There's no shortage of videos of her online. I find it interesting that she started her YouTube channel only a few years ago, and yet she's been able to grow it to a million followers."

"That doesn't seem so odd to me. She was hot, blonde, and had great cleavage. I'm guessing from looking at the clientele here at this conference, that most of her fans and viewers were men. She also loved taking sexy photos of herself. Who knows, maybe she had a side hustle, if you know what I mean."

Jack stroke his stubble thoughtfully. "You're probably onto something there. I did notice that most of the comments on her channel were from dudes. A substantial number of them mentioned how she looked, and some made rude comments or asked her out on dates. A few marriage proposals, too."

"Just what every woman wants when she's trying to be taken seriously while hunting Bigfoot."

"Do we know anything about her past? Anything about where she was born, where she lived, where she went to school?"

I shook my head. "We're not off to a great start, are we?"

Jack dismissed me with a wave of his hand. "It's early, and I'm sure we'll find out lots from this crowd. Probably too much. You'll see, by the end of the day we'll know so much about Kristi you'll feel like she's been your friend for years. You'll probably have more sympathy for her than you've felt for anyone in your life, and you'll simultaneously also dislike her."

"Is that what it feels like to investigate serial killers? Or their victims?" I'd never thought much about Jack's line of work, but now that he'd put it in such a personal way, I realized that it had to take its toll.

He nodded, but didn't offer anything more.

"Something tells me you know this from experience," I said.

"Looking into such darkness takes a toll. Talking to victims' families does, too." Jack was uncharacteristically serious. He shook his head, as if trying to clear the heaviness in the air. "What do we know about her activities in the hours before she was killed?"

"Not much. I saw her about half an hour before she joined the walk—that's when she was fighting with that Grant guy. That's all I've gathered."

"That reminds me"—he pointed at the notebook with his pen—"let's write down everyone we think is a suspect at this point."

"Okay, the guy is Grant P. Sanders. GPS," I said aloud as I wrote. "Did I tell you about the Bromies?"

Jack looked up with an expression that said *are you for real?* I plowed on, explaining the T-shirts and the term of endearment that Jack's fans had adopted.

"Okay, back to suspects," I said. "There's also the mysterious Mac M, whose last name we don't know, but we do know that he was threatening her, and talked about money in his text to her on the day she died."

"Very good," Jack said in a low voice that made parts of me heat up.

"There's also Dr. Jess Daws, I suppose."

Jack tilted his head. "Why would you add her to the list?"

"Because it seems like there was no love lost between Dr. Daws and Kristi. It's just a hunch. And from the conversation I overheard while in the hallway, she called

Kristi 'problematic.' Which is probably code for she hated her guts."

Jack stared at me for a beat, and I wondered if he was recalling how tight our bodies had been pressed together in that hallway. Because I sure was.

"Always follow your hunches. Anyone else?"

I pondered this for a minute in silence, sipping my coffee. "Oh! Alice the assistant. She seemed sketchy, going through Christie's pockets on the trail. I think that's it. There are surely more. But I found Alice's behavior at the crime scene weird and erratic."

We chatted about possible other suspects as we finished our coffees. We decided to split up, and canvas the convention floor. I still had an hour and a half before my talk. I figured I'd need a half hour to prepare, pee, drink water, pee again, and freak out about speaking to a group, which left me a solid sixty minutes for sleuthing.

I suspected a lot of people would attend my talk today, given my close proximity to the murder. That's what was making me nervous. I had to be prepared for some truly bizarre questions. Or worse.

"You take this right half of the room," Jack said. "And I'll take the left side. We'll reconvene here in an hour. How's that?"

I agreed and started off. At first I wandered, unsure of what I should do. I wasn't law enforcement, I wasn't a reporter. I wasn't anyone in a position of authority to start poking around. But by my third lap around my half of the room, I had an idea.

I'd return to the booths I'd visited yesterday, starting with the kind woman who'd sold me the catnip toy. What was her name? Michelle? She'd seemed eager to gossip and talk about Kristi, and I'd bet money that she'd have an opinion on the murder.

It didn't take me long to find the booth, mostly because she'd hoisted a giant flag with the iconic Bigfoot silhouette on one side of her table.

There were only two people in front of her U-shaped table when I walked up. They both appeared to be boys in their teens with oversized slouchy clothing and the paleness of kids who stayed inside and played too many hours of video games. Being into Bigfoot was possibly an improvement on that—at least the furry creature might inspire them to go take a walk in the woods.

Michelle's eyes lit up when she saw me. "Hey there! Quite a wild first conference for you, huh?"

For a beat, I considered playing stupid. But that probably wouldn't work. I nodded. "I don't know if you heard, but Kristi died on my walk yesterday."

I said this in a low, conspiratorial tone.

"I heard," she said, not even trying to hide the excitement in her eyes. "Are you able to share what happened? Or did the cops tell you not to spill the beans?"

"Um, well . . ." I hesitated. Alex hadn't ordered me to not talk about the crime. He'd just told me not to sleuth. "Sure, I guess I can tell you."

I gave her the abridged version, leaving out the part about the alligator.

When I was finished, Michelle was looking at me with wide, incredulous eyes. "Is it true they think she was murdered?"

"That's what the police say. As you know, I'm local, and my sister is, ah, close with the detective. Between us, Kristi was poisoned." I wasn't sure why I was being so secretive. Everything Alex had said earlier would eventually be in the local paper, if it wasn't already.

The woman's mouth opened to a perfect O. "Whoa," she whispered. This news was obviously unsettling to her, because her face drained of color.

"Yeah, it's pretty wild. I'm kind of curious. Do you know anyone who would have wanted to hurt her?"

She frowned, and I could practically see the wheels turning in her head. "Why do you want to know?" she asked matter-of-factly. "You some kind of cop? Thought you were a gator trapper."

Now it was my turn to look surprised. I hadn't imagined that she would give me pushback for asking questions. "No. Nothing like that. But some people online are saying that I might've had something to do with her death, because I was there at the time she collapsed. And they saw me on camera. I guess that's why I'm so interested."

She blinked her eyes rapidly as if she didn't believe me, or as if my answer was somehow inadequate. It kind of was, to be honest. "Are you doing your own investigation? I don't understand. Some things don't add up here."

No shit, lady. "Um, something like that. I'm asking around."

She hastily began tidying up—only her booth didn't

need organizing. It was as neat and accessorized as it had been the day before. "I don't think you should get involved with this. I'd let the cops handle it."

"Oh, of course! But I have some time to kill before my talk, so I thought I'd come by and say hi." It occurred to me then that I should've opened with that line and not come out all guns blazing with the questions about a murder.

She put her hands on the table, in between two large, squishy Bigfoot foot pillows, then leaned over, closing the gap between us. "Kristi was involved in a lot of really sketchy stuff. I think you need to stay away from any amateur sleuthing."

"Funny, that's what the detective told me."

Michelle shot me a nasty look, which made me feel as if I was being a vulture for asking questions. I rubbed at my forehead. "I'm sorry. I didn't mean to bust in on you this morning and ask all kinds of things about someone that I don't know, and that you probably don't know."

"No hard feelings. But just don't stick your nose where it doesn't belong."

I expected her to smile in a conciliatory way, or at least look pleasant. But she still wore the same dark expression.

"Yeah, that's probably a smart idea," I said quickly, while giving her a little wave. "Have a good rest of the day."

Feeling chastised for my curiosity, I slowly strolled the room, pausing at various booths and checking out the strange merchandise. Every time a vendor asked me if I'd like to see more of their stuff, I thought about mentioning Kristi. But my encounter with Michelle had sapped me of my courage.

Finally, I drifted to a booth that sold old plaster casts of Bigfoot tracks. This was actually interesting to me, mostly because I remembered Dad and I would go out into the woods and he'd point out various animal tracks. It was one of the first things he'd taught me, in fact. I learned the smaller prints of rabbits and foxes, the larger prints of coyotes, and in mud near riverbanks, the spindly, minimalist gator tracks.

These here looked like graphic images, all fat and rounded and big-toed. They were almost comical, they were so large. I pointed at one and asked the burly, bearded man behind the table, "Where did you find this? It's so huge."

"That's what she said." The guy chuckled, and I forced a smile in response. "Found that here in Florida, in the Ocala National Forest. There's a lot of Skunk Ape activity up there."

"Interesting." I bent over so I could peer at a second plaster cast. This one was even bigger. "I'm new to this whole world, and I've heard there's a rift in the community. Some people think Bigfoot comes from aliens, while others have a more scientific view of the origins. What do you think?"

The guy squinted one eye then tilted his head. Now that I stared up at him, he seemed to bear a resemblance to Bigfoot. He had the curly reddish-brown hair, the bushy beard, the hulking frame.

"You look really familiar," he finally said.

I shook my head. "I'm from Florida, but I've been away for years at college and then for work. I was living in Boston for a long time. I'm local to Wahoo."

The guy snapped his fingers. "That's it! You're Maggie Andrews. Logan Andrews's daughter."

A hesitant smile spread on my face. It wasn't a surprise that my father, a lifelong gator trapper, lover of '80s heavy metal music, and man of a thousand interesting stories, would know a bearded Bigfoot bro. "Where did you meet my dad?"

The man grinned, showing small white teeth that looked like Chiclets buried in a forest of hair. "You don't recognize me, do you?"

My mouth opened and closed. "I'm sorry, I don't."

"I'm your cousin Colby."

Chapter Twelve

I was both horrified that my memory was so poor and mystified that Colby Andrews was no longer the rail-thin boy I'd known a decade and a half ago.

His father was my father's half-brother. Which made us cousins, I guess. Or something. All I knew was that our grandpa had two families, and neither had known about each other until Paw-Paw's funeral. I was too young to remember, but Dad always told hilarious stories about the women meeting each other for the first time, during what he had endearingly dubbed "the funeral parlor skirmish."

Apparently it had devolved into a brawl in the parking lot.

Dad, Vera, and I had never been particularly close to that wing of the family. Frankly, they had been something of a joke between the three of us over the years, all because Colby's dad had found a potato chip that resembled St. Francis. They'd displayed it in a case, dedicated an entire room to a shrine—and then gotten a religious tax exemption and charged folks to see it.

"No way! Colby? I didn't recognize you with the beard."

"Yeah, everyone says that. And I've also packed on the pounds." He slapped his ample belly, which jiggled.

Colby wore a T-shirt sporting a silhouette of the state of Florida with a foot smack dab in the middle. "You're looking good, though, Maggie. So good that I tried flirtin' with you there for a minute. Come here and give your cousin a hug."

While shuddering inwardly with the thought that a blood relative had tried to put the moves on me, I obliged and quickly embraced him.

"What are you doin' here?" he asked.

I explained about my alligator talks yesterday and today, leaving out Kristi's death. For now.

"Oh, that makes so much sense. I guess this is the sort of thing your dad would've done."

I nodded, suddenly stabbed with grief. I'd give one of my small toes to get Dad's take on this conference.

"Hey. I'm real sorry that I wasn't able to make your dad's funeral." Colby stroked his beard and I could see his blue eyes were wet. "I was out west in Colorado, on an investigation. Was there for a month. When I got back, the funeral had already taken place. Damn. I really loved your old man. He was one of a kind."

A heaviness settled in my chest. I didn't want to think about Dad right now. It would make me too sad—not something I needed prior to talking to a group of people.

"He was," I said, then quickly changed the subject. "What were you doing in Colorado? What kind of investigation?"

Weird. When I was in Boston, Dad had always relayed the local gossip, but he'd never told me that Colby had a job as an investigator. Probably a PI, if I had to guess.

"Some tourist on a steam engine train captured a video of what they thought was a Sasquatch. I had to go out and poke around for myself. Did two weeks in the backcountry of the San Juan National Forest, then set up base at a motel to gather my thoughts."

Oh. *That* kind of investigator. "Did you find anything?"

"You're lookin' at it." He gestured to the plaster cast of the foot sitting in between us on the table.

I nodded slowly. I wasn't exactly sure how to proceed. Or what to say. My cousin was a Bigfoot believer. Huh. If there was ever a time when I wished Dad were alive, it was now. He'd be so entertained by this detail, I could practically hear him guffawing.

Given Colby's family's history, this news shouldn't have surprised me. But somehow it did. "Wow. That's pretty impressive."

I hoped I'd conveyed the proper amount of awe and wonder. Colby seemed like he was quite proud of whatever it was that he'd cast in plaster, even if it was merely an artistic rendering of what he thought a Bigfoot print should look like. Considering his family, it wasn't outside the realms of possibility to think that Colby might be lying to make a quick buck.

But this was a prime example of not my circus, not my monkeys.

Or, as Dad used to say, "not my swamp, not my gators."

Still, I wanted to pump my cousin for information, figuring he wouldn't mind. "Hey, do you know—"

"Oh my God! There she is! That's the woman who was with Kristi Klaus when she died."

Colby and I snapped our heads around to the sound of the woman's voice, which was closer than I was comfortable with. Standing in my personal space were two women. Both were middle-aged, and both wore white shorts, white sneakers with ankle socks, and matching hot-pink shirts that simply said *Bigfoot Babe.*

What was with the people in matching shirts here, anyway?

"You're that gator hunter, aren't you?" One of the women fiddled with her phone.

I nodded. Already I had a sneaking suspicion of what they were about to ask.

"Would you mind if we asked you a few questions for our Facebook page?"

"No, I'm not giving interviews. I'm sorry. The police told me not to talk to anyone."

The slightly taller woman shot me a look that said *yeah, right.* "Then why were you all chatty with Michelle?"

"Michelle . . . Oh. Uh." The woman in the booth. Had they been following me? What an unsettling thought. I didn't have a good answer for their question, though. I looked at Colby helplessly.

"Brian," Colby barked over his shoulder. "I need your help."

"Well?" the taller woman demanded.

"No comment," I said.

A skinny young guy emerged from the other end of the L-shaped table, grinning. He was missing a front tooth. "Hey, boss," he said to Colby.

"Hold down the fort. I'm going for a smoke with my

cousin. If Ella comes back, tell her I'm outside. Don't tell her about my cousin, though." Colby looked at me and gestured with his head. "Let's go."

He moved around the table and I scurried after him, not looking at the two women who were grumbling with disappointment as we left them in the dust.

"Thanks for getting me out of that situation," I said as we threaded our way through the crowds. It had gotten packed in the last half hour.

Colby put his finger to his lips, indicating that I should be quiet. Why, I wasn't sure, but I clammed up and followed him out of the hotel and around the building. There was a lone, thin guy with sallow skin puffing away near a potted palm.

Colby and I took a seat on a bench opposite him.

"You've gotta be careful about what you say in there. The walls have ears. And eyes." He pulled out a pack of Newports and offered me one. I declined, wondering why he was being so secretive. Then again, the smoking man nearby did look weird.

Good Lord, I was getting awfully paranoid.

"How's your sister?" he asked.

"Vera's good. Just opened her bookstore. She's here selling Bigfoot romance novels. They're quite popular."

He chuckled and lit up. "Yeah, they are. My girlfriend consumes them like Pringles."

For a solid thirty seconds, he relished his first drag. "You really stepped in some shit with Kristi."

"I didn't kill—"

"I know. I know you didn't. How could you? You'd just

met her and she keeled over in front of you. I saw the videos." He shook his head. "Can't say I was surprised to hear that it was murder, though."

"Really?" It dawned on me that I'd been given a great investigative gift, in the form of my cousin's undivided attention. "Did you know her well?"

Colby chuckled bitterly. "I know way too much, cuz. It's a cutthroat world in there." He gestured to the building with his cigarette.

I studied him as he puffed. He was exactly eight years older than me and Vera. Since our fathers had only discovered they were half-brothers later in life, we hadn't grown up together, nor were we close. Well, that and the fact that Dad had always been skeptical of the family because of their moneymaking, tax-evading, potato chip scam.

The Holy Chip. I hadn't thought of that in years. Dad had claimed the family made a million bucks from the St. Francis chip shrine. I never entirely believed him, thinking it was just some crazy story of his.

Still, when we were about ten, Vera and I had inspected every potato chip we ate, hoping to find a treasure. Vera, of course, wanted one that looked like Justin Timberlake and concocted an elaborate fantasy that once she found one that looked like him, the pop singer himself would come to Wahoo and ask her to marry him.

Always a romantic, that one.

I actually did find a Flamin' Hot Cheeto that looked like a manatee, but Dad had broken it to me gently that folks probably wouldn't pay money to see it. Our dog promptly ate the blob-shaped snack, then barfed it up.

"What do you mean by that? Why is it cutthroat?" I asked Colby.

"How long do you have?" Holding his cigarette in the air, he stretched. His shirt rode up, exposing a wide expanse of pale, hairy belly.

I averted my eyes and checked my watch. Forty-five minutes until I had to meet Jack. "Less than an hour."

"Okay, so the CliffsNotes version. Here we go. The cryptid world is small, and everyone loves to gossip."

"Kind of like Wahoo." We smiled at each other.

"I've been in this community for years," he started. "Since I was a teenager. Something about the idea of creatures like this living in the wild, it's fascinating to me. I saved up from my summer jobs and went to my first conference out in New Mexico when I was eighteen. I met so many experts and count many people here as good friends. I tell you all this because I want you to know that I'm not a fly-by-night scammer."

He looked at me pointedly, and I knew that he knew my dad had poked fun of his family for the Holy Chip.

"Of course."

"Kristi came on the scene a couple of years ago. She hadn't gone to any conventions, just started posting videos about her expeditions." He took a long drag and looked off into the distance, then exhaled a plume of smoke that seemed to hang in the air. "A lot of people dismissed her at first, mostly because she was young and beautiful, and a woman, of course. I didn't, though. I try to be welcoming to everyone. Hell, I think there needs to be a lot more diversity in the community and even ponied up money for a minority Bigfoot scholarship."

I wasn't sure if I wanted to ask what that entailed, so I merely nodded. "Good for you."

"Kristi and I became friends. More than friends, really. Fine, I'll tell you. We were lovers. We were passionate about everything together. Bigfoot, travel, science fiction, sex."

"Oh." I chewed on the inside of my cheek, trying to imagine the comely Kristi and my burly cousin together. To say I was afraid of where this conversation was headed was an understatement. Still, it did partially explain why all these women were into monster erotica.

They wanted a man who looked like Colby Andrews. At least my cousin was among friends and potential dates. Much easier than a dating app, I assumed.

"She was too much for me. Too wild, too . . . I don't know. She lived up in Vidalia—"

"Georgia?" I interrupted. "Where the onions are grown?"

"Yeah. That's where she was from. But she moved to Orlando—not that long ago, actually."

Okay, now we were getting somewhere. This was concrete information to bring back to Jack. I'd passed through Vidalia once, and it wasn't pretty. It was so hardscrabble and small that it was difficult to imagine the glamorous Kristi there. No wonder she'd decamped to Orlando.

"Why'd you break up?" I asked.

"I wanted to start a family." He hung his head. "She didn't want kids. She wanted superstardom."

How much "superstardom" could one achieve by hunting Bigfoot? I guess the world would never know. "Well. That sucks."

"It's okay. It was for the best. I met my girlfriend soon after and we're planning to have a kid next year." He lifted his head and beamed. "But Ella's a little jealous. Ella's my old lady. I had to promise to stop talking to Kristi, had to cease being her friend. Kristi didn't take it well."

It seemed unreasonable that Colby's new girlfriend was so jealous, but what did I know? I'd been in exactly one real relationship since college, and it had fizzled like wet fireworks on the Fourth of July.

"What did she do?"

He blew a breath out of his nose. "She showed up drunk at my house one night. The cops were called. There was a brawl."

The horrified look on my face made Colby wave his hands. "I didn't hit her. The brawl was between her and my girlfriend. It didn't help that Ella was drunk, too. I called the cops, and thank God they came because Ella was just about to get her machete off the wall."

I made a mental note to never piss off Ella. My lips involuntarily pulled back into a wince as I recalled the stench of gin coming off Kristi. "Did she have a drinking problem? Kristi, I mean."

"Why do you ask?"

"She smelled like booze yesterday during the walk and was rather . . . disruptive."

"She liked to party, let's put it that way. Booze, weed, and some other stuff." He tapped his nose.

Great, she was also a coke fiend. This case was getting more complicated by the second.

"Was she arrested when she showed up at your house?"

"No. She talked her way out of it. My girlfriend was the one who spent the night in the can, but that's because she brought out her nunchuks."

Charming. "How long ago was that?" I wanted to keep this discussion as fact-based as possible.

"About a year. I haven't seen or heard from Kristi since."

"Until this convention." Oh crap, was my cousin a suspect in her murder?

He shook his head mournfully. "My girlfriend's been with me almost the entire time. She doesn't usually come to these things, but when she saw Kristi was speaking, she decided to tag along. I don't mind or nothin', but I hadn't even *seen* Kristi. Thought I caught a glimpse of her yesterday but I was so busy with the booth that I couldn't get away."

I got the distinct impression that Colby was disappointed he hadn't run into his old flame. "Wow, that must've been a real shock to hear that she'd been murdered."

"Bruh, you don't even know." He scrubbed his face with his free hand. "If I knew who did it, I'd probably kill the guy."

"Well, don't do anything rash." I realized this might be like telling a hurricane to mind its manners. "Who do you think killed her, anyway? Do you think it was that Grant Sanders guy? The Bromies?"

My cousin tilted his head, a frown of confusion on his face. "Are you asking me if the Bromies killed Kristi? No, of course not."

"No, I meant Grant. Sorry."

He shook his head. "Grant didn't like her much. Weirdly, he never tried to sleep with her."

"Why is that weird?"

"He tries to screw everything that walks."

A little surge of triumph went through me. So I'd been correct in my initial assessment of Grant. *Go me and my douche radar.*

Colby took another long inhale, the ember of his cigarette nearly at the filter. I shoved an image of him and Kristi kissing out of my mind.

"Kristi and Grant had a professional relationship. I always thought it was like, game meets game." Brody swept his hand in an arc through the air. "No, I don't think it was Grant. I heard she had a run-in with another researcher two days ago. Didn't see it, but a lot of people were talking about it even before she went on that walk with you."

"Who did she get into a fight with?" Was this the woman from last night? Or someone else? How many people had Kristi pissed off?

"Dr. Jess Daws. The two of them have butted heads before, mostly because they believe two very different Bigfoot origin stories."

"Oh yeah? Really?" I wanted Colby to keep talking.

While shaking his head, Colby chuckled. "Dr. Daws is in the old-school camp. She believes there's a scientific explanation for Bigfoot. She's an actual researcher who went to MIT and worked as a zoologist, so a lot of people put weight into her opinion."

"And Kristi?" I already suspected the answer after watching that video with Jack in the bar last night.

"She believed there was an alien connection to Bigfoot. She embraced the more unusual theories about the origins of cryptids."

"Huh." I scratched behind my ear. "What do you think?"

"I've gone back and forth. I'm kind of bi on the issue—I can see the merits of both."

"Makes sense. But tell me, is Dr. Daws capable of murder?"

He huffed a little laugh. "Dr. Daws is capable of anything. And from what I heard, Kristi really laid into her the other day. Called her a fraud, told her she was peddling fake news, said she had no evidence to support her theory."

"Yikes. And what did Dr. Daws say in response?"

"That Kristi was a scammer. It was a total catfight."

"Was she?"

The silence that hung in the air was almost too much to handle. I was about to change the subject because the vibe was simply too awkward, but Colby spoke up.

"She had that streak in her. And trust me, I can spot that kind of person a mile away because of my parents."

My jaw dropped. "Didn't expect you to say that."

"I call it like I see it. Let's just say Kristi tended to

embellish. She found that she got more views and likes when she made shit up."

"And yet you still loved her?"

His face crumpled into misery. "I couldn't help it. She was just so damned hot. I felt like I hit the jackpot whenever I was with her. Like a Playboy model come to life. I mean, look at me and then look at her. Come on."

He had a point. "I see. Listen, I have to get ready for my talk. It's coming up soon."

"Oh, hell, cuz, I didn't even look at the program. You talking about gators?"

"Yeah."

"Right on. I'll try to attend, but no guarantees. What room?"

I told him the location and he nodded. We swapped contact info, and he said he needed to get back to the booth. Before we parted, he folded me into a giant bear hug. Colby smelled like dirt and faintly of oatmeal soap.

"You be careful in there, okay? Don't be surprised if some people show up to your talk and try to get you to discuss Kristi's last moments. She has some rabid, scary fans."

"Oh, that reminds me!" I pulled out of his embrace. "Do you know someone named Mac?"

For the first time, Colby's blue eyes hardened. "Why?"

"Yesterday, I happened to see Kristi's phone. There were some concerning messages from a person named Mac."

Colby jammed his hands into his jean pockets, his face pinched with . . . something. Worry? Anger? It was difficult to tell.

"When did he text her?"

"When did he not text her? There were dozens of messages."

My cousin shook his head. "I can't believe she was still talking to that guy."

"Why?"

He closed his eyes and shook his head. "I don't think I can handle this emotionally."

Oh, great. Now he was getting all sentimental on me, right at the time when we were close to a breakthrough.

"Tell me about Mac," I pleaded.

Colby opened his eyes. "Kristi was Mac's girlfriend for a while, before we started dating."

His mouth remained open, as if he was about to say more. I waited. And waited.

Nothing.

"Was their breakup bad? What's his last name? Is he in Vidalia?"

Slowly, Colby shook his head. "Mac McCracken. Bigfoot hunter from North Carolina. I'm sure he's here, since he was the original organizer of this convention. I hope I don't see him because there's no tellin' what I'll do to him. I don't think Mac ever felt that they really broke up. He sure didn't act like it. I thought he was a stalker . . . I really need to go. If Ella gets back and finds me not there, she's going to lose her shit. Let's keep in touch, okay cuz?"

"Yeah," I said slowly, trying to absorb his words. "I'll see you around."

I watched as he disappeared into the hotel. Who the hell was Mac? Was he really a stalker? And where could we find him?

151

Chapter Thirteen

Not wanting to pass Colby's booth and face a possibly awkward encounter with his "old lady," I took the long way around the outside of the building, savoring the bright sunshine.

If only I could be on the water, kayaking today. Instead, I had to give my talk in about a half hour. My stomach clenched. I'd have just enough time to debrief Jack on what I'd found. The automatic doors to the hotel glided open and I power-walked inside.

One guy in a khaki fishing vest stopped me and asked if I was the woman who saw Kristi collapse. I waved him off, annoyed. What was with these people anyway?

"You can't hide from the truth," the guy called out.

Great. I was pissing off Bigfoot believers.

As I made my way to the meeting point, I saw my sister's table from far away. At least I thought it was. It was so packed that I could barely see the Straight From the Heart sign. Well, I was glad someone was having a productive day.

Jack was already at the food court when I arrived. Two small coffee cups sat on the table, one in front of him and one in front of the empty seat. I plopped down with a heavy exhale.

"I'm guessing by that sigh that you either found something amazing or struck out," he said.

"I found out just enough to be frustrated."

Jack cracked a lopsided grin. "I feel the same."

I wrapped my hands around the cup. "Is this for me?"

Jack nodded. "You want to go first?"

"Sure. I'm not sure what's more surprising. That I found someone who knows who the mysterious Mac is, or that my cousin is a Bigfoot believer." I got out my notebook and a pen.

Jack snort-laughed. "Your cousin is here?"

"He sells plaster casts of Bigfoot tracks. I have to say they look surprisingly real."

"Uh-oh. Someone's turning into a believer."

I squinted at him. "I definitely don't buy any of this. Do you?"

Jack shrugged.

"Wait. You believe in Bigfoot?" My tone was incredulous.

He leaned in. "I don't believe in the commercial Bigfoot. Do I think that aliens landed and unleashed a posse of seven-foot-tall furry creatures into the wild? No. But do I think there are creatures that can't be explained out there, ones that are elusive and want to be left alone? You bet."

Now I was squinting so hard that I figured I'd need Botox for my wrinkles at the age of twenty-five. "What?"

He chuckled. "Maybe it's because I grew up reading science fiction and fantasy, or perhaps it's because I loved *Unexplained Mysteries* and *The X-Files* as a kid.

Dunno. I want to believe, as the slogan goes. It's more hope than anything else."

My expression relaxed. Like everything else about Jack, even this was endearing. "Okay, fair enough."

I then set aside my personal feelings on cryptids, and told him everything that I'd heard, seen, and discovered. Jack reached across the table for the notebook and pen, and scribbled as I spoke.

"Cousin Colby might be a suspect. We should also add his girlfriend to our list." I sat back in my chair, shoulders slumping.

"Interesting. Very, very interesting," Jack muttered.

When I was finished, I took a deep breath. "What did you find out?"

"I ended up having a long conversation with a stage-hand who travels around the country with the convention. Apparently this Bigfoot conference is kind of like a travel-ing, ah, circus, for lack of a better word. It goes from city to city, and a lot of the core speakers, like Kristi, show up at every event. There are also several spots for local cryptid experts. I use that term loosely, by the way, in case you think I've lost my mind."

Jack flashed his sexiest smile and continued. "Anyway, this guy—his name is Tom—said Kristi treated him like dirt. She was arrogant, demanding—oh, and get this. She put in her contract that at every event she requires a bouquet of fresh pink roses, locally sourced honey for her allergies, and Arctic Blitz Gatorade."

"I guess we've discovered that she was a diva."

"Oh, and she wanted one more thing: a small bowl

containing precisely three lemons, each cut into exactly eight pieces. Kristi believed the scent of fresh lemon helped clear her mind and enhanced her focus before her speeches."

I rolled my eyes.

"And Tom did give me another extremely important detail: he heard that Kristi may have had a criminal history. I texted Diego to find the reports."

"Really?" I practically yelped the word. I loved that Jack had found out such a juicy tidbit. "How do we confirm this?"

"Now that you've given me a few more details, like her hometown and where she moved, and about this mysterious Mac McCracken—whose name is unique, thank God—I can do some research while you're talking. I'll also pass along that information to Diego."

"Oh crap, what time is it?" I flapped my hands nervously. It always seemed like I lost track of time when I talked with Jack. Our conversations were that interesting. I checked my watch. Ten minutes until I went on. "It's almost time. Crap."

We toted our coffees to the Boca Grande Room, a small, windowless, beige hotel conference space. I had braced myself for a crowd. When I arrived, it was more like a small cluster of a few people, most of whom were checking their phones, looking bored.

Jack and I paused at the back of the room.

"I'm sure more people will come. There's still five minutes," he said.

I nodded, unsure of whether I should be happy that I

wasn't being swarmed with angry and curious Kristi stans, or disappointed that no one wanted to hear my talk on gators.

"I'll be back here." Jack drummed his fingers on the back of a chair. "Checking on some records in Georgia. Can I keep this notebook?"

"Sure. I'm going to talk to the tech guy. I think he's getting the equipment ready."

Jack scanned the room. "That guy up front? Oh, sweet, that's Tom. The guy I was chatting with."

We walked over and Jack introduced me. Like my cousin, he had a bushy beard, only his was dishwater blond and slightly less wild. I wondered if facial hair was a requirement for employment with the traveling Bigfoot show.

"Nice to meet you, Maggie. The slide deck you sent over is all ready to go. Here." He handed me a small remote and explained how to use it. "I'll be over to the side if you have any trouble. Good luck."

He scurried away. Jack wished me good luck and went to the back of the room, leaving me alone.

I surveyed the thin crowd. A few more stragglers had come in, mostly with confused looks on their faces. A woman in the front row raised her hand.

"Excuse me. Miss?" She had long, silvery-black dreadlocks and was sitting next to a younger woman who looked almost identical to her. "Is this the 'Combatting Sasquatch Skeptics' session with Dr. Daws?"

"No. This is the wildlife session."

"Oh dear." She reached for her purse. "This sounds

really interesting but we can't miss Dr. Jess Daws. She's only speaking twice this entire conference and isn't doing any meet and greets. I'm sorry." The other woman with her nodded and they both ducked out.

I tried not to appear deflated. Four more people trickled in. At one minute past the hour, a man with thick, coke-bottle glasses, a too-tight Mothman T-Shirt, and baggy jeans piped up.

"Are we going to start this thing or what?" he asked.

I stood behind the podium, glad for the block of solid wood separating me from everyone else. "Yes, let's start."

Ten people had showed up to my talk. I knew this because I'd counted each one. I started with a brief introduction, about how I'd grown up with my father, who was known around town as the Gator King. I gave a quick rundown of my experience at the Boston Zoo, and how I'd returned to Wahoo only a few months ago to take over my father's trapping business.

"I want to show you in photos what you can expect to see when you're out in the wilderness in Florida. There are a few creatures who have the potential to be hazardous, and I don't want you to—"

"We want to know about Kristi," the man in the Mothman shirt hollered. Others agreed loudly.

"Yeah!"

"Yes, talk about that! Please!"

I glanced at Jack in the back of the room. His face was buried in his phone while he simultaneously wrote furiously in my notebook. While I hoped that he was finding the detail that would crack the murder case wide open, I also wished he had a magic solution for me and this potentially unruly bunch of Kristi fans.

But this was my show to run, and I had to face the music.

"Okay okay, we can improvise a little here. Since there aren't many of you, we can have a more informal talk. Do you all want to come a little closer to the front so you can hear me?" I walked around the podium to perch on the edge of a long, sturdy table at the front of the room.

Everyone else clustered around me. I now counted nine people. When had I lost the tenth? Oh well.

Out of the corner of my eye, I saw Jack look up, startled. I shot him a little smile to let him know I was okay, and he went back to his phone.

I clapped my hands together gently. "I take it you all knew Kristi? Or knew of her?"

Everyone nodded somberly.

"I followed her videos from the beginning," the Mothman T-shirt guy said.

"I've met her at four conferences," a woman added.

"She was so nice. When my cat passed away, she sent me a card in the mail," a woman who appeared to be about eighty said.

Something about that last detail made my heart squeeze. "It sounds like she was really special to all of you."

Everyone's heads bobbed in agreement. Hmm. This was a unique opportunity. By now, Jack had crept closer to the group and sat one row behind, right in the middle of the room. So he was listening after all.

"What would you like to know? Unfortunately, I only

met her for the first time yesterday, right before the walk. I'm sad that I didn't get to know her. She seemed like a special person."

No one said a word. Sweat broke out on the back of my neck. Did these folks think I'd killed her? Or were they looking for some kind of informal grief therapy? It was difficult to tell, and frankly I'd rather have talked about gators. Why had I opened this weird door?

"I think you would've been friends," said one woman who I recognized as having been on yesterday's walk. "Kristi was a champion of women who worked outdoors."

A few people murmured in agreement, then everyone seem to talk at once. They told stories about how funny she was on her videos, how much she'd loved her dog, and how she had a true passion for Bigfoot.

That was the word they used. *Passion*.

I didn't interrupt anyone. I just sat on the table and listened. Every now and then I would look over at Jack, to see him scribbling in the notebook. Unfortunately, I didn't think anyone's memories of Kristi were all that interesting from a crime-solving perspective.

Mostly people just wanted to talk about the times they'd met her and gotten autographs. Or the kind emails they'd received from her. Or the funny things she did on video. Honestly, I wasn't upset by this. Their sweet words for Christie made her seem more human, and less weird and scammy.

Sure, these folks probably did have a slightly skewed parasocial relationship with her, but it had mostly been harmless.

Or had it been? Was one of these people here her murderer? My blood ran cold just thinking that. I studied each and every face, thinking about whether they were capable of poisoning.

"How did you all find out about what happened? Where were you when you heard the news?" I asked.

A little smile appeared on Jack's face.

"Most of us were at Grant's talk," said the Mothman T-shirt guy. He looked around, and five people nodded. "We're Bromies, after all."

Ahh, the ever-present Bromies.

"I was up in my room with my husband and daughter," one middle-aged woman said. "My kid had a headache so I was dealing with that, and I got a text."

A couple of other people said they were having lunch; apparently there had been a Bigfoot Burger special in the bar. The one woman who had been on the walk piped up and gave her account of what she had seen.

"You were so calm," she said, gesturing toward me. "I was so impressed at how you tossed that gator and took charge of the situation. You really tried to help her, and I hate that people here are accusing you of killing Kristi. It was also terrible how those two other people filmed everything. No respect for Kristi."

There were murmurs of agreement from the rest.

"Thank you," I said softly. Then, I dropped the bombshell question. "Why would somebody want to murder her?"

Everyone's eyes shifted nervously. An uncomfortable silence took over the room.

Chapter Fourteen

"We have our theories," said one woman. Half the group nodded.

"Care to share them?" I asked.

"We're worried about lawsuits," one man said. "The person we think is responsible is here at the con and she's . . ."

"Quite litigious," chimed in Mothman shirt guy. "She once sued a fan for defamation. The guy claimed she'd embezzled from a Bigfoot hunting group."

Yikes. This crowd was chock full of secrets and scandal. I frowned. "Oh. So it's a woman? Your main suspect is a woman?"

Everyone nodded.

"Another researcher?"

More nods. They had to be talking about Dr. Daws. I hadn't seen any other women on the list of panelists other than her and Kristi.

This was when I decided to shoot my shot. "Is it someone who has very different theories on cryptids?"

"Yes, and it's someone who might be speaking in another room right at this moment," one guy said. "She's extremely popular."

They were one hundred percent talking about Dr.

Daws. In my mind I replayed the conversation I'd over-heard last night outside the ladies' washroom. Yikes.

"Maybe we should get back to the gator talk," one woman said. "We're in dangerous territory here. Sorry to sound like conspiracy theorists, but the person we're talking about is powerful and she hated Kristi. If she finds out we've been slandering her . . ."

Several people shuddered. "Retaliation," one person whispered.

Dang. Right when we were getting somewhere. I didn't want to push it, though, or have word get back to Alex that I was asking questions and doing his job. I agreed to return to the topic of wildlife and resumed my place behind the podium, remote in hand.

Since my talk was only scheduled for forty-five minutes and we'd already burned at least twenty talking about Kristi, I focused mostly on one sexy beast.

The American alligator.

The mood appeared to lighten as I told stories of my father and I trapping alligators over the years.

I clicked to a slide that showed a riverbank at the break of dawn. "One memorable encounter," I began, "was with a feisty seven-footer lurking in a neighbor's koi pond. Dad and I improvised a lasso from some sturdy rope in our truck. It required patience and a stroke of luck, but we finally managed to loop it around the gator's jaws. Pulling with all our strength, we coaxed it into a crate."

The next slide showed the gator on the ground, its mouth taped shut.

"Whoa," said Mothman shirt guy. "What do you do with 'em after you catch 'em? Do you fry 'em up into gator nuggets?"

A chorus of *ewww*s and laughter erupted.

"No, my uncle owns a reptile sanctuary here in town. He does private tours if you're here for a while. It's an interesting place." I explained how and where to find my Uncle Burt.

I advanced the slide, revealing a faded photo of a younger me, radiant with pride beside my father and a securely bound alligator on a flatbed. "Another time we were called to a public swimming hole on a scorching summer day. The place was teeming with families, and panic was setting in fast because there was a pretty big ten-footer. Dad and I used a mix of distraction and a sturdy capture noose. We finally got him, but that was dicey."

The last slide showed a serene marsh at sunset, casting a peaceful glow over the waters. "But the catch that sticks with me the most wasn't our largest or most dramatic. It demanded the most creativity. A small gator, barely five feet long, had holed up in a cluttered backyard shed. The cramped space made our usual methods too risky. Dad had the brilliant idea to use a large mirror, putting it at the shed's entrance. The little gator was fooled by its own reflection, which it mistook for an intruder. The gator charged towards the mirror and right toward us. We gently and carefully rehomed it into another swamp. That day was a mix of psychology and patience, two things Dad taught me."

The group seemed to love that story, and by now I was awash in memories of Dad, as I always was when I told stories about our adventures in the Florida wilderness. My throat thickened at all the good times we'd had together.

"Where's your pa now?" one woman chirped.

"He passed last year," I said softly, willing myself not to cry. Sometimes the grief of his absence hit me with no warning, and I prayed that this wouldn't be one of those moments.

"He'd be real proud of you," the woman said.

"Thanks." I smiled at her.

At that point, someone's phone alarm went off, shattering the emotional moment.

"It's noon," Jack said aloud.

"Oh! Well. I guess that does it for my talk. Sorry it was a little discombobulated, but I'm happy to take questions. I have some brochures and business cards here, if you'd like to take one. Just remember: never approach, molest, or feed wildlife." I reached for my backpack, pulling out the stack of papers to set them on the table. "Also, I should put in a good word for my twin sister, who is selling books from her store Straight From the Heart here at the convention. She's in booth 312."

A few people approached and took a brochure. One of the women told me she'd already purchased a special edition of her favorite monster romance series from Vera. I thanked her.

Finally, it was just Jack and me in the room.

"You okay?" He reached over and rubbed my back.

"Yeah, it's just . . . talking about my dad. It's hard, you know?"

"I do know. I lost my sister as a teenager."

My mouth dropped open. "Really? Oh my God. I didn't know. I'm sorry. What happened? No, you don't have to tell me. Sorry. I'm an idiot."

"No, I was going to tell you. I didn't know the right time." He paused for a beat. "My sister was the victim of a serial killer. That's why I do what I do. I decided early that I wanted to figure out what makes people like that tick."

I sat in silence for a few awkward seconds as my heart hurt for him. "What an awful thing to go through. I'm so sorry."

"It's okay. Really." He put on a brave smile. "We can talk more about it later. Let's stay focused. Your talk went really well. Unfortunately, I didn't get much from my internet research. There weren't any Kristi Klauses in Vidalia. Are you sure your cousin had the right town?"

More than anything, I wanted to find out about Jack's sister. But he seemed eager to shift the discussion. Not that I could blame him; what a devastating thing to have had happen. "I'll ask again."

Jack flipped a page and studied his handwriting. "We got a lot of excellent info about Kristi."

I came around to the row of chairs where he was sitting and sank down next to him. "You think?"

He tapped the pen on the notebook. "We have a much fuller picture of who she was. It's a mistake in an investigation to only look at the negatives about the person. The positives are just as important. Those people adored her."

"It's true. I feel terrible for them. Some seemed really broken up. And what about that other stuff? Someone who would sue? Were they talking about Dr. Daws? They had to have been, right?"

"They were," boomed a voice.

Jack and I looked up. It was Tom, shuffling his skinny body toward us.

"Hey bro, what do you mean by that?" Jack asked.

Tom stopped at our row and gripped the back of one chair. "I don't think Jess Daws had anything to do with this. She's a good lady—a little prickly, but not a murderer. No, I think somebody else did this. A man. Out for revenge."

"Does the name Mac McCracken mean anything to you?" I suspected Tom knew more than he was letting on. If he'd worked the conference for years, he probably knew where a lot of the skeletons were stored. Being a behind-the-scenes guy, he was free to observe everything—and was easily ignored by flashier people like Kristi.

Tom snorted. "Does it ever. He was one of the founders of this whole shindig. Hell, he hired me a decade ago, when he first began."

"Can you tell us more?" Jack said in a friendly tone.

Tom sat in a chair in next row, twisting his body to face us. "Mac is a long-time Bigfoot researcher. He did it back before it was popular, back before it became a fad, back before all those social media stars. Hell, even before all the Netflix shows. He started this conference in North Carolina, and it used to be just a small gathering of guys who liked to go out in the woods and look for creatures."

"Is he still in charge?"

"Hell no. Grant P. Sanders came on the scene and weaseled his way in. And Kristi, too, but she did it in a different way. I didn't tell you any of this earlier," Tom said, looking straight at Jack. "I didn't think it was particularly relevant, but then those folks started disparaging Dr. Daws, and I won't stand for that."

"What was the relationship between Mac and Kristi?"

Tom huffed a laugh. "Mac's the one who got Kristi into the Bigfoot world. About six years ago, he met Kristi under some unusual circumstances and fell in love."

"Oh?" Jack's sexy right eyebrow quirked up.

"Kristi was in prison on theft charges."

"Theft? Do you know what happened?" If I had to guess, I'd assume it was shoplifting.

A little smile spread on Tom's face. I could tell he enjoyed being a keeper of secrets. "I happened to get my hands on her arrest record because I had a buddy who worked as a sheriff up in Georgia. She worked at a nursing home and stole from the patients."

I recoiled. "Really? Like jewelry and stuff?"

"Yeah, that and cash from trust fund accounts. Nearly thirty grand. It was her first arrest and the judge went easy on her, though. She successfully argued that she shouldn't be in prison long because she was beautiful."

Jack and I exchanged glances full of *yikes* while Tom continued.

"Mac went on one of those prisoner dating sites and met her. She happened to be behind bars in North Carolina, close to where he lived. He started visiting her, sending her money, taking care of her family in Georgia. I told him she was just using him, but he insisted they were in love."

I sat, frozen. Was Tom's story true? Kristi had been in prison? Then again, combined with the fact that Alex had told Jack he was looking into Kristi's past, this information made sense.

"Then things got weird," Tom continued.

Jack and I slid a glance to each other. Hoo boy.

"Uh-huh," Jack prodded. "How weird?"

"Kristi, whose name wasn't Kristi back then—she went by her real name—went on a reality TV program called *Cellmate Soulmates*. Mac didn't go on the show, but it turned out that she was scamming quite a few other guys from prison. The show followed some of those other guys and Kristi when she was released."

"Wha—how?" I said. "And why? And do you know her real name?"

Tom looked at me as if I'd just fallen off the turnip truck. "Money. Why else? I can't recall the exact spelling of her real name, but it's similar. Christine with a C versus Kristi with a K. That kind of thing."

I felt as though I were a few steps behind. How had Kristi spent money while in prison? Or had she saved it? Were prison savings accounts a thing? I suspected Jack knew the answer to this question, so I'd wait to ask him.

"So Kristi was using Mac for money, was using other

men for money, went on a reality show, then was released from prison and moved to Florida. Got it. What happened after that?"

"She bleached her hair blonde, changed her name, and became a famous cryptid adventurer. Mac had a vision, knew she'd draw all sorts of new people to the scene. And sure enough, she did. Attendance at these tripled within a year. Her videos got crazy views."

"What was her real name?" Jack interjected.

"Christine."

"Christine Klaus?"

"I think it was Christine Clauson. Not sure how Christine is spelled, though. Sometimes people spell names funny, you know?"

"A stage name." Jack stroked his chin. "Fascinating."

"But . . ." My voice trailed off because my mind was overwhelmed with questions. "Is this common knowledge about her scamming people from prison? Does the Bigfoot community know she was in prison? Why did they trust her if she had such a shady past?"

I couldn't believe I was casually tossing around phrases like "the Bigfoot community."

"Most people don't know, and the people who do didn't care. All they saw was a sexy woman who liked to prance around the outdoors in tight pants. Kristi adopted a few controversial opinions about Bigfoot, and then she went on some daytime talk show about Bigfoot hunters, and boom! She was a bona fide celebrity."

I felt that Tom's version of celebrity and mine were slightly different, but I wasn't here to quibble.

"Have you talked to the cops about this?" Jack asked gently.

Tom shook his head. "I hate cops."

"A common sentiment," Jack murmured.

"Wait, back up," I started. "When did Mac and Kristi break up?"

Tom tipped his head back and forth. "Don't know if they ever really broke up. They had a complicated relationship. He was kind of off the scene for a couple of years after his heart attack. Kristi took up with some guy who does feet casts after that, but that ended."

"Colby," I interrupted.

"That's him. Good guy. Another one of Kristi's victims." Tom shook his head. "This is Mac's first conference since his health problems."

We chatted a bit more about Mac, gleaning a few details such as his age (fifty-two, precisely nineteen years older than Kristi), his former profession (train engineer), and family (one grown daughter from a previous marriage).

"But the question remains: did Mac kill Kristi?" I mused aloud.

Tom curled his lip. "Hell no. Mac doesn't have it in him. He loves—well, loved—her with everything he had. I knew it would end in heartbreak, but not like this."

He then proceeded to tell us that he had to go take a leak, and wished us a nice day.

Now Jack and I really were alone in the conference room. We stared at each other, our eyes wide with shock.

"Holy crap," I exhaled.

"Right?"

"We really need to tell Alex this."

Jack nodded. "I should go find him. But we should also check out that reality TV show."

"You know, let's ask Vera about that. She loves all that crap. I wouldn't be surprised if she watched . . . what was it?"

"*Cellmate Soulmates.*"

I started to snicker while Jack tapped on his phone.

"Here's the synopsis: Cellmate Soulmates *dives into the tumultuous world of female inmates at the notorious Carolina Crest Women's Correctional Facility, who navigate the rocky road to romance with partners from the outside. This show combines the gritty reality of life behind bars with the sensational drama of love and relationships, offering viewers an unfiltered look at the complexities of connecting from the inside out.*"

"Yeah, that's totally Vera's jam."

"Wait, there's more," Jack said, holding up a finger. "*Each episode zeroes in on a few key inmates, revealing their backstories, their crimes, and their romantic entanglements with men on the outside who are drawn to their forbidden allure. From steamy love letters and emotionally charged phone calls to the tension-filled visiting hours where every glance and touch is charged with longing,* Cellmate Soulmates *pulls no punches in depicting the raw reality of these relationships.*

"Here we go. *Central to the series is Christine, a gorgeous and charismatic woman from Georgia.*" Jack glanced up with a knowing look. "*She's a manipulative inmate who becomes entangled with Jake, an older, recently divorced man seeking companionship. Their relationship, fraught with challenges and clouded by Christine's criminal past, begs the question: do cellmates make good soulmates?"*

We sat in silence for a moment, the gravity—and the absurdity—of it all sinking in.

"I think we should take another run at Alice, her assistant," Jack finally said.

"That's a good idea," I agreed, my mind racing with potential leads and questions. "If anyone knows what secrets Kristi was hiding, it's probably her. I hope she's still here."

"I'm guessing the cops told her not to leave town." Jack stood up, stretching his arms. "I'll start by touching base with Alex. See if he's heard anything or if he can discreetly ask around. He needs to know about this reality TV angle, and about Kristi's real name. Although I suspect he already knows those details. I'm going to guess that they've already matched her fingerprints to her criminal record in Georgia."

"Do you think the autopsy is finished?" I also climbed to my feet.

Jack snapped his fingers. "Good question. I'll find out."

A plan was shaping up. Sort of. It was more like an octopus trying to play the drums—lots of movement, much noise, but no guarantee of a tune.

"What if Mac killed her? Those texts I saw were borderline threatening. Maybe he got frustrated that Kristi had bled him dry for cash while sleeping with other people?"

"It's possible," Jack said as we walked slowly to the door. "But let's not forget about Dr. Daws. She and Kristi did have their differences. Competition does strange things to people."

"True. But Tom seems to think Daws is innocent."

"And Kristi's fans think she's guilty. Let's keep an open mind. Plus there's your cousin, I'm sorry to say."

I held up my hands. "No need to apologize. Tell Alex about him, and about Colby's girlfriend, too. Her name is Ella. Otherwise, we have a good plan. I'm going to find Vera. Send me the link to the TV show."

I pulled my own phone out of the side pocket of my backpack.

As we prepared to split up once again, I couldn't shake the feeling that we were on the verge of uncovering something huge. The pieces of this weird-ass puzzle were slowly coming together, but the full picture was still fuzzy.

We were at the door and agreed to meet at Vera's booth in a half hour. Jack's hand was on the handle. He paused before he swung it open. We could hear the din of the convention burbling on the other side.

"Be careful, Maggie," he said, his voice laced with concern for some unknown reason. "Please."

Before, I'd have dismissed this as Jack being funny, or adorably cautious. Now that I'd found out about his past, I suspected his concern was for a very different reason— one that made my heart crack in two.

Chapter Fifteen

Before going to my sister's booth, I decided to take a detour because I had more questions for my cousin.

His table was at the end of a row, not far from the back door and the smoking terrace. When I approached, I made eye contact with Colby, who immediately averted his gaze. He was standing next to a woman who was a few inches shorter than him. Her hair was scraped back in a severe ponytail, and she wore a hoodie, leggings, and UGG boots. I wondered if that was Ella, his girlfriend.

"Hey there!" I grinned wide. "Thought I'd come back by. Had a few more questions for you."

"Who the hell is this, Colby?" the woman asked.

"This is my cousin that I was telling you about, babe. Maggie, this is Ella."

I waved and smiled.

Ella didn't. She looked me up and down with an expression that told me she didn't quite believe Colby. It was then that I realized her eyebrows were entirely drawn on, in an odd red color. Oh dear.

"Our fathers are brothers," I offered.

"Half-brothers," Colby corrected. "Remember I told you how my pawpaw had two families?"

"What do you want?" she asked me.

I massaged the back of my neck. "I wanted to ask Colby a few more questions about, ah, the person we were talking about earlier."

"Is she talking about that bitch?" Ella turned to Colby. "What did you tell her?"

"Nothing, really. I swear! Maggie was there when Kristi died."

"I sure as shit wish I was there when she croaked. You want to know about her? I'll tell you about her. C'mon." Ella ducked under the table to come to my side. "Don't trust anything he told you about her. He's still in love with her. What a piece of work."

I wasn't sure if she was talking about Colby or Kristi. She grabbed my arm and pulled me away, which made me a little afraid, given all I'd heard about her. I figured I could take her, though, since I had a knife in my bag. Although I was definitely nonviolent, I would kick ass if needed.

Across the aisle were the bathrooms, and she dragged me into the one marked *Family*. I grew a little scared when she locked the door behind us.

"Are you screwing him?"

"Who? Colby?" I recoiled in horror. "No, he's my cousin. Or second cousin. Or half-cousin. I haven't seen him in at least ten years. More. God, no, I'm not bumping uglies with my cousin."

"People screw their cousins all the time." Her brows drew together. "I kind of see the resemblance, I guess. Are you the twin?"

"Yes! Vera's my sister."

"Ohhh, the one who opened that bookstore. I've been meaning to get over there."

I nodded and mustered a smile. The only reason I was entertaining this unhinged jealous woman was to get more detail on Kristi. Ugh, I hoped this paid off. I also hoped she didn't shank me and leave me for dead in this bathroom.

She slipped the purse off her shoulder, dug around, and extracted a vape pen. My eyes drifted to the NO SMOKING sign affixed to the mirror, but it was probably best I didn't point that out.

"What did he tell you about Kristi?"

I gave her the scantest of details, leaving out Colby's personal feelings. "In my opinion, he sounded like he's totally over her."

Okay, that was a bit of a lie. A whole lie, even.

"That wasn't her real, legal name, you know." Ella sucked on her vape pen and stood against the folded-up diaper changing table. She exhaled a cloud of smoke and the entire bathroom smelled like fruit punch.

I leaned against the sink. "I heard that, actually. Kristi sounds like she was something else. A scammer, a convict, a reality TV star."

She snorted. It dawned on me that Kristi and Ella kind of looked similar, although Ella seemed a little rougher around the edges. And with red eyebrows. Still, no wonder the woman standing in front of me had a bit of a complex about her rival.

"I know I sound like a crazy, jealous bitch, but Colby was obsessed with her. Honestly? I'm glad she's dead."

My jaw flapped open and closed. "Well."

She sucked on her pen and shook her head. "I didn't do it. Colby and the other guys who work the booth can vouch for me. I was at that stupid booth from six in the morning to five at night yesterday. Barely had time for a hot dog."

She snorted and shook her head.

"It's understandable why you'd dislike her."

"You know, Kristi and I did fight once. But that was because she was drunk and showed up at our house. The cops totally sided with her, though."

I nodded slowly, hoping she'd continue.

"Kristi didn't believe in any of this stuff." She waved the vape pen toward the door. "She was a scammer. She didn't even believe in Bigfoot. I hate when people do that—take advantage of gullible people. Bigfoot is real, but not like Kristi claimed."

"Do you think that's why someone killed her? They were mad she was scamming people? I assume she made money off her schtick."

"She did. A lot of it. Her YouTube channel had incredible views. She made a mint off that. Spent it all on surgery, though. Her ass cost twenty grand, I heard. But no. I don't think that's why she was killed. I think"—she pointed at me with her vape pen—"she screwed the wrong woman's husband. Or boyfriend."

"That's certainly possible. Listen, do you know anything about her being on TV? A reality show, when she was in prison?"

"Pfft. Yes." Ella rolled her eyes. "She scammed all sorts of guys while locked up. Got them to send her thousands of dollars."

"That's what Mac McCracken did, right?"

She nodded. "Poor Mac. She chewed him up and spit him out."

"What did she spend money on in prison, anyway? That's what I can't figure out."

Ella rolled her eyes. "She funded her post-prison life. Duh."

"Oh. Of course. Right. Uh, where is Mac now?"

"Somewhere here in the hotel. Or in the bar, crying over Kristi. She took him for thousands, tens of thousands, and he made her a star. All because he thought she'd marry him."

"Yikes."

"Yeah. And she strung him along, screwed with Colby, and then moved on to her next victim. I'm telling you, the world is a better place without her in it. She was like one of those praying mantis insects, the kind that eat the males after mating."

It was difficult to reconcile Ella's version of Kristi with the person those folks in my talk loved and admired. That was human nature, though. Even Hitler must have had some buddies, I supposed.

"Why are you so interested in her murder?" Ella eyed me suspiciously.

"I guess because she died almost literally in my arms. It was tough to see. And because people think I might have had something to do with it. Also . . ." My voice trailed off.

She sucked at her vape pen. "Also what?"

"This is going to sound crazy."

"Bruh, we're at a Bigfoot convention."

We both grinned.

"True. I helped solve a murder not that long ago. Asking questions, doing research, poking around. I kind of like doing this. Poking around. Sounds silly, I know."

"No it doesn't. What do you think all these people are here for? Because they love a furry creature? I mean, some do. But a lot of people want the thrill of accomplishment. Want the excitement of putting a puzzle together. I get it. No judgment here." She shrugged.

Oddly, Ella was turning out to be more reasonable and logical than most people I'd chatted with today. Life was such a surprise sometimes.

"Can you think of anyone else who had recent beef with Kristi?"

She shook her head. "I tried to keep my distance from her. Had to get a special dispensation from a judge to come here because technically she has a restraining order against me. But I heard this: she and Grant P. Sanders were hot and heavy."

"Whoa, really? Colby said they hadn't hooked up. I thought I read in the brochure that he's married with kids?"

She lifted her shoulder. "Like Kristi would care. I know that Colby says she never hooked up with Grant, but I don't believe it. He's notorious for screwing his fans. I believe they were together. He was always with her, with Kristi's assistant Alice trailing behind."

"Right. Well, maybe I'll take a run at him. Any tips?"

She studied my face for a beat, then gestured with her vape pen. "Flirt with him. Unbutton your blouse. Two buttons. Ask him out for a drink—he likes Jack Daniel's, thinks it makes him look more like a man. But really, he's a pussy."

"Eww." I gnawed on my bottom lip. "I don't know about all that."

"You gotta do what you gotta do. I need to get back to Colby. He's probably set the damned booth on fire in my absence. Here's my number. Text me if you have any more questions." She dug around in her purse and handed me a business card. On one side was a photo of a Bigfoot plaster cast.

"Thanks. I really appreciate it."

"You're welcome. Sorry I came on a bit strong there. Colby tests the limits of my patience. Hey, are you living back in Wahoo for good now? Maybe you and your sister can come over for a barbecue."

"Thanks, I'd like that," I said, smiling.

We walked out of the family restroom together and hugged goodbye. Were the pieces falling into place? I sure wanted to think so.

Chapter Sixteen

There were only a few people at Vera's booth when I walked up. Her face was pinched with worry as I slipped behind the table.

"How did the talk go? I was concerned about you. Why do you smell like chemical punch?" Her nose twitched. Vera had an extremely strong sense of smell. She leaned in and sniffed my neck.

"Vape pen." When I saw the look of confusion on her face, I added, "Long story. The talk went better than expected. I found out a lot about Kristi."

It was only when Vera fixed a nasty look in my direction that I realized I'd said something I shouldn't have. My mind was so jumbled with details about the murder that I'd forgotten that I was supposed to keep my sleuthing from my sister.

She brushed past me and hissed, "You promised."

Within a few minutes, the customers around the table had either drifted away or bought a book and then left. It was only the two of us now.

"So, what did you find out?" Her tone was as frosty as her favorite Oreo Blizzards from Dairy Queen. She no longer ate those, though, claiming she needed to "stay trim."

"Are you going to be mad if I tell you?"

She shook her head. "I have to be honest. I've been hearing people talk about Kristi for hours. It's kind of gotten me curious about her life and her death."

Excited that my sister was finally onboard with my investigation, I told her everything that Jack and I had discovered throughout the morning. It took me ten minutes, and she sold books to two people during that time. I helped by sliding the books into pink plastic bags with the bookstore's name on the front.

"You saw Colby? Our Holy Chip cousin? He's a Bigfoot hunter now? That actually makes sense."

I stared at her and folded my arms in front of my chest. "That was your takeaway from everything I said? Not the fact that Kristi had been in prison and was scamming guys? Not that she was on a reality show? Not that there are multiple people who deeply disliked her, and were justified in their dislike?"

"Does Colby make a living out of Bigfoot hunting?"

"Vera. Focus. We're in the middle of a homicide investigation."

"I'm not in the middle of any investigation. I think I'm the only one in this entire building who isn't seeking answers to a mystery."

Uh-oh. She'd saddled up and was about to climb onto her high horse.

"I'm trying to do my job, and go out on a date. That's all I want. Somehow, all of you"—she waved her hand wildly in the air at the throngs who were milling past—"are conspiring against me."

Maybe she wasn't down with the investigation after all. I'd have to tread lightly. "Okay, let's just not talk about it for now. How was your morning?"

She recounted how many books she'd sold (a surprising number), how many skeevy men had asked her out (also a shocking number), and that she'd heard something interesting.

"Yeah? About what?" I pretended to flip through a notebook. The cover was of a muscular man with tentacles embracing a redheaded woman. I didn't want Vera to think I was too eager for information.

"Don't pretend like you're not interested. You can't fool me." She rolled her eyes. "I overheard a couple talking about how Kristi had some fight with someone at a booth two days ago, when everyone was setting up here in this room."

"What was the fight about?"

"Apparently it was over a man."

"A man?"

"I was eavesdropping so I didn't hear everything. It sounded as though Kristi and the vendor lady were sleeping with the same guy. I thought that was hard to believe, but after hearing what you found out about her, I guess not. I guess Kristi got around. Anyway, I texted Alex as soon as I heard this."

Of course she did. Anything for an excuse to talk to him. But also, that was what normal people did when they got a clue about a murder. Unlike what I was doing. "Did you find out who the vendor was?"

Vera shook her head. "I was pulled away by a customer."

"Too bad, but thanks for telling me," I murmured. Did this mean we needed to add another person to our suspect list? I'd have to consult with Jack.

"What are you doing the rest of the day?"

I shrugged. "Jack's supposed to meet me here soon. I think we'll probably just hang out for a while here."

And gather information. I didn't say that out loud, but I didn't need to. Vera knew exactly what I'd be doing. As a twin it was difficult to hide anything from your sibling.

"I was kind of hoping you'd go home and pick something up for me."

I didn't really want to leave and drive all the way back into town, but I also didn't have much of an excuse to *not* help Vera. When I'd come home from Boston, I'd pledged to be the second-in-command at her new bookstore, while taking over Dad's gator business. She'd been so busy here at the conference that I would seem like a jerk if I didn't do her this favor.

"What do you need?"

"I wanted you to bring me a change of clothes. I think Alex and I might go out to dinner directly from here tonight."

"Vera, you don't need to be so accommodating with Alex. Let him do a little bit of the work. Make him pick you up."

Her face had taken on a sour expression. "Can you please not meddle in my relationships?"

I shook my head. Vera had notoriously bad taste in men. I actually thought Alex was the best of the bunch, but I also didn't want to see her disappointed. Maybe if she gave a little less at the beginning of every relationship, the men might give her more later on.

"Fine. I'll go home and grab your stuff."

She flashed a small smile. "Thank you."

Because she'd been working nonstop for hours, I encouraged her to take a break, go to the bathroom, and get some food while I ran the booth. She did, reluctantly.

Of course, I was hoping to have much the same luck that Vera had earlier—that throngs of people would come to the booth, gossiping about Kristi. But no such thing happened. The most exciting customers were two old men who seemingly wanted to joke about romance novels.

"I wonder if the authors who write these practice a lot with their boyfriends and husbands, wink wink," one guy said.

The other guy looked at me. "Do you write these? How do you do your *research*?"

"I'm just the saleswoman." I hoped my curt tone and steely eyes would deter any further salacious questions. They did, because the men wandered off.

A few minutes later, Jack strolled up. A little zing went through me when I saw him subtly swaggering over to the table.

Between helping customers, I quickly brought him up to speed about Ella.

He let out a long whistle. "Wow. The clues keep coming hard and fast. We should take a run at Grant."

"We should. But my sister needs me to run home and grab clothes for her. She thinks she and Alex are going out to dinner directly after the conference. Would it be okay if we drove home?"

"I think Alex is really looking forward to that dinner." Jack's lopsided grin was back.

"Oh yeah? Did you talk with him?"

"I ran into him in the lobby. He's headed back to his office to do some research. Was very appreciative of the things we found. Oh, and get this: the autopsy report is back. Kristi definitely died from tetrahydrozoline poisoning."

"Okay. Well, that's a concrete detail. You didn't tell Alex I was poking around, did you?"

Jack shook his head. *Good.*

By this time, Vera was back, toting an oversized, half-eaten corn dog and a giant beverage. Jack greeted her.

"I'm not talking to you." She waved the corn dog playfully in his direction. "You're caving to my sister's worst impulses."

Jack and I looked at each other and snickered. If only he knew about my worst impulses.

"We're going home to grab your stuff. And we'll check on Catsy, too."

"You're the best," Vera said in her normal, squeaky voice. I knew that getting some food into her would help her mood.

Jack and I wandered off.

"You don't have to come back here with me," I told him. "I can always take my car."

"We'll see. I've been curious about something, though. I think we should check out the trail again. We'll be looking at it with fresh eyes today, and hopefully no cops and paramedics. Want to do that now?"

"You think? Didn't the cops comb it pretty carefully? What are you expecting to find?"

We walked toward the lobby. "I'm not sure. But it's good to look at everything at least twice."

"Fair enough. Let's go."

We struck out under a cloudless blue sky. As we powered through the parking lot, we talked about the weather. Miami, Jack said, seemed hotter with all that asphalt. I mentioned that I'd felt like I was freezing to death in Boston every year, and the sensation never left until I crossed the Florida-Georgia line.

"This whole area has great parks," Jack said as we started on the trail. "I didn't know this even existed. How many miles of trails are here?"

We chatted for a bit, with me giving him details about the park's history. If we weren't going to see a murder scene, this would have been my idea of a fun date. Well, and if we'd brought tasty snacks, and maybe some wine, too.

At the little bridge where Kristi had tried to maul the turtle, I stopped at the top. "Did I tell you what Kristi did here?" I pointed out where the turtle had been. "She was hell-bent on petting a snapping turtle. Can you believe that?"

He shook his head, laughing. Then he peered over the bridge railing. "Hey, what's that?"

There were ripples in the water, then a bit of movement. "I think that's a couple of baby gators."

We watched as two cute hatchlings swam under a fern.

"Does that mean momma's around somewhere?"

I nodded. "Probably."

We scanned the banks, then moved to the other side of the railing.

"There," I said, pointing.

The large gator was half-submerged in the water, almost completely camouflaged in the foliage along the stream bank. "That's probably Mom."

"Wow, you're good." Jack's hand went to my back and rubbed. "I didn't even see it at first."

"They're great at concealing themselves."

We stood watching the bucolic scene. I could practically feel every muscle in my body relax, especially since Jack was gently massaging my shoulder.

"Being outdoors is so much better than that hotel. Ugh, I feel like my soul is dying every minute I'm under those fluorescent lights."

I especially enjoyed that there were no people around. Somehow, all the Bigfoot lovers would rather be inside than combing the countryside for the elusive creature.

"I feel the same." He looked at me, then reached for my hand. "Maggie?"

He pulled me into him, and our eyes met. I swear, it was like a fairy tale, us atop a bridge in the hush of the forest. Although these kinds of adorable moments were normally my sister's jam, I had to admit that this was pretty romantic.

"Yeah?"

"C'mere." He cupped my face in his hands. His gaze landed on my mouth. "I just wanted to tell you that you look really gorgeous today. And well, I wanted this."

He leaned in and pressed his lips to mine.

"Oh. Oh!" I said against his mouth. We kissed slow and lazily. "Was this walk a ploy to get me alone so we could smooch?"

"Something like that."

Jack went in for another kiss, something I was completely onboard with.

The world seemed to pause, the only sounds the distant murmur of the forest and the soft rush of water beneath our feet.

I melted into him, the stress of the past day fading into the recesses of my brain. Jack was such a good kisser that it was easy to forget the world when I was in his arms.

Cheesy, I know. But achingly, gloriously, true.

His thumbs brushed my cheeks in a way that sent shivers down my spine. I reached up, my fingers finding the back of his neck, pulling him closer, deepening the kiss. It was sweet and unhurried, a stark contrast to the chaos inside the convention.

As we finally broke apart, breathless and smiling, I couldn't help the laughter that bubbled up inside me.

"Jack, that was . . ." I searched for the right word, but all that came out was "Wow."

"Wow is right . . ." His eyes, half-lidded and sensual, snapped open. His gaze tore from my face and focused on something over my shoulder.

"What?" I gripped his biceps.

"I thought I saw something."

I turned so my back was against his front. His arms circled me in a protective motion. "Where?"

"To the left, near that tree stump." He pointed. "It's pretty far away. I'm probably wrong. It was a bird, most likely. The light isn't great in here."

My heartbeat sped up. Then, I saw it. A dark figure, flitting from tree to tree. "That doesn't look like any bird I've ever seen."

We waited for a few more seconds, then saw the dark blob flicker again. It looked like it was peering around a tree at us. Was there a person in the woods, spying on us? Or some kind of monster? I'd read online horror stories of Slenderman. Maybe I'd been listening to too many Bigfoot hunters. No, I couldn't let my imagination go wild.

But there it was, moving in a jerky, unnatural way from tree to tree.

"It kinda looks like a guy from the Blue Man Group. Only not blue," I whispered. "That's super creepy."

"I think we should probably get the hell out of here." Jack's voice held an urgency that I'd never heard.

He grabbed my hand and we turned in the direction of the hotel. We were walking at a fast clip when I heard twigs and leaves crackle and snap behind us.

Then, the ominous sound of footsteps.

Jack glanced over his shoulder. "Run," he growled.

We hauled ass down the trail and into the hotel parking lot.

"My car's right there," he yelled, letting go of my hand. He took out his keys and unlocked the door.

We dove in and roared off. Well, not roared, because it was an electric car. More like zipped.

Both of us were panting.

"What did you see when you looked back?" I gasped, more out of fear than actual exertion.

"A person in one of those stretchy, all-black costumes."

"What?" I was so confused.

"The kind they use in performances, like a bodysuit with feet and gloves and it covers the face and head. Also known as a zentai suit. Often used in theater performances or against a green screen. Sometimes they call it a disappearing man suit."

Even the name made the hair on my arms stand up. "It was a person, not a creature? You're sure? There are some bears in these parts."

"Definitely wasn't an animal. Seemed like a person in a costume to me." Jack checked the rearview mirror.

"Oh God. Is someone following us?" I twisted around, only to see a silver minivan.

"No. Well, I don't think so."

"That's not exactly the reassuring answer I was looking for."

"Let's just get home and we'll call Alex, okay?"

I nodded. My heart rate hadn't come down. Was someone following us? And why? Who had been in the woods spying on us? Or had it merely been a kid playing a prank with a creepy costume? Questions rolled through my mind like a news crawl on a billboard in Times Square.

We drove in tense silence back to the house. Jack parked his car around back, and for some reason we dashed inside his cabin.

Jack locked the door, then pulled his desk chair over and secured it under the doorknob.

"Just in case," he muttered, peering out the window.

"Is there anyone?" I paced his small living room.

"No. I think we're okay." He walked over to the sofa and sank down.

I joined him, sitting so close that our legs were touching. "What do you think is going on? Could this be what Kristi saw?"

He chewed on his full bottom lip for a while. "Dunno. It could be someone watching us. Could be someone who doesn't want us to investigate. Super creepy, though. I swear someone was following us on our way here."

Our eyes met. I'm not sure what I noticed first. How our breathing was in tandem? How his gaze flickered to my mouth? How I, without thinking, slowly licked my lips as if I was some sort of femme fatale?

He leaned in and pressed his mouth to mine. And with that one kiss, it was as if we'd unleashed all the tension of the day, all of our sexual chemistry, and said, *screw it, we're doing this at the absolute worst time.*

I wasted no time hopping into his lap, straddling him and running my fingers through his dark hair. Meanwhile, he consumed me, grabbing my butt and pulling me closer.

We kissed and kissed, each minute becoming hotter.

"Whoa," I breathed against his mouth as he slipped his hands under my shirt. "Is this a danger bang?"

With his fingers on my bra clasp, he stopped and tilted his head. "Do I dare ask what a danger bang is?"

"It's a romance novel thing." My entire body felt like it was on fire with need. "Usually in a romantic suspense. The heroine and hero get it on during a time of great danger."

He unfastened my bra, then flipped me on my back. I gave a little yip of happiness when he stripped off his shirt and I got an eyeful of his shark tattoo.

"Without question, this is absolutely a danger bang, Maggie."

That was the hottest thing any man had ever said to me. He pressed himself into me, urgent and hungry. Then he gave me everything I'd been wanting from him, and more.

It also made me realize that danger banging was better in real life than in any novel.

Chapter Seventeen

Sometime later, we were still tangled on the sofa. Only the sounds of our ragged breathing and the distant calls of birds in the yard were audible. I was lying half atop Jack, whose legs were surely in an awkward position—one foot on the floor, the other twined around mine.

It was Jack who broke the silence, his voice a low murmur against my ear. "You know, for a while there, I forgot about everything—the case, the weirdo in the woods, everything. Damn."

Still feeling a bit hazy and heady from the unexpected hookup, I pressed my head into his chest. "Same."

"We probably should call Alex, fill him in on what happened in the woods." Jack said this slowly. I wasn't sure if it was because he didn't want to get up, or because he was feeling awkward that we'd just done the deed on his sectional sofa and that his first thought was to call the cops.

I was feeling a mixture of both, to be honest. Even though having sex on a random afternoon while investigating a murder was a first for me, it wasn't totally out of character. But regret danced around the edges of my mind.

Was that the best idea, Maggie? I could practically hear my sister's chiding voice.

Jack kissed the top of my head. "In other news, I'm a big fan of danger bangs now. I'd rather skip the danger part next time, though, if we can. But with you, I'll take what I can get."

Thrilling tingles showered through my body.

"Noted." I eased up and off his body, my mood boosted by the fact that he didn't seem to be regretting our hookup. After all, even if this was just a one-off, we still lived on the same property. I wanted to retain our fun friendship at the least.

But a next time was A-OK with me.

We pulled on our clothes and tried to regain some semblance of professionalism. As I was looking for my sneaker, Jack—who was wearing jeans but no shirt—crossed the room for his phone. He dialed and peered out the window, then let the curtain fall.

"Anything?" I asked.

He shook his head, then spoke into the phone. "Hey, Alex, man. How's it going? . . . Yeah? . . . Oh, yeah? Great. Uh, we had an incident happen to us just now . . . Yeah. Maggie and me."

I listened as he gave a quick rundown of what we'd seen in the woods.

"Okay, cool, cool. See you then." Jack lowered the phone from his ear. "He'll be over soon. Sounds like he's now worried about your sister and is going to try to convince her to shut down her booth for the day."

My eyes scrunched up in a wince. "Vera's gonna kill me."

"Why? She's sold a ton so far." Jack scratched his chest

and yawned. "Hey, do you have any food at your house? I'm starving."

I opened one eye, my mind still on my sister's wrath. "How can you eat at a time like this?"

"You're seriously asking that after . . . after . . ." He waved his hand at the sofa.

I grinned. "There's stuff for sandwiches. C'mon."

He pulled on a shirt. We peeked outside and dashed across the yard to the main house, checking to see if anyone was watching us. Our property was as serene and bucolic as ever. Still, I double-locked the back door. It seemed a little silly, but also necessary.

"Can you do a quick check of the house, just to make sure no one's hiding? I'm feeling especially nervous. I'll start on the sandwiches."

Jack agreed, and as I was getting out the bread, cheese, and cold cuts, I wondered where Catsy was. She normally greeted me when I came home, and I wondered if she was confused because I normally came through the front door.

I headed towards the living room, calling softly, "Catsy? Catsy, where are you, tiny monster?" I expected to hear the jingle of her collar or see her tiny, floofy form slink out from under a piece of furniture, but there was no response. The house felt unusually still, the kind of quiet that made every creak and whisper seem amplified.

I didn't like this one bit. My mind began to work overtime. What if someone had broken in and kidnapped Catsy? Or worse? But the front door was undisturbed.

I checked her favorite haunts first: the sunny patch by the window, the back of the sofa where the sun hit just right in the afternoons, even the little nook behind the bookshelf where she sometimes squeezed herself in for a nap. But she was nowhere.

Worry set in as I went room to room, my tone becoming more insistent. It wasn't like her not to come when called, especially when I used a singsong voice similar to Vera's. Usually this was her cue that food was available, and she never missed a meal.

As I passed by the hall on my way to check the upstairs, I heard Jack's voice, low and serious, drifting from the spare bedroom. Curiosity piqued, I paused. He was on the phone, his tone way different from the professional banter he'd shared with Alex.

"I don't know, Dad," he was saying, a thread of frustration in his voice. "This job at the university is a great opportunity, but I'm just not sure it's the right time to make a move. I wanted to stay here in Wahoo longer."

I leaned closer, my heart tightening. What? He was considering leaving? He'd just mentioned being here for several more months. Weird.

"Yeah, I get that it's a once-in-a-lifetime chance, and that it's closer to you and Mom," Jack continued, the sound of him pacing back and forth on the hardwood floor barely audible. "But there are things here . . . people here . . . that are making me second-guess everything. And more than that, I'm getting a lot done here, writing-wise. I even have an idea for another book."

People. Was I one of those people? The thought sent a

ripple of both hope and fear through me. I wanted to burst into the room, demand answers, but I held back, my hand hovering over the doorknob. He didn't owe me anything. We weren't officially in a relationship.

"I know, I know. I haven't made any decisions yet," he concluded, his voice softer now, almost resigned. "Let's talk more about it when I see you next weekend."

Everything went silent, and for a moment, so was my heart. Somehow, I'd allowed myself to fantasize a months-long fling with him. I'd told myself it was just attraction and friendship, but the thought of him leaving for good sent a heaviness straight to my chest.

Shaking off these serious thoughts, I reminded myself there was a more immediate concern. "Catsy?" I called again, my voice echoing slightly in the quiet house as I made my way to the second floor.

As I reached the top of the stairs, the softest of purrs hit my ears. Following the sound, I found Catsy curled up in the linen closet. Someone, probably Vera, had left the door open. Catsy was nestled among the towels, her tiny body rising and falling in the most peaceful of slumbers.

If only I could sleep that soundly.

She looked utterly content, oblivious to the turmoil in the real world. "Found you, little ninja," I whispered, gently scooping her up. She stirred, blinking sleepily at me before stretching and letting out a tiny yawn that melted my insides.

Back in the kitchen, I set Catsy down and filled her bowl with her favorite snacks. She purred, nuzzling my hand in thanks before turning her attention to the food.

Watching her eat, a temporary calm settled over me. At least one member of this household was unfazed by the day's events.

With Catsy content, I turned my attention back to the sandwiches. I was laying out slices of bread when Jack's arms wrapped around me from behind, his body warm against mine. He planted a soft kiss on the back of my neck, sending a shiver down my spine.

"You're amazing, you know that?" he murmured, his breath warm against my skin. "Not just for rolling with the chaos today, but for everything. And these sandwiches are going to be incredible. Is that Gouda? I'm a lucky man."

His words soothed the raw edges of my worries—almost. I leaned back into his embrace, allowing myself this small moment of comfort. I wanted so badly to ask him about that conversation, but I couldn't bring myself to say a word.

As I was cutting a sandwich, the back door burst open with a force that made us both jump. Vera stormed in, her eyes wild with a mix of concern and fury.

"Maggie! What is going on? Alex told me to shut down my booth for the day out of a security precaution, which was fine because I'd already sold way more than yesterday, but he said something about you and Jack and a stalker in the woods? And now you're here making sandwiches like it's a normal day? While canoodling? What is going on?"

Her gaze flicked between Jack and me, taking in our still-disheveled appearance. Jack broke apart from me and leaned against the counter with a sheepish expression.

"'Canoodling' is an excellent word. Haven't heard that in a while," Jack said.

"You've also ruined my date. Probably." Vera slapped her purse on the island counter. "I'm going to freshen up. Alex will be here any minute; he was right behind me."

She stomped off, her footsteps thundering on the hallway's wood floor.

Jack winced. "Uh-oh. Is she going to be okay?"

"She'll be fine." In the face of the unfolding crisis—a murder, Jack's possible departure, the mystery of who had been stalking us in the woods—my sister's histrionics were small potatoes.

As I was finishing up the sandwiches, there was a knock at the door.

"That's probably Alex. I'll grab it," Jack said.

Hmm. It was three in the afternoon. I should probably offer a few more snacks. I was dumping some chips into a bowl when I heard the burble of conversation coming from the living room.

Thinking I'd impress the guests with some freshly made grub, I piled the sandwiches on a plate along with the chips and waltzed into the living room.

Jack grinned. My sister scowled. Alex scowled harder.

"Snacks?" I said, holding out the food.

Jack grabbed a sandwich, along with a napkin. The other two ignored me. Shrugging, I set the plate and bowl down and scooped up a sandwich, then settled next to Jack on the sofa.

"I'll get you some tea," Vera murmured to Alex, who looked at her as if she was the human embodiment of joy. She glided out of the room.

"All right, you two. What happened?" Alex stood in front of Jack and me.

Since we both had full mouths, we had to do that awkward thing where we chewed and swallowed first.

"We were in the park, on the trail," I started.

"Why?" Alex interrupted.

Mercifully, Jack took over and told the story of our stalker in the woods, leaving out no detail. It was actually pretty impressive how much Jack had observed about our surroundings, down to the direction of the wind and where the sun was in the sky.

Alex stood, his thick brows merging into a scowling unibrow.

"Are you absolutely sure someone was chasing you?" he asked.

Jack and I both nodded.

Vera, who was back without any tea, followed up with "Are you sure it wasn't a bear?"

Jack and I glanced at each other and shrugged. "That's exactly what Maggie suggested," Jack said.

"But bears don't come out in midday, usually. It doesn't make sense." I shook my head.

"It could've totally been a bear," my sister chimed in with her high-pitched voice. "You know how they raise themselves up and they hold their little paws in the air like this."

She held her hands up in the air, palms toward us, making little claw-like motions with her fingers. With her yellow floral dress, she looked about as menacing as a Care Bear.

"Exactly," Alex said. He, too, raised his hands in the air and mimicked Vera's stance. "They really do look like this, don't they?"

"But sometimes they look like this." My sister raised herself on her tiptoes and bared her teeth. "I think they do that to look bigger. I've heard they do that when they eat from garbage cans."

Alex nodded enthusiastically. As he and Vera discussed the various ways bears broke into dumpsters while both wiggling their fingers in the air, I gaped at them in semi-disbelief.

"It wasn't a bear," I shouted. "I'm the only person in this room that has a degree in animal biology. I know what bears look like. This was definitely not a bear."

Vera turned and walked out, muttering something about iced tea.

Alex lowered his hands. "Well, whatever it was, I want you two to stay home. Don't go to the convention tonight, or any parties, events, after-hours raves, what have you."

"There are raves here?" Jack said between mouthfuls.

"You two? Meaning me and Vera?" I retorted.

"Don't poke around. Just stay here and do whatever this is . . ." Alex waved his hand dismissively in our direction. "And no. You and Jack. Stay here and do . . . whatever you two do when you're not getting into trouble."

I couldn't help but snicker, considering we had just done a whole lot of frenzied *whatevering*, which earned me another glare from the detective. And my sister, who walked in with a tall glass of iced tea for her love interest.

"Thanks for the tea," I snarked. "What about Vera? She needs help with her booth tomorrow."

"We'll see," Alex snapped, while taking the glass from my sister. "Thank you, ma'am."

I swear, my sister curtseyed. What was going on between them? They certainly seemed to share the same goofy way of communicating. Blergh. I rolled my eyes.

"For tonight, I'm going to wrap up a few things at the station, then I'm coming back here for Vera in about two hours. We're going to Sunset Sizzler, because I heard they have new vegan options and I thought Vera would like that."

I could almost see waves of joy radiating off my sister. I almost made some pithy comment, but Alex continued. "I'm planning on having my first dinner that's not eaten in my car in a week, and I don't want anything, or anyone"—he fixed a hard stare my way—"to screw that up. You understand?"

I lifted my half-eaten sandwich to my forehead in a salute. "Yes, sir."

Chapter Eighteen

I was sprawled on the daybed in the Florida room, reading a new romantic suspense novel. This one involved a team of hot dudes who rescued pets during forest fires, and the heroine was a park ranger in jeopardy.

Just before the character's first kiss with of the firefighters, I paused to take a sip of my wine—Vera and I had bought a box of the finest that Julio Gallo had to offer at the local Publix supermarket—and cast a longing glance out the window at Jack's cabin.

It had been four hours since we'd gotten a talking-to from Alex. Three and a half since Jack had said he needed to take care of some work, and went to his place. Two hours since Vera and Alex had left for their romantic dinner at Sunset Sizzler.

I tried to get Vera to promise she'd bring back one of the restaurant's signature loaded baked potatoes for me, but she refused, saying that she wasn't sure how long her evening would go or when she'd be home.

"Planning on getting lucky and staying at his place?" I'd teased.

She'd stared at me stonily. "You are killing my vibe," she hissed.

So I'd taken my vibe-murdering ways to the enclosed porch to read for a while. Now, I was bored.

I was also thinking about the conversation I'd overheard between Jack and his father. It had revealed a side of him I hadn't noticed before. Doubt and hesitation: two things I'd never seen him exhibit.

His words echoed in my mind. *This job at the university is a great opportunity, but I'm just not sure it's the right time to make a move.*

And that mention of "things here . . . people here" had left me guessing. Was I one of those people influencing his decision to stay or go? The thought sent a flurry of mixed emotions through me. On one hand, the idea that I could be a reason for him to consider staying filled me with an unexpected happiness.

On the other, the reality that he might leave inspired a wave of sadness. I hadn't been looking for a boyfriend, but Jack had somehow wormed his way into my heart, mind, and other body parts.

I liked the guy. A lot.

As these thoughts swirled in my head, I saw Jack leaving his cabin and ambling in my direction, as if my thoughts had conjured him up. I met him at the screen door and carefully opened it so Catsy wouldn't escape— although I didn't need to worry about that, because the minute she saw him, she waited patiently on the daybed, swishing her fluffy white tail.

"Get a lot of writing done?" I asked.

By now he was stroking Catsy's head, making her purr so loud I could hear it from five feet away. The man had that kind of magic in his fingers.

"A little. I came over because I received an interesting text."

"Oh yeah, what about?" Maybe this was his way of breaking it to me that he was thinking about leaving town?

"It was from Tom. You know, the tech guy at the conference."

I perked up. "Oh yeah? Why? And how'd he know to text you?"

"I gave him my number because he's interested in serial killers. I was telling him about my book and said I'd send some articles to him." Jack smiled.

"Not sketchy at all." Now we were both petting Catsy. Jack's hand occasionally grazed mine.

"Tom suggested that if we wanted to meet Mac McCracken, he's out drinking with Grant tonight. Apparently, they're both drowning their sorrows over Kristi's death at the Shady Lady."

"The bar here in town? They're not at the hotel?"

"Yep. Just the two of them, at the bar. They invited Tom but he's back at the hotel. Apparently there's an issue with the screen in the main conference room, and they need it for Grant's big closing talk tomorrow."

"That's an interesting tip. Alex warned us not to investigate, go to the hotel or to the convention tonight."

Jack stopped stroking Catsy, which earned him a swat on the hip. He dug around in his pocket and pulled out his keys. "Alex didn't say anything about us grabbing a drink at a local watering hole, though."

"I'll put on some shoes," I said.

#

The Shady Lady was Wahoo's most notorious bar. It was the scene of countless hookups, fistfights, business deals, and drug transactions. On any given evening, you could have either a peaceful beer with friends or become embroiled in a life-changing fracas that ended in jail.

It was always a gamble. Jack and I had been here several times together, most recently when we were sleuthing the last homicide. That time, while we were sitting at the bar, a woman with a monkey—an actual live primate—had approached us with a hot tip in our case.

I hoped we'd get so lucky tonight.

But things seemed unusually quiet when we walked in. The place was about a quarter full, with a couple of women playing pool. Jack and I headed straight for the bar.

"Hey, Farah's here tonight," I said when I spotted the smiling bartender chatting with a guy at the end of the row of seats. We'd gotten to know her during our times here.

She spotted us and grinned. Farah was a beautiful woman who was not stingy with her pours of liquor. She usually wore a tank top, and I couldn't blame her, not with those toned arms of hers.

"Hey, you two," she called out. "Be right with you."

She leaned over the bar and kissed one of the men, then sauntered over. "My guy's back from grad school," she said, gesturing to the thin guy with glasses. He lifted a hand into a wave and we waved back.

"Nice," I said. "Everything calm tonight?"

"So far so good. I think everyone's laying low after the other night. Your usual?"

We nodded. Jack and I always had the same draft beer here—a hoppy local brew with an orange aftertaste.

"What happened the other night?" Jack asked.

Farah leaned in, a conspiratorial twinkle in her dark eyes. "Well, you know how things go around here. Let's just say the Shady Lady lived up to her name in a rather . . . unconventional way."

She paused for dramatic effect, glancing around as if to make sure no eavesdroppers were nearby, even though the bar was relatively quiet.

"Turns out, the karaoke machine got hacked. Not sure how, but apparently since it's hooked up to the internet, things like that can happen. Instead of playing the usual tracks, it started belting out sea shanties. People nearly rioted. You know how they love their eighties hair bands around here."

Jack and I dissolved into laughter, thinking about sea shanty songs in a place like this. Farah set our beers in front of us and Jack handed her his credit card.

"Keep it open," he said. "We might be here a while."

"Oh yeah? How come? Usually you two are one and done."

"We're looking for a couple of guys." I paused, then

lowered my voice. "We're investigating a murder at a Bigfoot conference."

"Cool!" Farah cried, then pretended to wince when a few people nearby stared in her direction. "Sorry. You're probably working undercover, aren't you? Tell me more. I love your stories. Y'all are wild."

Jack gave her the rundown while she poured the beer. Meanwhile, I scanned the room for Grant.

"There are two guys sitting around back, near the dartboard," Farah leaned in and whispered. "One's an older guy with a beard and the other looks like Brendan Fraser in *The Mummy*. But not as hot."

The Brendan Fraser description sounded exactly like Grant P. Sanders. "That's them." I slid off my barstool, clinging to my beer. Jack followed.

"Solve that Bigfoot murder," Farah called after us.

We threaded our way past tables and chairs, then around the corner. It never made sense that the dartboard was in a somewhat hidden spot, since it was the place where several dubious and dangerous discussions took place. I'd heard of more than one person being stabbed with a dart.

Intentionally.

Hopefully, that wouldn't happen to us tonight. Bu when I saw Grant sitting morosely with another guy, I realized I didn't need to be worried.

This was more of a wake. The two men looked miserable. An enormous, nearly empty, pitcher of beer was in front of them.

Grant was still in his budget explorer outfit, while

the other man was clad fully in camouflage. He was older than Grant, with a full white beard, white hair, and prominent teeth. He wore a too-tight black T-shirt with the conference logo on the front, and the kind of jeans that sit between a man's ample belly and his junk.

As I approached, Grant's attention turned to me.

"Hey, I know you," he said. "You're the chick from the conference. I didn't get your name."

Apparently, he wasn't that broken up by Kristi's death, because he leered at my chest. Jack was next to me, and I noticed that he straightened his spine a little and rested his hand on the small of my back.

"I don't think we formally met." I plunked down in an empty chair next to Grant, despite not having an invitation. "I'm Maggie Andrews, Gator Queen. I trap gators. That's my job."

"You're the queen of all gators?" the man in camouflage slurred, then chuckled bitterly. "This entire weekend has been a farce. A mistake."

"Why do you say that?" I asked. Maybe not the best opening question, but I had to start somewhere. "And you are?"

I knew it was Mac—I'd seen a photo of him online—but wanted to prod him into talking.

"Mac McCracken. Creator of the Bigfoot conference happening here in town. And I'm not in the mood. For anything." He shook his head and took a glug of beer. "My apologies in advance, ma'am."

I shifted to look at Grant, who flashed a lopsided

smile. I could tell he was incorrigible, and his entire flirtatious persona made me vaguely ill.

Before I could say anything, Jack interjected. By now he was sitting next to me.

"Listen, bro. We're doing a podcast. Well, my girlfriend here is a gator trapper. She's helping me out." Jack smiled.

I figured Grant would bristle at another man claiming a potential sex partner, but he stared at Jack with an equal amount of sauciness.

"Oh, really? You two are together? What exactly are you both looking for? Something professional? Or something more . . . personal?"

I would have sworn on my father's grave that Grant was flirting with Jack. What was going on here? Was he implying that he might want to be the filler in a Maggie-Jack sandwich? Oh dear. I was officially out of my league here.

The contents of my stomach also threatened to erupt in my mouth.

Jack laughed and slipped an arm around me. "Just professional, my dude. Thanks for the offer, though. Flattered from a guy like you."

This seemed to be just the thing to get Grant talking. He proceeded to ignore the inebriated Mac—who looked like he was nodding off—and scooted his chair closer to us.

"What's your podcast about?" Grant asked, again eyeing my cleavage.

Jack tightened his arm around my shoulders. "It's a true crime podcast. Normally we look into cold case crimes. But since Maggie was giving a talk about gators when—"

"You!" Mac thundered, his raspy voice bouncing off the paneled wood walls and the dartboard. It was as if he'd come alive after a centuries-long slumber. "You were there when Kristi died!"

"Yes. I was." Probably better just to rip the bandage off now.

Mac sighed, his whole body sagging with the forceful exhale. "What were her last words?"

I clutched my beer glass, recalling how she'd thought she'd spotted something in the woods. A chill went through me. "I think her last words were, 'Watch this.'"

Mac shook his head and chuckled. "That's my girl. She was so adventurous. So bold. So damned beautiful. A true star."

A tear leaked from his right eye and disappeared into his white mustache. We were silent for a moment, and I played back Kristi's last moments in my mind. It still bugged me that Kristi had seemed to be gesturing at something when she climbed down the embankment.

What was it? A drug-induced delusion? Or had something actually been in the woods—the same creature Jack and I saw?

"Man, it's okay." Grant patted the older guy's arm. "Did you two want to interview me for your podcast?"

"Eventually," Jack said. "Would you mind if we pre-interviewed you now? Just so we can get our notes straight. Maggie, do you have your notebook?"

"Of course." I was always prepared with a notebook and five pens. I reached into my bag and deposited everything on the table.

"Tell us about Kristi." Jack's voice was calm, as if he was encouraging a feral animal to eat from a bowl for the first time.

"She was my everything." Mac wiped his eyes with his fingers.

"Where did you meet her?" I piped up.

Well, that was all it took. Mac launched into a long and tortured explanation of his second divorce ten years ago and his quest to find love online.

"Not easy when you're an older guy who isn't a millionaire," Mac said, while Jack and Grant nodded. "I had a bad run of unemployment, and women just want purses and shoes these days."

Funny, I would've thought his dearth of dates had something to do with the fact that he looked like a demented Santa Claus. Or that he was an unemployed Bigfoot enthusiast. Or the casual sexism. But maybe age discrimination and the desire for luxury goods was the real answer.

"I was noodling around online," Mac said slowly while rolling a napkin into a ball. "And I saw a photo of a beautiful woman who just happened to be in prison."

Translation: he was looking for a woman who couldn't get away, so he trolled the prisoner dating website.

"Interesting. What happened then?" I glanced at Grant, who was staring into his beer mug. He looked up and winked at me.

Barf.

"Kristi responded, and I swear, it was like looking into my own soul. We had so much in common."

He started to cry again and I looked to Jack, helpless. It seemed like we were going too far. That this man's grief was way beyond our investigative abilities.

"We're sorry. Maybe we should do this another time," Jack said tenderly.

Mac shook his head. "Talking about her helps."

Grant sighed audibly. A curious thing to do, considering his friend was clearly devastated. If they were friends?

"How did you find out what happened?" Jack was so good at this.

Mac dabbed at his whiskers with the balled-up napkin. "I was in a meeting with my team. Had been all morning. We've been having problems with the projector setup at the hotel in the main ballroom, and everyone's been racking their brains on how to fix it. I'm no longer in charge of the entire conference, but I help out when there's a crisis."

"Hope it gets fixed before my talk tomorrow," Grant grumbled.

Mac waved his meaty hand dismissively. "You'll be in the spotlight. Don't you worry. But yeah, I'd been in that meeting for hours, since nine in the morning, when someone burst in with a video, saying Kristi had collapsed."

Kristi had keeled over around 12:30. Mac had been in the meeting since nine. Did that absolve him? "Tell me, had you seen her that morning?"

Mac shook his head. "I hadn't seen her all conference, if you can believe that. Well, saw her from across the room."

"Why's that?" Jack asked.

Mac swallowed, took a sip of beer, swallowed again, and sighed. "We broke up. A few weeks ago."

"Again. You broke up again. For the what, fifth time?" Grant said. His tone was unnecessarily mean, in my opinion.

"We had a rocky relationship," Mac told us. "Listen, I gotta take a whizz. Be right back."

With that, he hoisted himself out of the seat, hitched his jeans up higher on his ample belly, and shuffled off.

Jack and I glanced at Grant, who shook his head.

"That guy's been lovesick over Kristi for years. Poor man. I've told him for years that she was just using him for money."

"Was she?" Jack and I leaned in.

Grant rolled his eyes. "She soaked him for everything he had. Drained his savings account while she was in prison. And that reality show, my God. How embarrassing. When she got out, Mac brought her into the cryptid community. Gave her a different name, a new look, everything. He paid for her ass, literally."

"Is that common knowledge?" I asked. "Do people know that about her?"

Grant shook his head. "Only me and a couple of Mac's trusted friends know, but maybe rumors have circulated. I've hated Kristi from the beginning, but I buried my feelings about her out of respect for Mac."

"Oh, really?" I probably put too much emphasis on my words and came off as accusatory, because Grant held up his hands.

"I didn't kill her. I have a solid alibi."

"Oh yeah?" Jack said. "What is it?"

Grant put his elbows on the table and shifted his body toward us. "I was in bed with someone."

Chapter Nineteen

I blinked. Jack blinked. Grant grinned. "You want to know who?"

Jack and I nodded in tandem.

"Alice."

"Kristi's assistant?" I yelped.

"What?" Jack asked.

Grant shrugged. "Yeah."

"I thought you were sleeping with Kristi," I blurted.

The two men stared at me. Jack looked slightly terrified, with good reason. Grant seemed pissed.

"Sorry. That's what I heard."

Grant shook his head vigorously. "I'd never do that to Mac. Bros before hoes and all that."

Somehow, I suspected that Grant wasn't so selective, or that great of a friend. Kristi had been gorgeous, and he was the kind of man to want to screw anything that moved.

I rested my chin in my hands, perplexed. Still, sleeping with Alice was a solid alibi. Although the two of them could've conspired to kill Kristi, right?

"I can't believe she was poisoned," Grant said, his voice cracking. "Who would do that? I'd like to get my hands on—"

"You know about the poison?" I asked, alarmed.

He nodded. "Someone on one of the Reddit forums got a hold of a police report. You'd be surprised at the capabilities of the Bigfoot researchers. Not sure if that person obtained the report in an entirely legal manner, but it doesn't matter now."

I winced and tugged at my ear. It did matter, very much! Grant was a tool. That information might only be known to the killer, and I hoped Alex hadn't heard about this yet, if only to salvage my sister's dream date at Sunset Sizzler.

"And don't start thinking we poisoned her water," Grant added, seemingly reading my mind. "Kristi was fanatical about her water bottle. She had a Stanley Cup that she loved, and she wouldn't let anyone touch it. She kept it with her at all times. It was a special-edition hot pink, and she got a million views one time when she left it in the woods with beer for a Bigfoot and came back the next day. The liquid was gone."

I sat back in my seat, speechless. I wasn't even sure what I was more stunned about: that she'd left beer for some wild animal to drink and possibly poison itself, or that people believed a Bigfoot was drinking out of a Stanley Cup, or . . .

That I didn't see Kristi with the cup at all during our walk—and that she didn't take the cup she normally used.

"That proves Bigfoot exists?" I couldn't hide my skepticism now.

Grant, who had just taken a swig of beer, nodded, swallowed and grinned. "There's something about your eyes that's so alluring, Maisie. Has anyone ever told you that?"

Jack cleared his throat. "Her name's Maggie."

"Right. Right. Anyway. Kristi had the cup with her when I last saw her. We were in the vendor alley, talking about the program. I never touched the cup."

Which is when I'd seen them bickering. Perhaps Grant didn't touch the cup, but Alice . . .

"Interesting. I assume you told the police all this."

"Well, the part about me and Alice, yeah. But not the cup, because I didn't think it was relevant."

He paused to drink, and Jack and I exchanged wary glances.

"Anyway, we need to focus on the future. I don't want this to affect the conference attendance in St. Louis. That's where we're going next. Although not having Kristi around, that's going to screw things up. She was popular." He shook his head. "We've got to move on, though. I think we'll put a tribute to her in the St. Louis program."

"Who do you think killed her?" Jack asked, steering the conversation back to the case.

"You don't think Mac did," I followed up. "Do you?"

"Mac? Hell no," Grant said sharply. "He's a total idiot when it comes to women, but he'd never hurt one. And he didn't come within twenty feet of her. Here's why: his daughter told him she'd go no contact if he continued to have anything to do with her. Mac's daughter's about to have a kid, so he wants to be able to see his grandbaby. That's why. He'd been torn up about this, since he loved Kristi but he also loves his kid. He hadn't been near Kristi in a few weeks. I, for one, was happy about that. She did nothing but make that man miserable."

"Huh." Something wasn't adding up. "But did he text her?"

Grant wrinkled his nose. "Maybe. I wouldn't put it past him, especially if she asked him for something. Which she did a lot. Money, usually."

I didn't answer. Mac seemed to have an alibi. Kristi had definitely asked him for money. Nothing was adding up.

"If she was so terrible to Mac, and if he was trying to keep her out of his life, why was she invited to the conference?" This seemed like an obvious question, but Jack rolled his eyes.

"Mac and I have invested a lot of money into this show. Kristi was a big draw. She made money, we made money. We couldn't afford to not invite her, you feel me? I'm technically in charge of the conference. Mac sold the naming rights to me a year ago."

Jack and I nodded.

"I think Dr. Jess Daws did it," Grant declared, a hint of conspiracy in his tone. "She hated Kristi. They get into a fight every conference. Like freaking clockwork."

"But why?" Jack seemed to be playing dumb.

"Daws is an actual scientist. She's not like the rest of us. I believe in Bigfoot and cryptids, but Jess is a whole other level. She's done research, gotten grant money, published scholarly articles. And when she sees someone like Kristi, who was so obviously in it for the fame and the money . . ." His voice trailed off.

"I wonder if the cops are tailing her," I mused aloud.

"I hope so. Because if she's really the killer, I'm worried for a few more people. Daws has it in for several Bigfoot hunters. Well, the ones who think Bigfoot came from an alien race."

I was about to ask if Grant believed that himself, but by now, Mac was stumbling back to the table.

"Believe what?" he asked. "Are you talking about Mothman? Lemme tell you about the time I was in Angola and saw—" He coughed once.

Then he barfed all over the table, splashing everything in sight. Including me.

# # #

An hour later, I walked out of the bathroom and into my bedroom, brushing my freshly washed and blow-dried hair. Jack, who had showered at his own place but returned to mine for a debrief, held out a glass of wine.

He was sitting against the headboard of my bed in a fresh white T-shirt and delicious-looking gray sweatpants.

"I have to admit, getting puked on by a Bigfoot hunter who looks like Santa Claus wasn't on my bingo card for this weekend." I took a fortifying gulp. "That was the most disgusting thing that's ever happened to me. Well, other than the times I had to clean the monitor lizard cage at the Boston Zoo. They crap a lot."

"I didn't know that," Jack said.

I had hoped to ask Grant and Mac dozens more questions, but after Mac had deposited the contents of his stomach on us, I'd accidentally knocked over a beer and the two men had scurried out of the Shady Lady without as much as an apology to Farah.

She'd taken the situation in stride, and we'd helped her clean up—gross, but it had seemed like the polite thing to do. Jack and I had left immediately after, and came home to decontaminate.

An unspoken, inconvenient truth hung in the air: being puked on was not a prelude to a round of bed-rocking sex.

"Yeah, that was something tonight. Wow."

I crawled onto the bed and sat next to Jack, my back against the headboard. "Do you think either one of those guys did it?"

He shook his head slowly. "Mac? No. I don't think so. I could be wrong, of course, but he didn't seem to have the opportunity."

"But he did text her," I pointed out. "And clearly he was in love with her."

"You're right. But something's been bothering me about the method of murder since the beginning."

"What's that?"

"Men tend to kill in anger. They use their hands, their feet, guns, knives. Men are violent creatures. Women who kill are a different story. Women are seven times more likely to choose poison as a murder weapon. From that standpoint alone, I'd say neither man did it."

"What about Alice, though? She was with Grant. Does that absolve her?"

Jack sucked in a breath. "Sometimes people feed the victim poison over time, and the toxic substance builds up and then kills. It would make the most sense that Alice was the murderer, depending on the level of Visine in Kristi's blood. The autopsy has identified the presence of the chemical, but not the amount. That information won't be available from the toxicology report for weeks."

"So what you're saying is that if you were the head investigator, you'd be looking at Alice and Jess Daws, more than Mac and Grant."

"Yep. That's my take. Honestly, I think Mac is too genuine in his grief. He's devastated. The man can't even keep his bodily fluids inside. And Grant? I'm not convinced."

"He does seem too ambitious and greedy. Did you hear him talking about how not having Kristi around is going to mess things up for their next conference? Kristi was his cash cow. He wouldn't have screwed that up by killing her," I said.

We then talked for a bit about my cousin, and his girl-friend. They didn't seem like they were serious suspects, either.

"Tomorrow we'll take another run at Alice and Dr. Daws," Jack said, yawning and putting the wine glass on the bedside table.

I did the same, and was surprised when he clicked off the light and slid down into bed, covering himself with the duvet. With any other man I would have thought this presumptuous.

With Jack, I was thrilled. He wrapped a muscular arm around me and drew me close.

"What I can't understand," I murmured, snuggling

into his side, "is why you want to do all this with me. Why you want to spend your free time investigating murder."

He kissed my forehead and hummed, a low sound that tugged at something deep and wanton inside me.

"That's an interesting question. I'm intrigued by you and your life."

I snickered. "By me and my life? Because it's so different than yours?"

"Sure, that too. I'm boring. Spend most of my days in a classroom or behind a computer. You live an exciting life."

"Oh yeah, that's me. Ms. Exciting." I thought about all the nights I spent alone, with Catsy. Or sitting on the sofa watching Vera's terrible reality TV dating shows while stuffing Cheez-Its in my face.

"Maggie, there's something about you." He paused so long that I thought he might have fallen asleep. "I don't usually date younger women."

"Ten years older, big whoop."

"Since I'm a professor, I have a policy. Usually when I see younger women I think of my students and I get queasy. I'm hoping you don't think I'm a creeper, as the kids say."

"You're not a creeper."

"That's a relief. I have to confess, I'm captivated by you, Maggie. I'm . . . I'm probably not the best prospect. My ex-wife used to say that I had a hard time opening up to people, and it's true. I'm trying to get better about it. I've been in online therapy, and I think losing my sister did a real number on me when it comes to trusting others. I'm trying to get better, though."

I held my breath, wanting to know more but not daring to ruin the moment and ask. Maybe Jack wasn't Mr. Right. But Mr. Right Now was okay with me, too.

He kissed my temple and continued. "But I find you endlessly fascinating, tater tot. And funny. And smart. And gorgeous. You're kind of like one of those rare flowers in the Everglades. Gorgeous, elusive, probably a little dangerous if you lick it."

"You've already licked it." I softly bit his chest through his T-shirt. I wanted so badly to ask him about his conversation with his father, about whether he was going to eventually leave me and break my heart, but I couldn't bring myself to utter the words. Not while we were here, in bed in the dark.

"Then I guess it's mine. That's how it works, right?"

I couldn't ruin this magical moment between us. I shifted a little, seeking his mouth in the dark. "Mmm-hmm. That's exactly how it works."

Chapter Twenty

The sound of the old song "See You Later, Alligator" ripped me out of a sound sleep. It was my special ringtone for gator calls, forwarded from my business number. This was entirely unwelcome, because not only was it six in the morning, but I was nestled in Jack's strong and warm arms.

I grumbled as I flung off the covers and pawed around for my phone on the nightstand.

"What the hell is going on?" Jack whispered.

"Trapping call." I tapped on the phone screen. "Gator Queen, how can I help you?"

"Maggie Andrews?" The woman's voice on the other end was silky smooth, with a touch of urgency.

"That's me."

"Hey, this is Mrs. Gilman. Joy Gilman. Your third-grade teacher, remember?"

"Oh hey, Mrs. Gilman." She'd been my favorite teacher in elementary school, mostly because she'd had a living room setup in her classroom, complete with a comfy sofa and a shaggy orange rug. For reasons unknown, that had seemed terribly sophisticated to my eight-year-old self. "What's going on?"

She let out a long breath. "There's a gator under my car."

My mind snapped awake. "Oh dear. That's not good. Inside the garage?"

"In the driveway. It's pretty big, too. The critter's tail is right next to the tire. I don't even know how the thing fit under there. Can you come and get it out?"

I blinked the sleep out of my eyes. "I'll be there ASAP."

She gave me her address and we hung up. I poked Jack in the leg. "You awake?"

"Mmrpfh," he responded from under the covers.

"Want to go to a gator call with me?"

He flipped the covers down, revealing a deliciously muscular chest and a wide grin. "Do I ever? Hell yeah."

I laughed. "For this one, I've got to bring Vera. I might need trained backup."

I could have sworn that when I left the room, Jack was rubbing his hands together with glee. Between that and how he'd rocked my world last night in bed, I got ready while wondering if he was the perfect man.

My thoughts soon turned dark, as I went up the stairs to Vera's room. She'd said she'd help for the next couple of weeks, so why did I feel like I was imposing on her?

I knocked softly on her door, then opened it. Vera kept her room pitch-black and cool, with light-blocking curtains, a fan, and an essential-oil diffuser that let out timed puffs of lavender scent.

"Hey," I murmured. "I have a gator call. I think I might need help. Can you come? Or should I call Uncle Bert?"

"Mmph," she responded. "Did I say you could come in?"

We always ignored knocking in our family. "It's at Mrs. Gilman's house. You know, my old teacher?"

The sound of covers rustling filled the dark room and she flicked on the light.

There, in bed with her, was Detective Alex, sleeping as soundly as the day he was born. Thankfully he was mostly covered up, but I could tell he wasn't wearing a shirt.

"Oh, God, sorry, yikes." I stepped back, grimacing.

"I'll be right there," she said.

#

"It's too early," Vera whined. "I feel like a hag."

"It was a late night," Jack chimed in, making me grin. "I feel a bit haggard myself."

"I feel like Merle Haggard," I quipped, making both of them laugh.

We were in my truck, with Jack in the passenger seat and Vera in the middle. Alex had slunk out of our house with a quick wave and a red face that told me he wasn't accustomed to the walk of shame. I didn't want to ask about that situation in front of Jack, in case Vera was feeling private.

She clutched her coffee as though it were a life preserver while we drove over the potholes on State Highway 19.

"I'm excited." I was practically bouncing up and down in my seat. "This is the first time since I've been home that we've gone on a gator call together."

Vera let out a raspy squeak, which sounded more like something that would come from a chipmunk with a pack-a-day cigarette habit. She wasn't as excited as I was. "I called Diego and woke him up, asked him to open the booth at the convention since I'm not sure I'll be there in time."

Ignoring the Bigfoot murder situation because I was so eager and anxious to see the gator, I continued to babble about Mrs. Gilman.

"That was the first year that Vera and I didn't have class together."

"Hated that year," Vera said, adjusting her sunglasses.

"I loved it. It was the first time I'd felt like, I don't know, a person in my own right."

"Oh, come on." Vera snorted. "I remember you crying that year about how lonely you were."

"That's because Jasmyn West told everyone she could see my underwear on the monkey bars. I couldn't help it that we had Pioneer Day and I was forced to wear that stupid dress."

Vera shifted toward Jack. "Maggie was a wild animal on the playground. I swear she fell off the monkey bars so much that the ER doctors knew our entire whole family by name."

Jack laughed, and thankfully, so did Vera. This was really why I was taking a verbal trip down memory lane—to make her nice and comfy before trapping the gator. Unlike me, who could snap into action at any time, Vera needed to ease into stressful situations.

Also, I was dying to hear the details of her date with Alex last night—I hadn't heard her come home, but then again, I'd been busy myself. It was probably best not to ask about it now. She'd likely be self-conscious about dishing the dirt in front of Jack.

For the rest of the ride, Vera told a story that had become somewhat legendary in our family. "Remember the Great Frog Rescue Mission?"

I groaned, knowing exactly where this was headed. "Vera, noooo."

"Oh, come on," Jack said, grinning. "I need to hear this."

Vera wasn't about to pass up an audience. "When Maggie and I were kids, we had this obsession with saving wildlife. Any critter that crossed our path was in for a rescue, whether it needed it or not. We had cats, and dogs, and various bunnies. We even raised some squirrel babies." She paused for dramatic effect. "One summer, a pond near our house was teeming with frogs. Maggie decided they were all suffering from 'urban encroachment' and needed to be saved. We were about eleven."

"In my defense, we'd just learned about animal habitats in school."

"Maggie concocted this plan to relocate them to what she deemed 'a safe space,' which was actually our bathtub. We spent an entire afternoon catching frogs and transporting them to their new 'habitat.'"

Jack was laughing now. "Let me guess, your parents were thrilled."

Vera nodded, barely containing her own laughter. "Dad was so proud. Mom, who loved critters, was too—but she didn't want to deal with all the frogs. And then Mee-Maw—our mom's mom—told us she was going to make frog legs for dinner and we freaked out."

"Did she make frog legs?" I could tell Jack wasn't sure if Vera was joking.

"Thankfully, no. Okay, here we are." I turned down a street that looked like any other in Florida. Stucco homes, palm trees, vibrant green grass.

And, somewhere, a gator.

Mrs. Gilman's home was located not far from ours, in a neighborhood filled with blocky, one-story houses built in the 1980s. A nearby, man-made pond was probably where the problematic gator had originated from, or was headed toward.

Even though people thought gators wanted to be menacing nuisances to humans, really they were quite misunderstood. All they wanted was a nice, freshwater home with some fish, birds, and frogs. They wanted a cozy, hidden spot to raise their babies.

They definitely didn't want to park themselves underneath a late-model Toyota Corolla.

I found my former teacher standing on the sidewalk with at least a half dozen of her neighbors. I parked the truck nearby and the three of us climbed out and strolled over.

"It's been years since I've seen you, Maggie," said Mrs. Gilman. She was wearing a fuzzy pink bathrobe, pajama bottoms, and running shoes. She looked athletic and middle-aged, like a mom who was really into power walking. Which was odd, because I remembered thinking she was so old back when I was a kid.

It hit me that she'd probably been about my age when she was my teacher. I silently shuddered, thinking about what it would be like to teach thirty children under ten. Eesh.

She gave me a quick hug and said hello to Vera. They'd seen each other in recent years, mostly because Vera had been a librarian in town and knew everyone.

"I keep meaning to visit the bookstore," she said to Vera in an apologetic tone. "You know how I love to read spicy books."

"Can't do that if you have a gator under your car," I said, and everyone laughed.

Jack went and stood near the neighbors, and within a few minutes, he was chatting them up. There was a festive mood in the air, a feeling that something interesting and possibly dangerous was about to happen. I thrived on that vibe. Many Floridians did.

Meanwhile, Mrs. Gilman showed us the gator from the end of her driveway.

"I came outside to grab my briefcase so I could do some early morning grading, and that's when I saw the tail." She squatted down and pointed. "If you get down here you can really get a good look."

Vera and I mirrored her stance.

"Oh yeah, he's a big one," Vera said. "Do you think we should call Uncle Bert?"

Our father's brother not only held a trapping certification, he was the owner of Tropical Acres, a reptile sanctuary. Since gators over four feet usually weren't relocated to ponds or lakes because they'd fight other, larger gators, my family had always brought those to Bert.

The smaller ones, we released into a swamp or a river. This one looked like it was destined for Bert's, although we wouldn't know until we caught and measured it. It seemed fairly beefy from this angle, though.

"I think we should be able to lure it out. If we need help hoisting it into the truck, Jack's here."

I didn't tell Jack that he might be pressed into service this morning, but from his earlier glee, I didn't think he'd mind.

Vera and I went to my truck, getting out a snatch hook on a long pole, some rope, and two rolls of duct tape. Jack wandered over.

"What's the plan?" he asked.

I pulled out a small cooler and handed it to him. "Well, we've got some chicken here that we're going to attach to this fishing pole. Hopefully that will entice the gator to crawl out."

He popped open the top. "Do you always keep raw meat around for this purpose?"

"Yeah, actually we do," Vera said. "Usually we keep it frozen but I happened to unthaw some for Catsy."

I stopped what I was doing and sighed. "You're making her food again? The vet told us to feed the canned because she's so much bigger than normal kittens her age."

Vera rolled her eyes. "Are we really going to argue about this now?"

"No, I guess not." I took out the snatch hook.

"What do you want me to do?" Jack asked. I loved that he didn't shy away from stuff like this. My previous boyfriend—who Vera had dubbed "Literary Fiction Larry," because he was a pretentious, Boston-born author—had been squeamish when in close proximity to reptiles. He'd nearly stroked out when I'd brought a small turtle home one day.

I threaded a hunk of the raw chicken through the hook, attached it to the pole, and handed everything to Vera. Today I'd be wielding the handheld snare. It was one of several that Dad had built out of items he'd bought at the hardware store. He'd always kept at least two in the truck, so I did, too.

The snare was made out of a cable looped in a circle, attached to a swivel that looked like a crampon—and that was affixed to a thick, half-inch nylon rope that was about five feet in length. That was linked to another cable swivel and an adjustable painter's pole. I used some duct tape to stick the rope to the pole and noticed Jack staring with interest.

"It's easier to control the animal with the pole and the rope. The head goes in here," I pointed at the loop. "Then we drag it out and maneuver it with these." I patted the pole, then the rope.

"And then what happens?" Jack pointed at one of the aluminum cable swivels.

"You'll see in a minute," I said.

Once we had our gear in order, I approached Mrs. Gilman. "You and the other neighbors should stay back. We're going in."

She wrung her hands. "Please be careful, girls."

We approached the car cautiously, Vera leading with the fishing pole, the scent of raw meat wafting in the early morning air. The neighborhood was silent except for the distant call of a mourning dove. I gripped the snare tightly, feeling its familiar weight and texture.

The gator hadn't moved much, its massive body a dark, almost prehistoric presence under the car. I could see the tip of its tail and part of its back.

Vera cast the line carefully, the chicken landing with a soft plop near the gator's hidden snout. We stood next to each other, barely breathing. Time stretched, each second a drawn-out anticipation of what might happen next.

This was always the part that inspired anxiety. The waiting. When would the creature emerge? Would it take the bait?

Sometimes they didn't.

Suddenly, there was a rustle, a low, guttural hiss, and the gator began to crawl, drawn out by the promise of a tasty snack. Its movements were slow and deliberate. It almost looked as though it was assessing the situation, its primitive, tangerine-sized brain working through the puzzle we'd laid out.

Jack, wide-eyed, stood a safe distance away, ready to assist but also unsure of his role. Hopefully we wouldn't need him to help at all.

Vera and I exchanged a glance, a silent communication honed over years of trapping with Dad and our family. This was the moment of truth.

As the gator inched closer to the chicken, I saw my chance. The reptile was halfway out from under the car.

With a swift, practiced movement, I maneuvered around Vera and positioned myself with the snare. The gator, fixated on the raw meat, didn't notice my approach.

A critical mistake, but reptiles weren't known for being brilliant.

With precision honed from countless catches with Dad, I slipped the loop of the snare over its massive head, right behind the powerful jaws, and pulled tight. The cable cinched snugly, securing my hold on the creature.

The gator's reaction was immediate and fierce. It whipped its head and body back and forth, trying to dislodge the snare, but the loop held fast. Vera quickly dropped the fishing pole and rushed to my side, grabbing the length of rope attached to the snare.

Together, we began the precarious dance of dragging the reptile from under the car and onto the open lawn. The gator thrashed and rolled, its tail sweeping through the grass with enough force to crush the delicate blades.

But with each twist and turn, the gator's energy began to fade. Its movements grew slower, more labored, as the snare's grip and our persistent tugging took their toll. It looked as though we were hurting the thing, but really, we weren't. Still, I always felt bad about stressing the creatures at this point—but knowing we wouldn't kill them was a bit of comfort.

Eventually, the resistance faded to a half-assed attempt at escape. Then it stilled for a few seconds.

Sensing our opportunity, I nodded to Vera, and with grunts of determination we gave one final pull. Exhausted from its struggle, the gator lay panting on the grass, its sides heaving.

This was my moment. I took a deep breath, and before I could second-guess myself, I leaped onto the gator's back. The sudden weight of my body atop the creature immobilized it further, and I quickly grabbed its powerful jaws, pressing them shut with everything I had. The gator started to thrash, and I tried to cover its eyes with my forearms.

Vera was right there with a long piece of black electrical tape. This size gator was a two-person job, and this was why. With the efficiency of a seasoned nurse in an ER, she wrapped the tape around the gator's mouth, ensuring it couldn't snap at us with its deadly jaws.

This was why we needed each other. We worked in tandem, instinctively knowing what the other needed at precisely the right moment.

"Not too tight," I warned. We used electrical instead of duct tape because it was water-repellent. I eased my hands back to the gator's neck, making sure the tape held. She wrapped a second piece of tape around the broad snout. Then a third.

The gator let out a low growl from its throat, and I heard a gasp from someone nearby—but I couldn't pause to look. The reptile still had powerful claws and a tail that needed to be immobilized.

Then, working quickly, we bound its legs, rendering it incapable of the powerful thrashes that could knock a grown man off his feet.

Panting from the exertion and adrenaline, I finally allowed myself to relax just a bit, sitting atop the subdued gator like a conquering hero, though I felt more like a caretaker ensuring the safety of both the animal and the people around it. I was sweating my ass off.

Vera, with hands on her hips, couldn't hide the grin on her face. "We did good."

I couldn't stop beaming. "We still got it, don't we?"

Jack, who had been watching with his mouth agape, approached. "I can't believe you just wrestled a freaking gator. I think my sphincter tightened a little just watching you."

Shrugging, and climbing off the gator, I replied, "This was an easy one."

I glanced down at the prone creature on the ground. It was about five or six feet long, and easily a couple hundred pounds. I suspected it was female, but it was difficult to tell. "I think we can probably hoist this in the truck with Jack's help."

Jack was standing a few feet away, a look of awe still on his face.

"You want to touch it?" I waved him over.

As Jack ran his hand over the gator's tough hide, I glanced over at the neighbors, who spotted us and cheered. I gave them a thumbs up, pumped full of adrenaline from the capture.

Mrs. Gilman walked over.

"I livestreamed that on Facebook," she gushed. "You two were incredible."

Was I the only person who wasn't going live online, constantly posting, always updating? I smiled and thanked her.

Vera had gotten out a measuring tape. Jack helpfully held one end.

"We'll haul it out of here in no time," I told Mrs. Gilman.

She scrunched up her face. "Are you going to kill it?"

I shook my head and explained what we did with larger gators. "This critter will live a wonderful life at Tropical Acres."

Chapter Twenty-One

It didn't take long for Jack, Vera, and I to bring the gator to Uncle Bert's. He was there waiting, along with Aunt Lolo and a couple of the sanctuary employees. They were two beefy local guys who had worked for him for years.

They hoisted the gator out of my truck while the three of us talked to Bert and Lolo. Somehow, they hadn't met Jack yet.

"You're the serial killer writer," Lolo said to him. Instead of her usual muumuu, today she wore a hippie peasant skirt and a neon-green Tropical Acres–branded T-shirt.

"And you must be the woman who bikes around town with her chihuahua," Jack said with a smile.

That, of course, tickled Lolo. She prided herself on her eccentricity and was well known around town for her pink beach cruiser and her little dog's matching pink outfits.

"I got a new dog, you know," she said, poking Jack in the ribs. Like us, Lolo was always taking in stray critters.

We all chatted about her new Min Pin named Todd for a while, then Vera piped up. "We have to go. I need to get to the convention."

"Oh, the Bigfoot thing?" Uncle Bert sucked on his teeth. "I heard about that in the paper, what with the murder and everything."

Jack, who towered over me, Vera, Bert, and Lolo, nodded thoughtfully. Apparently Jack was a giant, or we were just a clan of short people. "Maggie was there when the woman died."

That touched off another fifteen minutes of conversation, with Vera getting more and more worked up as every minute passed.

"Guys, we really need to go. I still have to shower and get ready, because I smell like gator," she said, shifting from one foot to the other. "I feel gross."

Eventually, the three of us climbed back in the truck and headed for home.

"I knew Lolo would want to talk our ears off. She never shuts up. If we hadn't left we'd have been there for hours. I'm already late for the convention." Vera's mouth turned down at the corners.

"Calm down," I said. "You're never on time for anything anyway so don't sweat it. We'll be there soon enough."

"We? There is no we. You're supposed to stay away from the hotel and the con."

I shook my head. "Alex said not to go there last night. He didn't say anything about today."

Vera let out a little huff of displeasure. "Do you have to poke your nose where it doesn't belong?"

I glanced at Jack, who was biting his bottom lip, probably to keep from laughing.

"In fact, I do."

My sister and I shot each other nasty glares, and it felt just like old times. I couldn't help but giggle, and eventually, Vera was smirking. I elbowed her and she finally grinned.

When we arrived home, Jack said he was headed to shower at his house, leaving Vera and I alone in the kitchen. While I made us English muffins with her favorite kumquat jelly (a Wahoo specialty), I leaned against the counter and smiled. Vera was assembling a snack bag for her day at the conference.

"That was killer this morning, wasn't it? Us working together, trapping like we used to with Dad."

She held up a hand. "Don't."

"Don't what?"

"Don't try to guilt-trip me into trapping. I only went today because I promised I'd help you in the next few weeks."

"But Vera, I thought you loved this. Thought you wanted to carry on Dad's legacy. This is what the Andrews family does, we—"

"No," she hollered, slapping a box of granola bars on the counter. The package flew open and the bars went everywhere. "Oh, fluff. You and Dad were trappers. You and Dad loved it. It was your thing. I only went along with it."

Her ferocity stunned me and I gaped, open-mouthed. "But . . . but . . ."

"Dad was your favorite. You two were like peas in a pod. Look, Maggie, I'm happy you've found your calling in life. But I'm still looking for mine, and I hope the bookstore is it. I hate trapping. I hate the smell of gators, I hate the sun and what it does to my skin, I hate how the critters thrash around because they're stressed. I'm sorry."

She swallowed back a sob, grabbed her lunch bag, and left me standing stunned with six granola bars on the floor, two uneaten English muffins, and a whole lot of confusion.

#

An hour and a half later, Jack and I strolled into the convention. Once again, he'd driven. I'd been going to rant about my fight with Vera, but considering his sister had been murdered by a serial killer, I wasn't sure if it was the best thing to discuss.

We stopped near the water fountain so I could fill up my Nalgene bottle. Unlike Kristi and half the planet, I didn't like the trendy, cute, or expensive bottles. Mine was a beat-up gray thing that I'd had since high school. Recently, I'd slapped a Gator Queen sticker on the front, right next to a sticker that said DEVOUR THE PATRIARCHY.

"Whoa, it's way busier today," Jack said, surveying the crowd.

"Probably everyone wants to get their Bigfoot merch while they still can."

I took a sip while scanning the room, then offered the bottle to Jack. He reached for it and took a swallow.

Jack wiped his mouth with his sleeve, which should have been at least vaguely gross. On him, it looked hot and rugged. "Where should we start?"

He flashed a smile and my heart, stomach, and other body parts fluttered. Yeah, I had it bad for this man. Warning lights and bells flashed in my brain.

"Well . . ." I spotted Michelle, the weird vendor I'd chatted with twice. I waved. Naturally, I'd expected her to wave back, but instead she scowled and turned away. "God, people are so weird here. Let's try to find Dr. Daws. I think I remember that she was supposed to give another talk today."

Jack fished the program out of his back pocket and unfolded it. "Says here she's in the Sabal Palm Room, doing a talk called 'Bluffing with Bigfoot: Mastering the Art of Cryptid Camouflage.' Ooh, there's a barbecue farewell dinner tonight, too."

"Okay, let's go into that session, then corner Daws afterward. How late are we?"

Jack looked at his watch. "It started over an hour ago. Should be ending in about fifteen minutes. Let's do it."

It took us a while to find the room, mostly because four people stopped us to ask about Kristi, and what I'd seen in her last moments on earth. At first, I tried to be kind and polite. But after the second person, it all seemed salacious and icky.

"Are you sure she's really dead?" the fourth guy asked me. "I think this is all a hoax. I think if she was really dead, we'd know it. And what did she see in her last moments, hmmm?"

I stared at him, my mouth contorted in a WTF grimace. "A hoax? What are you talking about? Would she appear as a ghost? Is the official word from the police saying she's dead not enough for you? Is me saying she wasn't breathing not enough for you?"

Jack tugged at my sleeve. "Maggie, uh, it's okay. C'mon."

The guy shook his head. "You're one of those who doesn't see the truth. It's okay. Hopefully you will someday. Peace out."

I stomped off, sputtering. "Can you believe these people?" I hissed to Jack.

He assured me that it was best to ignore everyone. I promised I'd try.

We arrived at the room, but not without further incident. Jack held the door open for me, but as I tried to sneak inside, the strap of my backpack caught on the handle, and I was pulled back like a slingshot. I let out a little *oof* noise, and the entire packed room—including the presenter—paused to stare at us.

Dr. Daws looked more than a little annoyed.

"Sorry," I muttered, holding up my hand. This was my cue to sit quickly in a chair, but every single one was taken.

My cheeks warm with embarrassment, I dove for the floor and sat with my back against the wall. Jack followed, but with a lot more grace.

Daws resumed her talk. She stood at the front, commanding the room with an ease that spoke of years in academia. She was wrapping up her presentation, her voice a smooth alto that floated above the murmur of the crowd.

She wore plain khaki pants, hiking boots, and a simple

yellow T-shirt. Oversized glasses, the kind that turned dark in the sunshine, covered half her face.

"In conclusion," she said, her eyes sweeping over the audience, "the essence of Bigfoot, or any cryptid for that matter, isn't about proving or disproving their existence. It's about what they represent: the unknown, the untouched parts of our world, and the endless possibilities that lie in the unexplored. Thank you." With that, she nodded, signaling the end of the session.

The room erupted into a mix of applause and chatter as people gathered their belongings. Jack and I exchanged a nod. It was now or never. We hauled ourselves to our feet and made our way through the dispersing crowd.

A few people were waiting to talk to the professor, and we stood patiently while everyone filed out.

"Dr. Daws?" Jack called out as we approached. She was packing up her notes and laptop, but she paused to look up at us.

"Yes?" Her gaze was inquisitive, a slight furrow between her brows. If ever there was a professor from central casting, Daws was it.

"We were hoping to ask you a few questions, if you don't mind," I said, trying to sound casual but probably failing.

Her eyes narrowed slightly. "Are you two with the police? You don't look like it."

Translation: *you look like all the other lunatics here.*

Jack shook his head. "No, we're not. We're . . . podcasters. Working on a show about Kristi Klaus. We're just trying to understand what happened to her."

Dr. Daws closed her laptop with a soft click, a long sigh leaking from her mouth. "Why is everyone a podcaster these days?"

"Good question," I said.

Her expression turned guarded. "You two were in the dance-off. Second place."

We nodded.

"Why are you asking me about Kristi? What makes you think I have anything to do with her . . . situation?"

I took a deep breath. "We're talking to everyone who was here, trying to piece things together. You're a respected figure in this community, and we thought you might have noticed something off that day."

Dr. Daws leaned against the table, folding her arms. "I don't know why my opinion about Kristi matters at all."

"We couldn't help but overhear that there was some kind of disagreement between you and Kristi during the convention setup. Would you mind sharing what that was about?" Jack's tone was diplomatic, yet direct. He did a long, slow blink of his eyes.

With those dark lashes of his, I'd have confessed every one of my sins. But Dr. Daws was obviously made of stronger stuff.

A flicker of irritation crossed her face. "Ah, yes, that unfortunate spectacle. Kristi and I had long disagreed on our interpretations of Bigfoot's origins. I advocate for a scientific approach, seeking natural explanations within the realm of undiscovered species or misidentified animals."

"And Kristi?" I prodded gently, already knowing part of the story.

the story.

"She was convinced Bigfoot was an alien, or at the very least, connected to extraterrestrial activity. Pure nonsense, but she was quite vocal about her theories." Dr. Daws shook her head, her distaste for the idea obvious.

"So, what happened the other day, the first day of the con?" Jack asked, leaning in slightly.

"We had a heated exchange, as we often do at these events," Dr. Daws admitted, her tone laced with regret. "Kristi was promoting her alien theory, and I may have publicly challenged the validity of her claims. It wasn't my finest moment, but I stand by my scientific principles."

"And where were you on Friday, when Kristi collapsed?" I found an opening and took it.

Dr. Daws raised an eyebrow, a hint of suspicion in her gaze. "I was out in the field, collecting data. I had no reason to be at the convention center, especially after that altercation. Unfortunately, some of Kristi's more zealous fans like to harass me. Why do you ask?"

Jack and I exchanged a quick glance, weighing our words carefully. "We're just trying to understand what happened to Kristi, that's all. If there's anything you remember that might help . . ."

Dr. Daws considered us for a moment, then nodded. "I understand your concern, but I assure you, I had no part in Kristi's demise. Our disagreement was purely professional, despite its heated nature. I've told the police everything I know, and they also have copies of the receipts I kept from that day."

"What kind of receipts?" I probed, even though I guessed she was a minute or two from getting security here. Her hand hovered over her cell.

"Lunch," she sniffed. "I had a lovely lunch at a place called Cheesy Does It, in downtown Wahoo. That was right after I gathered evidence at Whispering Pines Park. I have the admission receipt for that, as well."

My mouth opened, formed an O, and froze. Both the park and Cheesy Does It were miles from this hotel. Did that mean she had a solid alibi? Sure seemed like it.

Dr. Daws's eyes met mine, a glint of something unreadable flickering in their depths. "You see, I keep meticulous records of my whereabouts. It's a habit one forms when their work is often scrutinized by skeptics and believers alike."

Jack nodded. "That's very thorough of you, Dr. Daws."

She began to gather her belongings again, her movements deliberate. "In my line of work, one must always be prepared to defend their research . . . and their reputation." Her gaze lingered on us for a moment longer than necessary. "I suggest you do the same with your podcast."

As she shouldered her bag and walked away, her parting words hung in the air like a fog, thick with weird vibes.

"Do you trust her?" I whispered as we watched her walk through the door.

"Not even a bit," Jack said.

Chapter Twenty-Two

It was time for a snack. Jack wanted to try the Bigfoot pretzel, and I had my eye on a Mothman muffin, a sinfully tasty chocolate baked treat with two red cherries on the top.

"I don't get the cherries. What are they supposed to be?" I plucked one off and plopped it in my mouth.

Jack and I were sitting on a bench, watching the parade of people stroll by.

"Mothman's eyes. They glow red." He tore off part of the heel of the pretzel, little chunks of salt falling everywhere.

"Mmm-hmm," I hummed while chewing. "You know a lot about cryptids."

"Stayed up late the other night reading about things. It's quite interesting. I actually have an idea for my next book." He took a sip of his soda.

"Oh yeah? What's that?"

He waved the half-eaten foot in the air. "This. Cryptid connoisseurs. Bigfoot hunters. Skunk Ape detectives. The entire world. I'm fascinated."

I thought back to the conversation I'd overheard. Was now the time to ask about it? "That would require a lot of research, right?"

He nodded.

"Is that what you really want to do? Write?"

"Ideally, yes. But teaching brings in a steady paycheck." He glanced at me, a hint of something unreadable flickering in his eyes. "Why do you ask?"

I took a deep breath, deciding to let it all hang out, for better or for worse. "I accidentally overheard heard you and your dad talking last night. About you leaving town . . ."

Jack set his pretzel down on a napkin, his expression turning serious. "Maggie, I—"

"No, let me finish," I cut in, my heart pounding against my ribs. "I know we haven't put a label on whatever this is between us. Which is cool. And we're just getting to know each other. But hearing that conversation, well, it just made me wonder where you see this going. If you see it going anywhere. I mean, it's okay if you don't. I'm—"

He looked at me, his gaze softening. "I didn't realize you'd heard that. And I'm sorry if it made you worry. The truth is, I've been doing a lot of thinking."

The crowd around us seemed to blur into a backdrop as the moment stretched between us, charged with an unspoken question. This was it. He was telling me he was leaving. My muscles stiffened.

"About?" I said softly.

"My life. The future. You." He picked up the pretzel and inspected it. "I didn't expect—hell, didn't want—to meet anyone right now."

I held my breath. This sure sounded like we were about to put things on hold. Or something.

"But I'm freaking crazy about you," he said, his words almost inaudible. A sheepish grin spread on his face. "I barely know you yet, but I like being with you. A lot."

His surprising admission hung in the air, almost jarring against the cacophony of the convention's hustle and bustle. I felt a jolt of shock, mixed with a warm rush of something I dared not label just yet.

"You do?" I managed, my tone a mix of disbelief and joy.

"Yeah, I do." It was then that I noticed the tension in his shoulders easing. "And I know this whole situation is unusual. I'm older, I've got a job in a city four hours away, I'm working on one book, thinking of another. You moved back home and are starting a new business. It's a weird time for both of us. My dad would like me to take a teaching job up in Tampa so I'll be closer to them. My parents are older, and they moved north to the Gulf Coast, so I have to give that a lot of thought. Since my sister was killed, I'm all they have left."

"Totally. I completely understand. Honestly, I don't want to put a label on us, and I'm not ready for marriage or anything super serious, but I also don't want to get my heart broken, you know?"

"Um. It means I don't want to make any decisions without considering this—us. I want to keep exploring what's between us. See where it leads. If that's okay with you."

"It is, absolutely. Yes. Makes sense." The words tumbled out in a relieved exhale.

"I like your mind. No, I love your mind. And you have this weird and wild sense of adventure. Since I've met you, I've investigated two murders, pulled an iguana out of a toilet, and helped with a gator rescue. And of course, there's Catsy to think of. I think we've grown quite attached."

Now I was cracking up.

"And," he leaned in, his lips close to my ear, "I love your ass, too."

I mock-gasped, covering my mouth with my hand.

"Oh, don't pretend you're shocked," he teased. "You know exactly the effect you have on me."

"Perhaps." I took a sip of my water.

We sat in companionable silence for a few minutes while we finished our snacks.

"So, about Kristi's case . . ." Jack finally said.

"Yes." I wiped my mouth with a napkin, eager to steer the conversation away from romance. "Let's do a rundown of our suspects."

"Okay. We've got Mac. He was in a meeting all morning. Then we've got Dr. Daws, who claimed to be at a park and at lunch."

"Both places are a bit of a drive from here," I pointed out. "And there's my cousin and his girlfriend. Also, Grant."

"Who allegedly was sleeping with Alice."

"We should try to find her." My gaze roamed over the crowded room, as if I half expected her to emerge from the crowd. "But wait, I have a question. Is it really possible that Kristi was poisoned over time, and not just one big dose on Friday morning?"

Jack nodded slowly. "I've thought of that. But you said she was out of it during the walk. Almost as if she was drunk."

"She did smell like gin."

"My guess is that she was boozing it up, and someone dosed her that same day. Alcohol plus the Visine likely worked in tandem and killed her quickly. Most of the people here are from different states, according to the brochure. Mac is from North Carolina, Dr. Daws is from Washington State, Grant is from New Hampshire. Kristi lived in Orlando—who here would have access to her every day? If she was poisoned over time, it would have to be someone close to her."

Jack and I looked at each other and said one name at the same time.

"Alice."

# # #

We weren't having any luck finding the elusive Alice. We made several laps around the convention floor and asked a half-dozen people, all of whom had seen her that morning. Somehow, we kept just missing her, and I was beginning to think she was giving us the slip.

Twice, we strolled past Vera's booth. She and Diego were steadily busy, but not so busy that she didn't have time to shoot me a nasty look.

On our third trip around the convention floor, Vera waved me over. Jack went to chat with Diego. I hesitated whether to go over, considering how our conversation earlier had ended. Maybe she was going to apologize.

"Why don't you go home?" she suggested, her tone still frosty.

"Why should I?"

"Well, what are you doing?" She folded her arms. "You have no business here."

"That's not your problem. I'm looking for someone."

She wrinkled her nose. I did, too.

"Stop mimicking me."

"Stop telling me to leave. Hey, how was your date last night? I guess it ended well." I raised my eyebrow, hoping to make her laugh. More than anything, I wanted to put that fight behind us. But awkwardness hung in the air, something that seemed out of place and foreign with my twin.

Vera straightened a stack of books, her face morphing from pinched and angry to soft and dreamy. "Super nice. We shared one of those Onion Blossoms."

That was the signature appetizer at Sunset Sizzler, and I had to admit I was a little jealous because fried onions were among life's greatest pleasures. Vera usually wouldn't allow herself to eat such a culinary travesty, though, since she was always on a diet. "Ooh. It must be serious if *you're* eating fried food."

"He's really sweet."

"You say that about all the guys." When I saw her crestfallen expression, I quickly added, "But that's cool. I'm glad you had a good time. You two seem to share the same sense of humor."

Vera was easy to tease, and she usually gave as good as she got. Still, I knew how much this meant to her. Knew that she wanted a life partner, even if he was a slightly stiff, by-the-book detective. Better than so many other possibilities, including her last several boyfriends. I had to go easy on her.

"It was the best date I've been on in years, so I'd appreciate it if you didn't screw it up by getting arrested. I'm trying hard enough not to screw it up myself."

I shook my head, as if trying to shake loose some logic. "Wait. How could *you* screw it up? Vera, that man is smitten with you. He acts like he'd walk through fire for you. What are you talking about?"

Her nose twitched. "I haven't chosen the best men, you know. I assume something's wrong with me, or I'm a magnet for jerks, or I'm just a loser. I dunno. I seem to screw up a lot. I'm waiting for him to screw up. Waiting for the other shoe to drop."

She heaved a sigh. Vera sometimes got in a defeatist mindset when she was feeling unsettled or anxious. I was one of the few who could pull her out of it. Me, and Dad and . . .

Well, Dad was gone. So just me. And sometimes I refused to coddle her. Today I was feeling more charitable, probably because I kept thinking about Kristi's sister, the one I'd read about in the online news article. And Jack's sister, too.

"Vera." I reached for her wrist. "You have been through a metric crap ton in your life. A rare skin thing with your vitiligo at thirteen. Mom dying. Dad dying. Okay, yeah, you do have an ex who's serving a hard ten in federal lockup for election fraud. You've also graduated from college, worked one career at a library, and opened a business that's already successful. Just remember: the world might want to chew you up and poop you out, but never forget."

Vera giggled. This was one of Dad's pearls of wisdom. I wasn't sure if she'd want to revisit it, but I was already committed to the bit, so I plowed on.

"What aren't you supposed to forget . . . ?" I teased.

"The world might want to chew you up and poop you out, but you are corn," she said, laughing. Then her laughter turned to a smile. "Seriously. I don't want you to get arrested. I'm not fluffing around, Mags."

I pressed my hand to my chest and opened my eyes wide. "Do you see me doing anything illegal? By the way, where is Detective Alex right now?"

I was hoping Vera knew his whereabouts, mostly because I wanted to stay far out of his way.

"He's around," she said. "Doing his job as a law enforcement professional. Which is what he's paid to do. Unlike some people."

"Did he tell you anything about the case last night? Any pillow talk?"

"Maggie."

"Come on. What did he say? I should've told you to pump him for info. Use your feminine wiles to get it out of him. He adores you. I can tell."

"You're terrible." She shook her head. "You really think so?"

I nodded. "He looks at you like Catsy looks at her catnip bird."

She scoffed, but the pink tinge in her cheeks told me that she knew the effect she had on Detective Fun Stealer.

"Did you find out how old he is?" It was a question I'd been curious about since meeting him.

"He's twenty-nine."

I nodded, trying to paste on a thoughtful expression. Damn. Law enforcement sure aged a guy.

My sister scowled at me, probably because she was good at reading my mind. I quickly responded with "He looks really adult. Serious. Like he's dealing with serious things. But handsome. Very handsome. And muscular. Like an action figure."

He wasn't my type, but still.

"Maggie, he's got a stressful job." She paused for a beat. "But when he relaxes, he's so funny and charming. Almost shy. By the end of the night, I'd forgotten all about the homicide and what he does for a living. Did you know he loves to read science fiction, just like Dad did?"

She let out a happy sigh and inspected her nails, which were painted a perfect shade of ballet-slipper pink.

"Come on, Vera." I stood a few inches from her, in the annoying way only a sister could. "You're just as curious as I am about what happened to Kristi. You watch more true crime than I do."

Her eyes flitted around, almost as if she were checking to see if Alex was nearby. She was definitely close to spilling some choice information. I knew my sister as well as I knew myself.

"Please," I whispered. "Give me something."

"Fine. He said that he'd cleared a couple of suspects. Kristi's ex-boyfriend, some gross older dude who used to give her money. He has a solid alibi. And"—she shiftily glanced to the left and right—"our cousin is no longer a suspect, but his girlfriend might be."

"I knew it. She seemed sketchy. And almost certainly violent. Did Alex happen to say anything about Kristi's assistant?"

Vera's cheeks turned pink. "She was . . . she . . ."

"Spit it out."

"The assistant was in bed with someone when Kristi collapsed."

Of course Vera would be shy when it came to talking about bumping uglies. "I knew that."

"If you know all this, then why are you pumping me for information? What the fluff?" She stared at me pointedly and moved away to help a customer.

My sister was sick of this entire investigation thing, I could tell. And probably Bigfoot in general. I was sure she wanted this entire weekend over so she could take her relationship with beefy Detective Alex to the next level. I wondered if he knew that Vera had probably already picked out names for their kids.

Not my swamp, not my gators. Still, it was unsettling to me that she seemed to feel such anger about how close Dad and I had been. That wasn't something I could fix now, or possibly ever, which left me feeling frustrated and a little edgy. I had to get out of this booth.

I found Jack perusing some books. "Let's move along," I muttered.

We eventually ran into my cousin's girlfriend, who was a bit more friendly and less bulldog-like today. She even hugged me, which was only a little frightening. Vera's information loomed large in my mind, though.

"Have you seen Alice Oates?" I asked her. "We want to chat with her."

"That little mousy assistant of Kristi's? Yeah, I just saw her sitting in the Green Room. It's where all the speakers can go before and after their sessions."

She explained where to find the room, and Jack and I hustled off.

Chapter Twenty-Three

The Green Room was down a long hall, tucked away behind a nondescript door. It was a place easily overlooked amid the chaos of the conference.

"I always feel weird at events like this," I said. "One time, I went to the International Congress of Zookeepers. It was in New York, in a huge hotel, bigger than this. By day three I felt like I was hallucinating from the fluorescent lights and the lack of windows."

Jack nodded. "These places are unsettling. It's like the uncanny valley. It seems real, but isn't quite."

"That's it. You're really observant, you know that?"

We were at the closed door, and Jack paused. "You ready?"

He pushed open the door. A hush fell over us, a contrast to the cacophony in the main hall.

The room was bathed in a soft light, filtering through sheer curtains, casting everything in a soothing, sunlit hue. The light came from a window that overlooked a small tropical garden. Okay, maybe it wasn't a garden. Upon further reflection, it was merely the landscaping that ringed the parking lot. Still. I felt a lot more grounded now that I could see the natural world.

Plush, moss-colored sofas were arranged in cozy

clusters, with a few scattered armchairs upholstered in deep shades of forest green.

In one corner, a small buffet table was laid out with an assortment of snacks and refreshments, and as I always did, I scanned the offerings.

Ooh, they had those granola bars I liked. I stopped myself from reaching for one.

The gentle clinking of glassware punctuated the quiet murmur of conversation. Jack and I paused at a table with some brochures. They were for local attractions—things like airboat rides, mini golf, and . . . my uncle's reptile sanctuary.

"I guess Bert must have a contract with the hotel to hand these out," I murmured, pretending to be extremely interested in the brochures while Jack scanned the room.

"I see her," he whispered. "Far corner."

She was perched in an armchair that seemed to swallow her small frame, her hands fidgeting with the hem of her cardigan. Her eyes, wide and darting, were fixed on a point in the distance, lost in thought or worry. Or something more nefarious, like guilt, if you asked me.

Alice was now my number one suspect. Frankly, it was shocking that Alex wasn't here with handcuffs, dragging her off to county lockup.

As we approached, she seemed to shrink further into the chair, as if trying to blend into a fake ficus tree that stood next to the chair.

Jack cleared his throat softly, not wanting to startle her in the serene atmosphere of the Green Room. "Alice?" he began, his voice gentle.

She looked up and I could almost see her eyes focus. "Uh, yeah?"

Jack crouched, while I dragged a chair over. She spotted me. "Oh. Hey. It's you. The person who was . . ." Her words dissolved into a shuddering breath, one that told me she was trying mightily not to cry.

"Hi there," I said softly. "We're really sorry to bug you, but we wanted to ask some questions."

She rubbed her eyes. "What? Why? I've told the cops everything."

I looked helplessly at Jack.

"I'm a podcaster," he said, easing his butt onto the floor in a fluid motion. "Maggie's my . . . friend."

Alice's eyes shifted from him to me, then back to him, probably wondering (as I had) how many podcasters were in this place. "Okay. You want to interview me about Kristi. I get it." She heaved a sigh. "We should probably go somewhere quieter."

"Absolutely," I said, while wondering how we'd explain our lack of audio equipment.

"Would my room work?" She wrung her hands.

Jack nodded. As we followed her out of the Green Room, I couldn't help but notice the handful of other people eyeing Alice as we walked past. What did they know that we didn't?

It occurred to me that detectives really did have a difficult job—everyone seemed to harbor secrets, lies, and sketchiness. Also, we were going to a secluded location with a murder suspect. *Should I be worried about this?*

I pondered this while in the elevator, trying to ignore

the thick tension in the air. Then again, perhaps the unsettled vibe was coming from me, because I was imagining all sorts of ways the petite Alice could kill Jack and me in her hotel room.

"Nice weather we've been having," Jack said, obviously in a desperate attempt to make us all more relaxed.

Alice shot him a look. "It's too hot for me."

I seized on this as an opportunity to find out more about her, and to take my mind off all the dark thoughts. "Where you from, anyway?"

Somehow my accent had morphed into Deep South, as if I was channeling Uncle Bert. Next thing you know I'd be throwing around words like "kinfolk" and "bless your heart."

"St. Paul, Minnesota."

The elevator stopped on the sixth floor and the doors slid open. Alice got out first, then me, then Jack, who held the door so it wouldn't close on us. He was a gentleman like that.

"I'm right here." Alice pointed at a nearby door. "Kristi and I always get a suite with an attached room. I get the small room, of course. She was over there."

She gestured with her key card at the neighboring door, then tapped it against the lock. With a snick, it opened, and we trooped in.

"See, Kristi's suite is right on the other side of this door." She knocked on a door that was almost opposite the bathroom. I wondered what was in Kristi's room now—had detectives hauled all of her personal belongings away?

I filed the question away for later.

The room was typical hotel fare: a queen-sized bed with an overly plush headboard, a desk crammed into one corner, and a TV bolted to the wall opposite the bed. The color scheme was best described as Fifty Shades of Beige.

It immediately made me feel sleepy, which was probably the point.

What wasn't typical was the array of items scattered across every surface.

The desk was buried under a mountain of papers, sticky notes, and what looked like three different types of planners. But the real showstopper was the life-sized cardboard cutout of a Sasquatch standing guard by the window, wearing a party hat and a sash that read *Squatch of the Year*.

Alice noticed our stares and let out an embarrassed giggle. "That was a joke gift from Kristi last Christmas. She knew I love all the cryptid stuff from the conventions, so she thought it would be hilarious. I bring it to every convention."

Jack smiled. "That must have been fun, bringing it through an airport."

"It's a conversation starter, that's for sure." Alice sighed and set her purse down on the bed. It was unmade, which gave this entire scene an awkward, too intimate feel.

I moved closer to the Sasquatch, half expecting it to spring to life. "It's certainly got a presence," I said, giving the cardboard creature a tentative pinch.

Alice flopped down onto the bed, the weight of the world seemingly on her shoulders. "Yeah, well, Kristi was good at making things . . . memorable. Hey, do you want some water? There's some in the fridge."

I was about to say yes but then remembered that she might have poisoned Kristi. "Thanks, but I'm hydrated."

Jack declined and took a seat in the room's only chair, a utilitarian brown thing that looked like it had seen better days, while I opted for the edge of the desk, keeping a respectful distance from Alice. The room felt cramped with the three of us in it, the air thick with humidity, a faint smell of mold, and a cloying coconut perfume scent.

"So," Jack began, his voice gentle but firm, "How did you meet Kristi?"

Alice's face crumpled for a moment before she caught herself. Her gaze skittered to me, then to Jack. "Where's your podcasting equipment?"

I scratched my neck. "This is really a pre-interview."

"Oh."

"But we probably should record this, right Jack?" I held up my phone. "So we can refer back to it later?"

"Absolutely."

I swiped and tapped to the voice recorder, then nodded at Kristi. Whew. That was a close one. If Jack and I were going to continue investigating, we probably should pick up a cheap microphone at least. Then again, I hoped the case would be closed soon.

As in, as soon as we got out of this hotel room and called Alex to make an arrest. I pondered whether I should quickly text him, but Alice was already talking.

"I started getting into cryptids a few years ago, after watching some videos online. I stumbled upon Kristi and noticed that she was coming to a convention near me. I loved her whole aura so I had to see her in person. We met and had dinner together, and she asked me to be her assistant. That was two years ago."

"What did that entail, anyway?" I asked.

Alice blew out a breath, her cheeks puffing like a chipmunk's. "Answering emails, uploading videos, doing graphics, managing her schedule, traveling to conventions, sending out merch. So much. Too much."

"Wow, that is a lot. How often do you travel?"

"I try to come to as many conventions as I can. It's difficult with my day job, though."

I tilted my head. "Day job? You do, or did, all that for Kristi and have a day job? I hope it's something easy."

She shook her head. "I'm a dental hygienist."

Wow. How did she have time for all that?

"My job with Kristi was unpaid." Alice stared at her hands in her lap. "I know that's bad, but I really enjoyed it. Usually. We were, ah . . . It's complicated. I was her assistant, but it felt like more sometimes. She could be kind, but then she'd turn around and be so cold. I never knew where I stood."

Whoa. This was a lot to unpack.

"You received no compensation from her?" Jack's voice was laced with disbelief.

"Well, no. I mean, she paid for the airline tickets and the hotel room. Meals were on my own, unless she was buying." Alice licked her lips. "She told me I was getting exposure and experience, and that I'd someday have my own cryptid-hunting business and social media accounts."

Yikes, yikes, yikes. *Never work for exposure.* I wanted to shake Alice by the shoulders.

She continued, her voice gaining strength.

"But things were tense from the second I arrived. This convention has been a weird vibe from the beginning." She paused, as if weighing her words carefully. "Kristi was mad because I didn't arrive until Friday morning. I had to work late at the dental office on Thursday, and I couldn't get an earlier flight."

"That sounds rough." It must have been difficult for Alice to maintain that delicate balance between her day job and her indentured servitude to Kristi.

"It was," Alice admitted. "Kristi had scheduled a meet and greet for Thursday evening, and she was furious when I told her I couldn't make it. She said I was letting her down, that I wasn't committed enough."

Jack's eyebrows knitted together. "Did she say anything else? Anything that might indicate she was worried or scared about something?"

Alice shook her head, her hair swaying slightly. "Not really. She was angry. More than usual. I thought maybe it was the stress of the convention, but now . . ."

I reached out and placed a gentle hand on her shoulder. "Alice, if there's anything you remember, no matter how small, it could help us understand what happened to Kristi. Tell us what you know about her final days."

Alice hesitated, biting her lip as if debating whether to share more. Finally, she let out a long sigh, her shoulders slumping. "She told me about something weird that happened on Thursday," she said, her voice barely above a whisper. "Of course, she blamed me, for not being here, for not taking the time off work."

"What happened?" Jack leaned in. I marveled at the way his expression seemed genuinely concerned.

"Kristi got into a fight with someone here."

Jack and I perked up, our detective instincts kicking in. "What kind of fight? Physical?" I asked.

"No, nothing like that. More of a . . . disagreement, I guess. It was with a vendor, one of those selling water bottles and other eco-friendly stuff. Kristi wanted a water bottle, which was odd because she always carried her signature bottle around—you know, the hot-pink one with her logo on it."

I frowned, puzzled by this detail. "Why would she want to buy a new one? Was something wrong with hers?"

"That's just it, I don't know. And she wouldn't tell me. Probably she saw something that was cute. Or she got tipsy and lost hers. I know she has a bunch like it at her house, but maybe she didn't bring a backup. Anyway, the vendor—a woman, I think—refused to sell her one, said she hadn't unpacked. Then apparently the vendor relented and went in the back and gave Kristi one of the bedazzled bottles for free. But here's the thing, I get why a vendor would be upset—Kristi comes to these things and demands everything for free. Everything. Food, drink, merch."

Alice slapped her hand on the bed. It made a dull *thwack*. "Even though the woman gave her some free stuff,

Kristi was still angry. She didn't explain why, and I didn't see it happen, but she called me and yelled for a while. She was still fuming when I got in early Friday morning."

Jack and I exchanged glances. This was getting curiouser and curiouser. "Did Kristi say why the vendor was nasty to her?" I asked.

Alice shook her head, her expression a mix of confusion and concern. "Could've been anything. A lot of people love Kristi. Like, *love* love. But a handful of people really hate her, too. They think she's too stuck up, too full of herself."

"That happens with women who are unapologetic," Jack said, and I could've climbed him like a tree just for uttering those words.

Instead, I nodded seriously, hoping Alice would continue. She did.

"Kristi was always upset about something, but this seemed different. She kept mumbling about how it was 'unprofessional' and 'bad for business,' and how the booth vendor was a 'supreme bitch.' Those are the exact words she used on the phone after it happened. I thought maybe she'd calm down after a while, but she was still angry about it the next day when I got here. And some fans resent that she spends a lot of time with Grant, so that could've been it, too. The women go wild over him and are super protective. So, who knows."

"So, Kristi has a signature water bottle, tries to get one for free for some reason, gets denied, then actually gets the bottle, and is still upset about it. That doesn't add up," I mused aloud, trying to piece together the puzzle.

"Exactly," Alice agreed. "But that was Kristi. She got worked up about stupid stuff. I couldn't keep track of all her beefs. She was irrational and had a temper. And with everything else going on, I didn't get a chance to ask her more about it. I wish I had, though. Maybe it was important."

Jack jotted down a note on our little pad that we'd been sharing. "We should talk to this booth person, see if she remembers the incident and can shed some light on why she wouldn't sell a bottle to Kristi. You're sure you don't remember who it was?"

Alice shook her head.

"You know, it's strange." I was pacing now. "That day on the trail, Kristi had only a plastic water bottle, the kind you buy in the store for ninety-nine cents. Earlier I saw her with a pink cup, actually. But she didn't have it on the walk."

"Oh. Yeah." Alice sighed sadly. "That was the bottle she'd gotten from the vendor, the bedazzled one. She had that when she was arguing with Grant about her placement in the convention program. Then she handed it to me and I accidentally put it in my bag. I, um, went somewhere for a while and I guess she bought some water somewhere before going on the walk."

"Somewhere" meaning *Grant's pants*, I figured. "And then?"

"Or maybe she came up here and grabbed some of the bottles in her room. She always has water, is a freak about hydration. Was. I was sure she was going to yell at me for keeping her water bottle. That's the other reason

I was so worked up when you saw me on the trail. I went there anticipating a tongue lashing."

We all looked at each other. Considering the water bottle at the scene and Kristi's body had contained traces of the Visine, this seemed like a solid lead to follow. Alex was probably already on top of it. But did he know about the vendor?

"Interesting," I agreed, already formulating a plan in my head. "Anything else, Alice? Anything at all that struck you as odd?"

Alice hesitated, then sighed. "Not that I can think of. But honestly, this whole convention has felt off from the start. Maybe it's just me. Maybe it's hindsight."

"You've been through a lot, Alice. Um, but I do have another question."

"Yeah?" Alice looked despondent.

"Why were you so intent on getting things from Kristi's bod . . . from Kristi that day on the trail?"

"It must have looked strange, I know," she began, her voice steadier than I'd expected. "But there was a reason, I promise. Kristi was . . . well, she was very particular about her belongings, especially during events like this. And it was my responsibility to help her keep track of them."

It seemed to me that Kristi had asked a lot of an unpaid helper.

Alice paused, glancing at the cardboard Sasquatch as if it were a source of strength. "She always carried a small notebook with her, sort of a mini-journal where she jotted down ideas, observations, even cryptid sketches. She was convinced it would be crucial for her next big project. She'd been acting even more protective over it these last few days—almost paranoid."

Alice shifted uncomfortably on the bed. "When . . . when everything happened, my first thought was that notebook. Kristi would've wanted it safe, not lost or—worse—taken by someone with less than honorable intentions. There are plenty of rivals and . . . well, let's just say not everyone here plays fair."

Everyone here is so weird, I wanted to scream.

Jack nodded. "So, you were trying to secure her notebook? To keep her work safe?"

"Yes, exactly!" Alice's relief at being understood was palpable. "I know it might not justify going through her pockets, but in that moment, all I could think about was protecting what she valued most. It felt like the best thing I could do for her. The last thing I could do for her."

I mulled over her explanation, weighing the sincerity in her voice against the nagging doubts in my mind. "So that's why you were looking through Kristi's pockets after she'd collapsed?"

Alice nodded. "Yeah, but she didn't have the journal on the trail. I found it in her things. In her room. The cops took it. And since I had her pink water bottle, I gave them that for testing, and showed them her water stash in her room. They took all of it away."

Crap. I would've liked to read that journal. The room fell silent for a moment, at least until another lingering thought fought with my brain cells to emerge.

"Did Kristi drink?" I blurted.

"What do you mean?" Alice asked, her voice on edge.

"Did she like to get hammered? Booze? She smelled like gin on the walk, and it was only noon. That seemed unusual to me."

"She was starting to. I mean, she'd always liked to party. That's what she called it. Partying. But lately she'd been drinking in the day, too. She bought a big bottle of gin. The cops took that, too." Alice shook her head. "I dunno. Everything has gone to hell so quickly."

"Um." Jack stroked his chin. "Where were you when she was on the trail? When she passed."

Alice swallowed. Jack and I seemed to hold our breath while waiting for her to answer.

"I was in the hotel. In a room. I told the police about this." A long pause. "I'd rather not talk about it."

I paced over to my phone, which was on the bureau about a foot and a half from where Alice was sitting on the bed. I tapped the recorder off and showed her the screen.

"Between us," I said, "who were you with?"

She shut her eyes. "Grant P. Sanders."

"You two are friends?" Jack's tone remained kind. By now, I guessed we were doing the good cop, bad cop thing.

I kinda liked being the bad cop.

"We're dating," Alice said with a shy smile. "He and his wife are separating and they're getting a divorce as soon as his son graduates from eighth grade. That's in two years."

Oh, honey, I wanted to say. But I didn't. My track record of getting women to forget about terrible men wasn't the best. Okay, I'd only tried with my sister, and I'd done a rotten job of steering her away from jerks so far. I didn't have hope that I could counsel Alice out of dating Grant, either.

She had The Look. You know the one. The one that Taylor Swift had when she adoringly gazed at Travis Kelce after his Superbowl win.

Yeah, it was best if I ignored the love affair part of her story. I turned the recorder back on. "Can you run down what happened from the time you arrived at the hotel—what was it? Friday morning?"

She nodded and inhaled deeply, like she was summoning the will to carry on. "Okay, the flight here was awful. So much turbulence and it was running hours behind. I was flustered when I got here, and Kristi didn't make it any better."

"How so?" Jack asked.

"She kept ranting about the person who'd given her the bottle, then she was upset that Grant got better billing. She always wanted the biggest photo in the program."

Okay, so that aligned with the conversation I'd overheard on Friday. I ran my tongue over my teeth, wondering if I should ask a highly inappropriate question. Ah, screw it. I'd probably never get a chance with Alice again.

"Did she know about you and Grant's, ah, relationship?"

Alice's expression fell even further and she shook her head. "Grant wanted us to keep it on the downlow. He and Kristi fought a lot, and he believed Kristi might fire me, or worse."

"Or worse?" Jack repeated.

"Someday, I want . . ." She raked in a breath. "I want to start my own cryptid channel. Grant thought Kristi would go ballistic if she knew he was helping me do that. She'd have considered me a traitor."

This certainly gave Alice another reason to kill her boss, on top of the no paycheck detail, which was total BS in my book.

"So you got here and what happened?" I asked.

"I was starving, and all I wanted was to have coffee and a muffin. Kristi and I went to her room and she ranted for a while about vendor who gave her the water bottle she'd gotten for free. Then she went off about Grant for a while, then Mac."

"Why Mac?" Jack settled back into his chair.

"Mac was texting her nonstop, probably because she was asking for money."

"Were they broken up? Or just in a fight? And didn't she make enough of her own money?"

Alice scrunched up her face. "Hard to tell with them. They fought a lot, but who didn't Kristi fight with? Mac loved her and gave her lots of cash, at least until she started earning off her social media channels. But she still asked him for stuff. No amount of money was enough for her." She checked her watch and stood. "How much longer are we going to be? I'm supposed to meet up with Grant soon to go over his keynote speech. We can continue later."

I glanced around wildly. There was so much I'd love to ask her, but my thoughts were jumbled. I didn't trust that she'd want to chat later, especially if she told her married boyfriend about how we'd been poking around.

"Any chance we could take a peek into Kristi's room?" I said in my slowest, folksiest, southern accent.

"I guess? The cops already went through it." Alice seemed unsure. "Right now?"

Jack jumped up and crossed the room, placing his hand on the door that connected the two rooms. "You can just let us in through here, close and lock this door, and we'll let ourselves out of Kristi's room when we're done."

"Um, okay, whatever. But don't tell anyone I let you do this. Promise?"

"Absolutely not," Jack said.

"No way, won't say a word," I chimed in. We were overlooking the obvious: if we really were podcasters, and broadcast some audio from the room, we'd be telling the world.

But we weren't going to broadcast anything, and since we weren't actual podcasters, I stayed silent. Alice went to the door, unlocked it, and made a sweeping, ushering motion with her hand.

"There you go. I hope I could help with your show." She looked up at Jack, and for the first time, smiled. It was a flirtatious, surprised expression, as if she'd been caught off guard by his good looks.

Girl, same.

"We're really sorry for your loss," I said. "I hope things get a lot better for you, and you're able to start your cryptid hunting, ah, business."

"Thanks. Grant says he's going to help. He might make me a co-host."

With Alice's awkward personality and her thin voice,

this seemed about as likely as me becoming the lead dancer for the New York Ballet, but we all needed to have a dream. Still. I felt terrible for her, because it was obvious (at least to me) that Grant was stringing her along.

Ass clown.

Jack and I went through the door and we both waved at Alice. She waved back and shut her side, leaving us in a dark room. The heavy blackout curtains were drawn, allowing only a thin sliver of light into the space. It seemed eerie, being in a dead woman's room.

Chapter Twenty-Four

We both exhaled. Jack came over and murmured into my ear, "Good call asking if we could come in here. Nice job, tater tot."

I refrained from reaching around and pinching his butt in a moment of silliness. Or taking his face in my hands and kissing him. We needed to focus.

"Okay," I whispered. "Let's look around. First, let's open the drapes."

"No." Jack moved away from me and a light flicked on. He was near a brass floor lamp. "I don't want to risk anyone outside seeing us in here, so let's keep the curtains closed."

"Ooh, good point." I put my hands on my hips. "Where do we start?"

"Anywhere. You take one side, I'll take the other."

I gravitated towards the desk, while Jack went into the bathroom.

The desk was a picture of chaos. Makeup brushes lay scattered like fallen soldiers beside an eyeshadow palette. A gold-plated compact was open. Without touching anything, I inspected the cosmetics.

Jack walked back in. "Bathroom's been cleaned out. Nothing but bottles of shampoo and conditioner."

"Well, I can tell you that Ms. Klaus probably had a Sephora addiction."

"What does that mean?" Jack moved a pillow off the bed and checked underneath.

"Sephora. The cosmetics store. Vera's really into makeup, and because of that, I know Kristi's stuff wasn't bought at a drugstore. She's got at least a thousand bucks' worth here."

"Guess hunting Bigfoot pays well."

"Or Mac did," I muttered.

I moved on, my attention caught by a stack of Bigfoot-themed romance novels on the nightstand.

"Wow. I wonder if she got these from Vera?" I slowly went through the stack.

The titles were as absurd as they were intriguing, ranging from *Sasquatch Seduction* to *Mystic Moons and Monstrous Hearts*. I couldn't help but laugh. "Jack, you've got to see this."

Jack came over, an amused smile on his face as he read the spines. "Let's ask your sister if she carries these."

I quickly snapped a photo of the stack and sent it to Vera. *Do you recall selling these exact books to anyone this weekend?*

Her reply came within a millisecond. *Where are you?*

Oh Lord. She was going to be difficult. *None of your business. Just answer the question.*

I sell all of these books. I've sold a thousand books this weekend. I can't honestly remember, Mags. Faces are blurring together. I barely know my own name at this point. Overwhelmed. Sorry.

The fact that she'd ended with an apology took the sting and disappointment out of her message.

Next, I was drawn to the window, where a large, plush Loch Ness Monster sat perched on the sill, its soft green fabric catching the dim light. It was one of those squishy pillow things.

I picked it up, the stuffed animal's cartoonish eyes and friendly smile oddly comforting amid the tension. "Jack, have you ever seen a cuter Nessie?" I asked, holding it up for him to see. I waggled it in the air.

Jack turned from his inspection of the closet, a smile breaking through his focus. "I can't say I have. That's one cryptid I wouldn't mind running into in the wild." He took the plushie, giving it a gentle squeeze. "Feels like Kristi had a soft spot for more than just Bigfoot. Wait, what's this?"

He fiddled with a tag tied around the monster's neck and read the cursive aloud. *"To Kristi, from Johan. Keep Squatching! Love you."*

"A suspect, or an admirer?" I asked.

"At this point, is there any difference?"

Our search then led us to a collection of novelty socks draped over a chair, each pair adorned with a different cryptid: Bigfoot, Mothman, even a Chupacabra. I held up a pair with a particularly dashing Bigfoot sporting a monocle and top hat.

"Kinda cute. Doesn't really go with the luxury clothing in the closet, though." Jack gestured toward a door.

"Oh yeah?" I strode over and opened the door.

Inside the closet hung a row of what I could only describe as "haute couture wilderness."

There were sleek, tailored jackets made of fabrics that probably repelled rain, wind, and common sense, given the brand.

I ran my fingers over a vest that looked as though it was spun from the silk of golden orb spiders, lightweight yet shimmering with an iridescence that seemed to mock the very idea of getting dirty.

"Jack, look at this," I said in a stage whisper, holding up the vest. "It's like Gucci decided to make a line for paranormal sleuths. I can't imagine Kristi trudging through the mud looking for a stinky creature in this."

He came over, then bent down to examine a pair of boots with soles so pristine, it was clear they'd never kissed the earth.

"These boots were made for walking," he joked, "but only on perfectly manicured trails, it seems."

He stood and we shut the door. "None of these things are clues, though."

"Sometimes that happens." Jack went to the small, cylindrical trash can in the corner.

While he plunged his arm into it—gross—I peeked in the bathroom. Like Jack had said, there were only two bottles of haircare products. I recognized them as the kind sold in salons, the ones that were like thirty-five bucks per bottle.

"Aha," Jack cried.

I rushed out, excited. "What? What did you find?"

With a flourish worthy of a magician, he extracted a crumpled piece of paper, holding it delicately between his fingers. "This could be something. Or maybe not, considering the cops left it here and didn't seize it as evidence."

He passed me the treasure—a business card for Giggles-N-Ghoulies. As I smoothed it out, *Michelle Newman, Owner* stared back at me in orange Comic Sans font.

One chilling detail replayed in my mind, and I gasped as I recalled the conversation.

She'll get hers someday soon. I believe in karma.

I looked into Jack's brown eyes and shook the crinkled card in his direction. "I think we've just found something important."

No sooner had I opened my mouth to explain about my encounter with Michelle than Jack held his index finger over his mouth. His eyes were round and large.

WHAT, I mouthed.

He pointed at the door linking Kristi's room with Alice's. Then, I heard voices. Slowly, we crept toward the door and pressed our ears to the wood. I slid the crumpled business card into the back pocket of my jeans.

"Those podcasters are really digging deep into Kristi's background." That was unmistakably Alice's voice.

"Mmm-hmm," came the male baritone.

"I'm worried about what they'll find out about her. I don't want all her skeletons to come out."

My mouth formed an O as I stared at Jack, whose face was only a few inches from mine. It sounded like they were right on the other side of the door.

"Mmm, baby, you look so hot in those khaki pants."

I clutched Jack's forearm. *GRANT*, I mouthed, lifting

my hand as an unspoken question. Jack reached over and put his index finger over my lips.

"Grant, we should talk about the presentation. Maybe we should go downstairs."

"Baby, we only have a few minutes. C'mon, let me make you feel good. Don't you want some of Daddy's sugar?"

Jack's lips pulled back into a wince and we continued to eavesdrop.

A few long and interminable seconds of what could only be described as moist smacking sounds ensued. I stuck my tongue out, pretending to gag.

We listened for a couple more beats, and when Grant—in a husky, desperate voice—told Alice exactly where he wanted to put his "All-American sausage," I let out a single snort.

"Did you hear that?" Alice said.

Eek. Surely she knew the sounds were coming from us.

"I can only hear the sound of your desire," Grant replied.

Apparently Jack knew I was about to lose it, because he grabbed my wrist and pulled me away, toward the door. We burst out of the room and dashed into the hallway. When we got to the elevators, we stopped.

And laughed hysterically. For at least a minute. Tears streamed down our faces.

Jack pressed the button and we continued gasping with laughter, unable to speak. When we were in the elevator and the doors closed, he came to me, cupping my face in his hands.

"I can only hear the sound of your desire," he murmured in a low, growly tone.

That set us off again. We chortled until we arrived on the ground floor, then attempted to sober when we saw the crowds.

I wiped away tears as we collected ourselves in the lobby. "Seriously, we need to talk about what we just found."

Jack nodded. "Want to get some fresh air?"

We wandered outside, where bright sunshine greeted us, and parked ourselves on a bench near a man in cargo pants, a white T-shirt, and red suspenders. He was smoking, wore mirrored sunglasses, and stared at us a few seconds too long.

Probably he recognized me as the woman who'd been with Kristi when she died. I angled my body so my back was to him and faced Jack.

"I didn't tell you about Michelle because she didn't seem significant. Until now. I think we have a serious lead here." I went on to explain how I'd met the vendor on Friday, and bought a catnip toy for Catsy at her booth.

"She was sweet and pleasant when I met her on Friday, but the next day, she was cold and standoffish. I didn't think much of it, since it's a busy convention and I assumed she was busy. But then she gave me a dirty look. And now this." I pulled the business card we'd found in Kristi's room out of my pocket. "Michelle sells bedazzled water bottles. She disliked Kristi, because she thought Kristi was bonking Grant."

"Who, as we know, was sleeping with Alice, Kristi's assistant."

"Exactly. We have motive."

"And we have opportunity and method. The timeline adds up." Jack bit his lip, something I noticed he did when he was thinking. It was terribly sexy, so I didn't interrupt.

"I think we should check out her booth before we call Alex," he said finally.

"Maybe you should. She knows me, and clearly thinks I'm up to something."

"Which you are." Jack squeezed my knee.

"I wonder if one of us could distract her with conversation while the other pokes around." My mind raced with thoughts, most of which were ridiculous.

"You want to create a distraction?"

I nodded.

"Any thoughts on how we might do that?"

I tapped my fingers on my lips and did a mental scan of the convention floor. When I recalled a booth selling Bigfoot costumes, a wicked grin spread across my face.

Chapter Twenty-Five

"This is batshit crazy, you know that, right?"

Jack and I were in the family restroom. I'd just spent $109.99 plus tax on a Bigfoot costume. I figured I'd use it at Halloween, or at the Wahoo Wild Days, which was an annual gathering where folks dressed up (usually as pirates, but people had branched out in recent years, I'd heard). Or maybe I'd entertain Vera and wear parts of it around the house.

Either way, I felt it was a solid investment. I slipped one leg into the furry outfit, then the other, pulling it over my skinny jeans. Jack stood and surveyed me while I tugged it up to my bellybutton.

"It's a little large," he said.

"Eh, that's okay. I'm a Lady Bigfoot after a season of hibernation." I shoved one arm, then the next, through the fur-covered sleeves.

He narrowed his eyes. "Do cryptids hibernate?"

"Your guess is as good as mine." I turned. "Can you zip me?"

I watched in the mirror as he focused on my back, carefully enclosing me in the outfit. He looked up and met my eyes in the mirror.

"You're the sexiest Bigfoot I've ever seen."

"That's the best compliment I've had maybe ever. Okay, now for the head."

Jack went to the unfolded baby changing station, where we'd laid out a towel we'd unearthed in his car. Atop that was the costume head, along with the separate gloves and booties.

"You're sure you don't want the hands and feet first?"

"Well, okay."

He helped me into all four appendages and I studied the glove, which was made of rubber-latex-fur. "It looks oddly realistic, like I have claws."

Jack patted my chest, like he did with Catsy. "I gotta say, the quality of this Bigfoot costume is impressive."

"They used the best fake fur money could buy." I lifted one foot, then the other. The booties fit loosely over my Converse.

He reached for the head. "Are you ready?"

"As I'll ever be."

Carefully, he lowered the oversized head over mine, and onto my shoulders, adjusting it until my eyes aligned with the mesh-covered eyeholes. I blinked a few times, getting used to the limited field of vision. The interior smelled faintly of new plastic and stale air.

"I feel like I'm in a different world," I mumbled through the headpiece, my voice muffled. I leaned over the sink, peering into the mirror. The beard on the costume's head seemed much longer now.

"My Dad had a beard kinda like this," I yelled while touching it with one claw. This, of course, made me wish Dad was here. He'd have loved this entire absurd plan.

Jack chuckled, his voice sounding small and distant. "You look like you're ready to lead a cryptid parade."

I attempted a twirl, nearly losing my balance in the process. Jack steadied me by grabbing my upper arm.

"I just hope I don't trip and give us away. That would be the end of our covert operation."

He steadied me with his hands on my shoulders. "Just take it slow. Remember, you're a majestic creature of the wild, not a runway model."

"Got it. Majestic. Wild." I nodded, the headpiece wobbling.

I caught sight of myself in the mirror and preened, touching my gloved claw-hand to my furry face.

"How does it feel?" Jack asked.

"A little heavy. And I'm already hot. Oh, wait, I want to take a photo. We probably won't have time afterward."

I went to my bag and fumbled around with the bulky, clawed gloves. After a moment of clumsy attempts, Jack gently took over.

"Here, let me help you with that," he said, amusement clear in his voice. He reached for the phone and positioned it in front of us, flipping the camera to selfie mode. The screen displayed a surreal image: me in my full Bigfoot regalia, towering next to Jack, who was grinning from ear to ear. The toilet was in the background.

"Say 'cryptid'!"

"Cryptid!" I managed to growl through the costume, trying to sound as Bigfoot-like as possible. Whatever Bigfoot sounded like. I idly wondered if anyone had ever captured the creature's voice on audio, then had to remind myself, *Bigfoot isn't real, doofus.*

It was surprisingly easy to think that he was while here at the convention, though. Maybe that was the real reason people came to these things: to believe in the unknown. Everyone needed a hobby, I guess.

The camera clicked, capturing the moment. We looked at the photo together, our laughter echoing off the restroom walls.

The image was absurdly delightful. There I was, a not-so-ferocious Bigfoot, with Jack's arm slung around my furry shoulders like we were old pals just hanging out. We were making peace signs. The contrast between his casual attire and my elaborate costume made the scene even more comical.

"Let's take another one, but this time, try to look menacing," Jack suggested, barely containing his laughter.

I attempted my best Bigfoot snarl, holding my hands in the air like I was about to claw someone to death. Jack leaned in, feigning terror, his eyes wide and mouth agape. He snapped another photo, and we erupted into giggles again.

"Send it to Vera," I said.

Laughing, he did. Seconds later, my phone pinged. Jack flashed the screen at me.

I swear on Mom and Dad's graves that if you get arrested I'm not bailing you out. You will sit in jail for weeks. Maybe until trial. Do not fluff around.

I snickered. Vera would lose it if she knew what we were about to do. "No need to respond. You'll bail me out, right?"

"You'd better believe it." Jack checked his watch. "It's showtime. You remember the plan?"

"Head to Michelle's booth, cause a distraction, you sneak a peek behind the table. I'll meet you at the rendezvous point."

The rendezvous point was his car. Now that I was in the costume, I wondered how I'd quickly get to the parking lot, and if I could actually run in this costume. Eh, I'd deal with that when the time came. If worst came to worst, I'd slip off the feet and haul ass.

"Exactly." He opened the door a crack, peeking outside. "Coast is clear. Ready?"

I took a deep breath, the suit's fabric trapping all the heat from my body, causing the inside to feel a tad swampy already. "Let's do this."

I stepped out of the family restroom and stopped. My head had shifted so I could only see out of one eye.

"What? Do you want me to hold your hand?" Jack stood in front of me.

"Can you adjust my head?" Jack shifted it to the left. "A little more. Yeah. Like that."

"Oh, wait. There's Velcro here to hold it in place. At least I think that's what it's for."

While Jack fiddled, I saw a few people grin and point. "Hey, I found Bigfoot," one guy yelled.

"Ha. Ha. Ha," I muttered aloud, knowing no one could hear me from inside the mask.

You'd think that this crowd wouldn't be amused by a person in a Bigfoot costume. But when Jack finished and we walked toward Michelle's booth, I realized that was an incorrect assumption.

"OMG, can we get a photo?" two teen boys said.

Jack responded before I had a chance. "Uh, I guess."

As I posed with the teens, more people clustered around us. We hadn't anticipated this, but we also didn't want to disappoint the cute five-year-old who was staring up at me with unabashed glee, either.

"Say something, Bigfoot," one woman yelled in my ear.

"Sorry, Bigfoot doesn't speak," Jack responded, grabbing my hand (claw? paw?) and dragging me away.

He led me down one row of booths, through throngs of people. Michelle's booth was one of the larger, probably coveted, end caps, positioned to the right of the entrance.

Jack leaned in, probably thinking he was close to my ear. Really, it was my cheek. "I'm going over. You wait a few minutes, okay?"

I nodded, or tried to.

"Maggie? Did you hear me?"

"I did, and okay," I shouted, suspecting that through the costume and over the din of the crowd, he couldn't hear me at all.

"Stay here by this garbage can in the meantime." He squeezed my furry arm and walked off.

Several people tried to accost me, but I wagged my claws and shook my head. Eventually, they got bored and wandered off. It helped that a nearby booth was giving away samples of cinnamon-flavored nuts, adorably named "Nessie's Nuts."

Wait, wasn't Nessie a girl? I racked my brain for long buried childhood knowledge about the Loch Ness Monster.

Focus.

I took a deep breath. It felt like time to approach the booth, although it could've been anywhere from thirty seconds to ten minutes since Jack left. I glanced at the people lining up for the nuts.

Sweat formed on my neck. This was a terrible plan. But we needed to check out Michelle. I was more sure than ever that she'd killed Kristi, and I feared that Alex wouldn't believe us, even with the business card we'd found in Kristi's room.

I surged forward, almost tripping on my feet (paws?). Jack and I had walked slowly to get to this point, and he'd held onto my arm the entire way. Now alone, it was a bit more difficult to manage. The booties kept snagging on the cheap carpet underfoot.

The Giggles-N-Ghoulies booth was now in view. I could see the back of Michelle's head, and had a clear view of Jack's face. It appeared that they were having a conversation. I slowed my walk so I could observe a little more.

Jack laughed, tipping his head back as if Michelle had told the funniest joke ever. She also seemed delighted. I could now see her face in semi-profile, and she was positively beaming. No doubt because Jack had that kind of effect on women. Not that I minded; I wasn't the jealous type, and it was totally understand-able that someone would find him hot and charming.

I took another step, then another. I was a couple of feet from her U-shaped table. I was about to launch my planned chaos—doing a little dance and then holding up some of her merchandise, hoping the crowd would get involved—when someone bumped into me.

Hard.

Even if I hadn't been in costume, I'd probably have been knocked off my feet. But since I didn't have stability to begin with, the body blow sent me flying.

"I'm so sorry," the man who'd plowed into me said, but by that time, my legs and feet were in the air and I was soaring toward the table. I fell, back first, toward a pile of squishy cryptid pillows atop Michelle's table.

Saved by a Squishmellow, was my only thought before I crashed and crushed the cheap merch.

I slammed into the pillows and the table, literally snapping that section in half, and taking all of the mer-chandise with me.

Shouts of "Oh my God!" and "Is Bigfoot okay?"

Dazed, I realized that I hadn't actually broken the table—I'd landed at the exact part where two tables con-nected. Flailing around the plush pillow pile, I looked up and realized two things that sent a chill down my fur-covered back.

One was that I was staring straight into the furious eyes of Michelle Newman.

And two, my Bigfoot head was gone. Oh shit.

"I can explain," I said. Out of the corner of my eye, I

spotted Jack behind the booth table, going through a garbage can.

"You. You bitch," she hissed, and that's when she grabbed a canister of Mothman pepper spray on display and squirted me with a stream of liquid.

As it hit my fur-covered body, I struggled to climb to my feet. Then the substance hit my eyes. It sizzled and burned, sending waves of pain coursing through me. The stench of the unknown stuff filled my nostrils, making it hard to breathe.

Gritting my teeth against the searing agony, I fought back with every ounce of strength left in me. Using my clawed hands, I swiped at Michelle's outstretched arm in an attempt to knock the canister from her clutches.

But she was relentless. With a snarl, she lunged forward once again, aiming a powerful kick at my midsection. I felt the impact reverberate through my gut, and although it was painful, the blow was subdued by the furry outfit.

Eff her. Summoning every bit of resilience, I retaliated by pulling off my gloves and taking a swing with my real fist. One connected with Michelle's leg, causing her to stagger backward. Now I was standing atop a small pile of squishy pillows like some hybrid King Kong. She slapped my face. I punched her.

Blood trickled from her split lip, and that seemed to further enrage her.

The fight heated up as we exchanged blows, neither willing to back down. I managed to call for help, but no one stepped forward. Where was Jack? The chaotic scene around us only fueled the frenzy, as people stopped to form a circle and watch. The sounds of gasps and murmurs merged with our grunts.

"Whoa, this is better than WrestleMania SmackDown," one guy said with glee to his buddy. "Are you getting this on video?"

Somehow, amid the chaos and struggle, I spotted Jack. He was now kneeling at the metal garbage can, a small box in hand. He placed it on the table, then dumped the entire contents of the can on the floor.

Michelle squirted me again while calling me a highly improper name that began with a C. She squirted a third time. The crowd surged backward and I cried out, collapsing to my knees in the most pain I'd ever felt. Even a scratch from a diseased iguana at the Boston Zoo hadn't compared to this inferno melting my face off. My sinuses felt like they'd snorted a ghost pepper.

Through my burning tears, I heard Jack let out a primal grunt. He swing the metal garbage can at Michelle's shoulder.

The wastebasket made a sickening smack against Michelle's bones, sending her staggering to one side, dazed and disoriented.

I was on all fours now, retching and coughing and weeping. I thought I saw Luke the bad boy reporter, even, but that might have been a hallucination. Or not, since he looked absolutely horrified.

"Help me," I gasped in his direction, extending a furry arm.

As I writhed on the floor, hoping to die so that I'd be put out of my misery, I saw Vera.

"Maggie! Maggie! What the fluff happened? Oh dear. I'm sorry about what I said earlier. I love you," she cried, getting down on all fours and patting my furry back while I wheezed and hacked onto the rug. My entire respiratory system seemed to be shutting down.

"Pepper . . . spray," I rasped, pointing at Michelle, who was now swinging the wastebasket at Jack's legs.

"Who pepper-sprayed you?" Vera yelled.

I gestured toward Michelle, who was tussling on the floor with Jack. Vera stood up.

"What have you done to my sister, you freak?" she hollered.

"Hell yeah! Git 'er done, girl," someone in the crowd shouted. "Cat fight!"

The last thing I saw was Vera tying her blonde hair into a ponytail, then leaping through the air to hurl her small body atop Michelle's.

#

Meep, meep.

I came to in the back of a golf cart. Wait, was it a golf cart? It was more like a mini truck, and I was lying on the flatbed, still in my Bigfoot costume.

Jack was next to me, sitting upright. He groaned a little, and I noticed he was holding an ice pack to his head.

"Hey," I muttered.

"Shh. Just stay calm. We're taking you to the hospital," he said.

"What? Why?" I wiped my face, which was wet with

tears. At least I hoped they were tears, but I suspected there was some snot in there, too. Lovely.

Meep, meep.

I struggled to sit up, but Jack pressed me down. "Don't move, Maggie."

"Where are we going? What happened back there? How long have I been out? Why . . ." Suddenly I felt nauseous, and it was probably best if I didn't talk.

"It's all going to be okay," he said as we whizzed through the crowd. Whoever was driving the cart was doing an excellent job not mowing people down.

Meep, meep.

"What is that weird beeping noise?" My voice was the audio equivalent to sandpaper.

Jack smiled and smoothed the hair back from my forehead. "It's the driver. He's beeping at people to get out of the way."

"Where's Michelle?"

"Alex took her into custody."

"Oh, thank God."

He leaned over and dabbed my forehead with a cool, damp washcloth. My face still stung, and I sucked in a breath. "I found empty Visine bottles and cartons in her trash."

"You did?"

He nodded. "Our plan worked perfectly."

It did, with the exception of . . . Vera. I asked where she was.

Jack lifted a shoulder and that's when I noticed a bruise blooming around his right eye. Michelle must have gotten to him. "I think the Wahoo Police Department is trying to determine if they should charge her for assaulting Michelle. Vera's got quite the right hook. I wouldn't mess with her."

I allowed my eyes to close and smiled. My sister always had my back, and it was one of a thousand reasons why I loved her more than anyone on the planet. If she was thrown in jail, I'd definitely bail her out. Even if she didn't want to trap gators with me.

Chapter Twenty-Six

I settled back on the sofa, my feet propped up on the chaise, my legs covered with Vera's special pink fuzzy blanket. We'd just arrived home after hours in the hospital.

"Here, let me snip that off," Vera said, reaching for the plastic ID band around my wrist that contained my name, birthdate and the words WAHOO MEMORIAL HOSPITAL.

I held out my arm as she came at me with scissors. "Thank god I didn't have to stay overnight."

"Yeah, I was worried there for a bit, but I guess when they saw our terrible insurance they figured it wouldn't be worth it."

I rasped out a bitter laugh that led to a cough. While in the emergency room, I'd had oxygen, a nebulizer for asthma patients, and oddly, my face had been wiped down with milk of magnesia. Apparently that neutralized the pepper spray.

Add that to my useless knowledge pile.

"Do you want tea? Coffee? Water? Orange juice?" Vera stared down at me, worry creasing her smooth brow.

"Tea, I guess. Thanks."

When she left the room, Catsy sauntered in, unfazed

by my near-death experience and subsequent home-coming. She jumped up, sniffed my arm, then began to lick herself.

A few minutes later, Vera returned, carrying a mug. "It's my new chamomile, with some honey."

"Thanks." I took a long sip, the warm liquid soothing my still-raw throat. "That tastes so good. Wow. We should sell this in the store. Where'd you get it?"

Vera sat perched on the other end of the sofa, wringing her hands. "Maggie, I'm sorry about the trapping thing."

I shook my head. That argument we'd had seemed like it was a hundred years ago after the bananas scene at the Bigfoot convention. "Don't worry. Really. I'll figure something out. It's no big deal."

"No, it is a big deal. I was wrong. I exploded on you about Dad and Mom and my big, stupid feelings." Her eyes started to water. "While you were in Boston, I got used to being my own person, and not a twin. When you came back and wanted to trap, it brought back all those old memories of you and Dad, and feeling the pressure to be like you. Who he adored."

"Dad adored you, too," I said softly.

She nodded. "I know. But he had a special bond with you because of your shared love of the outdoors. I was more like Mom, who went along with the trapping and fishing and canoeing, but would rather have stayed home with an iced tea and a book."

I smiled. It was true. Mom had been naturally athletic, just like Vera, but her happiest moments were often spent at a used bookstore, or a junk shop, poking around. I'd always been bored when she brought us along, but Vera had loved that stuff.

"Vera, no. I probably ignored your feelings all these years, and that's not good. Dad and I were so enthusiastic about trapping that we shoved your concerns aside. You told us you didn't want to go out in the sun because of your skin. You always liked indoor stuff—books and the gym and more controlled environments. Not that there's anything wrong with that. I'm sorry. It wasn't fair of Dad, or me. And I get it, as a twin. I want to live my own life, too. But damn, I love working with you, like we did when trapping that gator."

"Mrs. Gilman's gator was only this morning," she said, a small smile spreading on her face.

I tipped my head back and laughed. "It seems like fifty years ago. Holy crap."

She sniffled and wiped away a tear rolling down her cheek. "I was so worried about you when I saw you rolling around on the floor at the conference. I honestly thought you were dying. You sounded like you were gasping for your last breath. I felt like a big fluffing jerk that we'd gotten into a fight right before. I'm so sorry."

"Is that why you decided to open a can of whoop-ass on Michelle?" I laughed through the tears that were forming.

Vera giggled. "I was ready to kill her for doing that to you. I'd never forgive myself if you died while we were in the middle of an argument."

My left eye was still watering a bit from the pepper

spray, and the lid drooped with a round of fresh, genuine tears. "Aww, Vera. I could never be that mad at you."

"We'll discuss the trapping later, okay? When all this"—she waved her hand in the air—"dies down."

She clicked on the TV and tuned it to a reality TV baking show, the one where everyone was kind to each other. A good, soothing choice after today. We settled into a companionable silence, the two of us and Catsy's purr.

After a while, right when the cake-baking segment was starting, there was a knock at the door. Vera hopped up to answer.

"Oh, hey guys! Wow, you brought so much stuff. Thanks, Jack." She stood aside and I saw Jack and then Alex walk in. Vera and Alex exchanged secret smiles.

I suddenly remembered that Alex had spent last night with my sister, here in the house. Somehow I'd glossed over that detail with all the bonkers goings-on.

Life comes at you fast.

"Hey, you," Jack said. He was carrying a bag with twin handles and set it on the coffee table, then leaned in and kissed my cheek. "How are you feeling?"

"Better." I adjusted myself so I was sitting a little straighter. "How about you?"

"Just a bruise. I've been in worse fights." He grinned. "Glad to see you looking better."

I appreciated the lie, knowing my eye was still watery and half-shut from where Michelle had squirted me directly.

Jack reached for the bag and opened it. "The owner of Cheesy Does It says hi."

He took a foil-wrapped sandwich out of a Styrofoam container. "Gouda, right?"

"You are amazing. Thanks." My stomach rumbled and I realized I hadn't eaten in hours.

While Jack unwrapped the sandwich for me, Vera and Alex came into the room. Vera was carrying an empty plate and she handed it to me, along with a stack of napkins.

"You're looking a lot better, Maggie," Alex observed. "I was kinda worried about you."

"Thanks. What's the latest with Michelle and the case?" I was dying to know.

"Michelle's being booked into the county jail. We're charging her with one count of second-degree murder and two counts of aggravated assault, for what she did to you and Jack." He paused. "We almost charged her for attempting to strike Vera, too, but since she didn't actually make contact, and because Vera got in a few punches herself, we declined to pursue that."

He smiled at my sister. She smiled back.

I was about to make a pithy comment about Vera's future as a prizefighter but Alex continued. "Michelle confessed everything the minute we got her into custody."

"No shit?" I said with my mouth full, then hastily wiped my lips with a napkin when Vera shot me a narrow-eyed look. "Why'd she kill Kristi?"

Alex made a clicking noise with his tongue. "She was jealous. Thought Kristi was having an affair with Grant, because she always saw the two of them together at conferences. What she didn't know, of course, was that Grant was carrying on with Kristi's assistant, Alice. Oh, and we found out that Grant and Michelle had, er, relations, during a Bigfoot conference in Montana last summer. That's what touched off Michelle's obsession with the guy. And with Kristi."

"Jealousy. One of the main motives of murder." Jack shook his head. "So she dumped the Visine into Kristi's water—why wasn't that first-degree murder?"

Alex's brows scrunched together. "We're not sure if we can prove premeditation. Michelle claimed that she only wanted to give Kristi diarrhea and derail her talk. She really hated Kristi and said she made a split-second decision, when Kristi demanded a free blinged-out water bottle, to dump water and Visine into it. Apparently she initially refused, then decided to give it to her free, but with the tainted water, along with another regular bottle of tainted water"

I scrunched up one eye skeptically, which made me wince in pain. "Hunh? I get that Kristi drank from the poisoned bedazzled bottle. But she also had a plastic bottle, the kind you buy in a store. How did Michelle tamper with a sealed bottle?"

"Michelle explained how she'd managed to melt the flip tops off empty plastic bottles for some of her creations, so the tops and seals would stay intact. Said she learned the technique for taking booze on cruise ships. She grabbed a sealed bottle, unscrewed it, dumped the eye drops in, then screwed on a top that looked like it was sealed. So Kristi ended up drinking quite a bit of

Visine over the course of a day or so. A couple of bottles, at least."

"Why'd Michelle have so much eye drops?" I asked, picking a piece of cheese off my sandwich.

"She said she got it on sale. But I'm sure prosecutors will take a hard look at that. I wouldn't be surprised if her charge is bumped up to first-degree murder eventually."

"All that over a Bigfoot hunter," Jack said softly.

The room went silent for a heartbeat.

"That's the thing about jealousy," I said, setting half my sandwich on the plate. "It blurs the lines between reality and the stories people tell themselves."

I felt pretty pleased with myself for that analysis. I'd have to remember that if someone did a true-crime podcast of this case.

Alex nodded. "And the real tragedy is, it was all a figment of her imagination. Kristi and Grant were never together."

"No, because Grant was screwing Alice," I said. My sister shook her head and stuck out her tongue.

"Oh, and guess what else we found out?" Jack said. "Tell them, Alex."

"What?"

Alex chuckled and shook his head. "The figure you and Jack saw in black? That turned out to be a few Bigfoot hunters filming a promo for their social media channels. I heard about it during my questioning and tracked the guys down and talked to them. Saw one guy's costume and everything, which was weird. Something about Slenderman, whatever that is. I confirmed they were in the woods when the two of you were on the trail yesterday."

"So there aren't cryptids in Wahoo. Too bad." I shrugged. "I wonder if that's what Kristi saw, too?"

"Probably," Alex shrugged.

"We'll never know," Jack added, then whistled the opening bars of the *X-Files* theme song. We all laughed.

Vera leaned in. "If there's one thing I've learned from this," she mused, "it's that holding onto our own version of reality can be more dangerous than facing the truth. We all need to let go of old narratives. Right?"

She stared at me as she said this. I stretched out, feeling the tension ease from my shoulders.

"And maybe write new ones," I said, sharing a look with Vera that spoke volumes about second chances and fresh starts.

Catsy, ever the queen, leapt onto the back of the sofa, surveying her kingdom with languid disinterest. She flicked her tail in Jack's face. Little flirt.

Jack chuckled. "Well, for now, let's just enjoy the fact that you're both safe, the perp is behind bars, and we've got Gouda sandwiches to devour."

The conversation shifted, lightening as we ate and talked about meaningless things like the weather, the baking show, and the deliciousness of Cheesy Does It.

Vera and Alex shared secretive glances, and I spied their fingers twined together.

Catsy jumped down and curled up half on my lap, half on Jack's. He was next to me, and I sighed pleasurably as I gently leaned against his shoulder. He kissed my head and a shower of fireworks went through me. Even in my rough state, I was attracted to him. The man was that magnetic, and the fact he still wanted anything to do with me after witnessing me barfing on a hotel carpet on all fours while in a Bigfoot costume—well, that was something special.

Still, I wasn't sure what would happen between us. Would he leave or stay? When would he let me into his world and his mind? Did we have a future together?

Those weren't questions I could answer tonight. I was in no rush for anything to change, not after all I'd been through these past few days.

No, for now, everything was about as perfect as it could get after the weekend's weirdness. We were home, safe, and cozy. Although Kristi's chapter was sadly closed, our stories—Vera's, mine, Jack's, and Alex's—were still being written. Who knew how, or if, they would end?

I looked around at the four of us, feeling a sense of contentment that was rare and hard-fought—similar to how I felt after trapping a gator.

Most importantly, Vera and I would be just fine. I needed to hold space for her feelings, and leap into my own unknown.

Epilogue

Heartfelt Haven: "Straight from the Heart" Bookstore Opens in Wahoo
Florida women trap gators, sell books, solve murders
By Luke Carrington
The Sentinel

WAHOO, Fla.—In the quaint, historic downtown of Wahoo, Florida, a new chapter unfolds for book lovers with the opening of Straight From the Heart, the only shop in central Florida dedicated exclusively to romance novels.

Owned by 25-year-old twin sisters Maggie and Vera Andrews, this unique haven for romantic literature is quickly becoming a must-see destination, blending the charm of small-town life with the universal allure of love stories.

Nestled among the palm tree-lined streets of Wahoo, Straight From the Heart offers a cozy retreat for those seeking a good book. The Andrews sisters, who are fourth-generation Wahoo residents, have meticulously curated a collection that spans the breadth of the romance genre, from historical romances that transport readers to bygone eras to contemporary love stories set in bustling modern cities. They also offer various sub-genres, including paranormal, science fiction, and monster romance.

"We wanted to create a space that celebrates love in all its forms, including LGBTQ+ stories, and books by BIPOC authors," said a smiling Vera Andrews. "Romance novels have the power to uplift and inspire, and we believe there's a story here for everyone, regardless of color, sexual orientation, or gender identity."

Both women are graduates of Wahoo High School. Vera worked at the Wahoo Public Library prior to opening the bookstore.

The shop's interior is as inviting as its collection, with plush reading nooks, vintage love seats, and walls adorned with romantic movie posters. The scent of new books mingles with the aroma of freshly brewed coffee from a small café corner, making Straight From the Heart an ideal spot for readers to pass an afternoon.

Already, the store is getting national attention; it was recently mentioned in a *New York Times* article, and the sisters say a TV station from Miami is scheduled to visit for a video segment next month.

But Straight From the Heart is more than just a bookstore; it's a testament to the diverse talents and backgrounds of its owners.

Maggie Andrews, besides being a bookworm, is also one of the few female alligator trappers in Florida. Her unique occupation adds an intriguing layer to the bookstore's charm, and has become a topic of fascination among the patrons. Prior to opening the bookstore, she lived and worked in Boston, where she handled reptiles at the Boston Zoo.

"Maggie's adventures as an alligator trapper and zoo-keeper bring a sense of excitement and a touch of the unexpected to our bookstore," Vera explained. "She's a reminder that love and adventure can be found in the most unlikely places."

When asked if either sister has a special someone, both demurred and paused before answering.

"Yes, but I'd rather not jinx it and discuss it publicly," Vera said. "It's still early."

Maggie added, "I'm not putting that in the paper."

The sisters' decision to open a romance-only bookstore was driven by their shared passion for the genre and their desire to create a community space where people could come together to share their love of reading.

Vera explained that their mother, who passed away several years ago, was an avid romance reader. She passed along her love of the genre to her daughters. Their father, Logan Andrews, was known around town as the Gator King—that's why Maggie's named her trapping business Gator Queen—and he enjoyed science fiction.

"Our parents both loved to read, and Dad taught us we could do anything if we put our minds to it," Vera said. "He always believed in both of us."

Interestingly, that self-confidence might have paid off in other ways, too. The sisters also recently solved two murders in Wahoo. One victim was a local gator trapper, Gene Robinson, and the other was Kristi Klaus, a noted Bigfoot hunter.

When asked by the *Sentinel* about this unusual turn of events, the sisters declined to comment.

"We'd rather keep the focus on the bookstore," said Maggie, while Vera nodded.

The impact of Straight From the Heart extends beyond the walls of the shop on Main Street. In a digital age where independent bookstores face numerous challenges, the Andrews sisters are proving that there's still a place for niche bookstores that cater to specific interests. Their success is a beacon of hope for small bookstores everywhere, demonstrating the value of creating specialized, immersive experiences for customers.

Straight From the Heart hosts regular events, including author readings, book clubs, and workshops on writing romantic fiction, fostering a community of readers and writers.

On June 6, the shop and the sisters will welcome best-selling author Gabrielle Hart, whose book, *Postcards of Love*, was recently optioned by Sony Pictures.

Local residents and tourists are embracing Straight From the Heart, drawn not only to its unique focus on romance novels but also to the warmth and passion of its owners.

"This bookstore has brought so much joy to our town," said City Councilor Emily Johnson, a Wahoo resident and regular customer. "It's more than just a place to buy books; it's a community hub where love—in all its forms—is truly celebrated."

As Straight From the Heart continues to grow, Maggie and Vera Andrews look forward to expanding their collection and reaching even more readers. Plans for themed scavenger hunts, happy hour, and an expanded snack menu are in the works.

Their dedication to celebrating romance literature and building a bookish community is a testament the enduring power of love stories to connect and inspire us, the sisters say.

As Straight From the Heart continues to weave its narrative into the fabric of Wahoo, Maggie Andrews reflects on the journey with a smile, her eyes twinkling with the same adventurous spirit that guides her through the swamps of Florida.

"In the end, whether I'm wrestling gators or sorting through love stories," she said, "it's all about embracing the unexpected twists of life."

About the Author

Tara Lush is a Florida-based author and journalist. She's an RWA Rita finalist, an Amtrak writing fellow, and the winner of the George C. Polk award for environmental journalism. She was a reporter with the Associated Press in Florida, covering crime, alligators, natural disasters, and politics. She also writes contemporary romance set in tropical locations under the name Tamara Lush. Tara is a fan of vintage pulp fiction book covers, Sinatra-era jazz, 1980s fashion, tropical chill, kombucha, gin, tonic, seashells, iPhones, Art Deco, telenovelas, street art, coconut anything, strong coffee, and newspapers. She lives on the Gulf Coast with her husband and their dog.